Joanne Sefton lives in Bath, with her husband and two children, where she is a working barrister. She is Scottish and has an MA in creative writing from Bath Spa University. Joanne has been long-listed twice for the Bath Novel Award, and this is her second novel.

You can follow Joanne on Twitter @Joanne_Sefton

By the same author:

If They Knew (also published as The Mother's Lies)

The Guilty Friend

Joanne Sefton

avon.

A division of HarperCollins*Publishers*

www.harpercollins.co.uk

Published by AVON
A division of HarperCollins*Publishers* Ltd
1 London Bridge Street
London SE1 9GF

www.harpercollins.co.uk

A Paperback Original 2019

A catalogue copy of this book is available from the British Library.

ISBN: 978-0-00-829447-2

Typeset in Birka by Palimpsest Book Production Limited, Falkirk, Stirlingshire
Printed and bound in UK by CPI Group (UK) Ltd, Croydon CR0 4YY

For my family.

Chapter 1

Karen
2019

The recipe book was well thumbed throughout, but there was one page that it naturally fell open to every time: *Crespelle con Pollo*. The Italian chicken pancake dish had been a family favourite for years. So much so, that Karen only really used the book out of habit – if needed, she could have made it blindfolded. The recipe took some time, granted, what with having to make the thin pancakes, cool them, and then stuff them with the chicken mixture, before pouring over the cream sauce and baking in the oven. She enjoyed cooking, though, and she particularly liked meals like this, which she could put together during the peaceful daytime hours. When the girls came back from school, she could focus on them, drinking her daughters in just as enthusiastically as they would inhale the tantalising, savoury aroma that would, by that point, be filling the kitchen.

A glance at the wall planner told her that Tasha's friend Claire would be coming over. Just as well she checked so she could bulk up the quantities a bit and make a generous salad and then Claire could stay if she wanted to. She probably

1

would. Karen prided herself on the fact that both Tasha and Callie's friends seemed to enjoy spending time in the house. Her eldest daughter, Evie, was at university now, but she would doubtless bring a whole new set of friends home come the holidays.

Tasha and Claire would do their homework together and then probably hang out upstairs; their GCSEs were looming in a few months and they were both conscientious girls. Callie would get home around the same time as her older sister, but then would need a lift to her dance class after dinner. Karen frowned. There was little point in coming home during the class, and she always intended to kill the time by going for a run, but now, halfway through February, her January fitness resolution was fading fast, and she'd never really liked running in the dark.

She always found herself getting impatient at this time of year. Although the days were creeping longer, it felt like they'd never actually get to spring. Perhaps she'd just take her book instead. The reception area was comfortable enough, and you could glimpse the girls through the glass door. It was sweet that Callie still liked to catch her watching and would happily break her drill to give Karen a cheery wave and a grin full of braces. Yes, that's what she'd do.

The TV on the wall wittered on as she collected the ingredients for the pancake batter. She didn't listen really, but she liked something on in the background. She considered turning it off but checked the clock and realised it would be the lunchtime news in five minutes so decided to leave them be. Without really thinking, she whisked together her eggs and milk and methodically weighed the flour, adding a pinch of salt. The key was to add the liquid gradually and beat it well;

that way you avoided lumps. As the opening notes of the news programme sounded, she picked the bowl up, nestling it in one arm while she whisked with the other, taking a few steps across the kitchen to catch the headlines.

It was clear from the newsreader's frown and sombre tone that something bad had happened.

A bomb on a tube train.

She put the bowl down for a moment, to notch up the volume, then picked it up again. She resumed her stirring automatically as she listened to the report.

'... *an incident was first reported on the Northern Line, between Highgate and East Finchley, at around half past nine this morning.*'

The presenter in the studio handed over to a windswept journalist standing in front of the station. An 'East Finchley' sign, with the distinctive, round London transport logo, was prominent in the background.

'... *several injured but no reports of fatalities on this quiet service, which was travelling out of central London. We can only speculate on how much more serious this incident could have been if the device had detonated earlier, on the train's inbound journey, at the peak of rush hour. The police have made no comment yet, but there is clearly conjecture that we are dealing here with a terrorist incident, which has – thankfully – not gone according to plan. Nonetheless, we saw scenes of panic as the train was evacuated at East Finchley station earlier this morning. This footage and photography comes from public mobile phone recordings, so we apologise for the quality, but it gives a sense of the scale of the incident here earlier today ...*'

The visuals cut again, this time to a jerky recording of people fleeing the station. The whole place was filled with smoke and debris, along with people running, seemingly in every direction. The phone had captured cries and shouts. Karen wondered who would pause to start recording in such a moment, but then there was always someone.

Briefly, she set the bowl down to add a splash more milk, then picked it up again. In her head, she ran through whether anyone she knew would be on that train at that time. She didn't think so. It made her shudder, nonetheless. The coverage went back to the studio now, where someone had taken the best of the amateur camera shots and turned them into slick backgrounds to head up the various aspects of the report. As the presenter commented on 'The Emergency Response', there was a picture of an ambulance crew arriving, one paramedic frozen in mid-air, jumping from the vehicle in his rush to get to the scene. The next segment was 'The Injured' and a different picture flashed up. This one showed a woman leaving the station building, a white burn mask covering her face and another paramedic guiding her by the shoulder. Karen took a sharp intake of breath at the scene; the bomb might have done less damage than those responsible had hoped for, but it didn't look great for that poor soul.

As the presenter continued to talk, striving to eke out a paucity of information into something that was meant to sound meaningful and authoritative, Karen squinted at the screen. There was someone else in the picture, just behind the woman in the burn mask. At first glance, this other figure, darkly clothed and covered in dust, almost merged with the background, but, as soon as Karen turned her attention away from the arresting image of that mask and really looked at the rest of the picture, the second woman jolted into focus.

With a clatter, the glass mixing bowl dropped out of her

hands, slopping creamy mixture down her dress and all over her suede slippers. For a long, frozen moment, Karen stared at the screen, ignoring the slow drips of batter sliding from her hem to the floor.

The other woman in the picture was Alex.

Chapter 2

Misty
2019

She'd been doing the job for twenty-two years, but the sting when they lost someone never hurt any less.

The couple sitting in front of her – knees touching, hands clasped – had strong rural accents that sounded out of place in the busy London clinic. They were from somewhere in darkest Dorset, driven here by desperation and internet research that had given them a glimmer of hope that, here, something could be done to help their precious Bella.

Over the last few months, Misty had come to like them, which wasn't always the case. She respected Alan, with his weathered farmer's hands and the pressed cotton handkerchief he put in his jacket pocket for trips up to town. His wife Ruth, with her wide, disarming smile and her scent of freesias, inspired a feeling of warmth that Misty knew was shared by all the staff who'd worked with Bella. Today, though, they were visiting for the last time.

'I never believed it would come to this.' Ruth sniffed, and Alan squeezed her hand where it lay in his. 'I knew it in my head, but I never believed it in my heart.'

Misty nodded, careful to allow the woman have the space she needed to speak.

'She was such a live wire, you know, when she was a little one. I wish you could have known her. These last few years, it's been like a flame going out. Maybe she was just too bright for us ... too bright for this world. She just faded away, and there was nothing we could do to keep here ... nothing ... nothing we could do.'

The short speech subsided into sobs and she leant into her husband's embrace, knocking awkwardly against the small cardboard box of Bella's things they'd already collected from the ward staff. Misty fought back a lump rising in her own throat.

People quite often talked of it in that way, their daughters fading away. It sounded quiet, almost holy, echoing the legacy of those wretched Italian heroines who starved themselves to sainthood in the Middle Ages. But Misty knew only too well that the fading was only a part of the story. Even as her patients' bodies diminished, so the presence of their disease grew – it entrenched itself in families, sucking up everything they had to give and more. Daily routines would turn into battlegrounds, education and prospects would be devastated, siblings would be left confused and neglected, marriages would founder. Anorexia was a tyrant. And, in the case of Bella Durnton, a killer.

After today, she wouldn't see Alan or Ruth again. They had declined, with their usual dignity, the clinic's offer to send staff to the funeral. Lyme Regis was too far, they said, it wasn't right to keep the staff from their work, far less to encroach on their time off. Misty knew that the funerals were often lavish and well attended, the privilege of those who die young.

What would come after that for Ruth and Alan? They had the farm – two hundred head of rare-breed cattle, as Alan had told her proudly when they first met two years earlier, and also the farm dogs that slept in the kitchen though they should be outside. Both were from families long established in the area. There were plenty of relatives scattered around, but no other children. Misty imagined Ruth doing flowers for the church and spoiling nieces and nephews. She wasn't the sort to let her tragedy define her, but, as Misty knew only too well, it would always be there. Would they blame her? She'd probably never know.

*

By the time the Durntons left for cardboard coffee at Waterloo and a lonely journey on the crowded train home, her afternoon ward round was still waiting for her and she had at least four emails to reply to that wouldn't wait until tomorrow. It was nearly 8 p.m. when she finally said her goodbyes to the night sister, collected her things, and made her way outside.

The chill evening air bit at her cheeks. It was February, the time of year when winter has long lost its glamour and spring seems little more than a fairy story. There had been an attempted terror attack earlier in the day – she'd caught bits and pieces of it on the news and on her phone through the day. A man with a homemade bomb in a plastic paint container tried to blow up a tube train on the Northern Line. No fatalities, thank God. There had been sporadic alerts and closures on the tube, which wouldn't affect her directly but meant the bus would probably be even busier than usual. She hoped the Durntons had got to Waterloo without disruption;

they didn't need travel chaos to deal with on top of everything else they'd been through today.

There was a crowd at the bus stop and she decided to walk, at least the first part. The streets seemed to have a skittish, febrile atmosphere as they always did on such days. But then, perhaps it was nothing more than her imagination, filling in what she expected to see. In the waiting room of the clinic, she'd noticed more people watching the twenty-four-hour news channel on the overhead TV than on a normal Tuesday afternoon. The screen showed familiar faces intoning sombre thoughts in front of police cordons and rolled shaky mobile phone footage of smoke and dust and a small crowd rushing from the doors at East Finchley. It was the parents in the waiting room, mainly, looking at the screen. The kids beside them were locked into their phones, so not everything was different.

She strode briskly, shoving her bare hands deep into her pockets, and the bite of the cold weather receded a little. They'd had a mild spell, but it was definitely back to gloves for tomorrow. Still, it was nice to be outside. The air in the hospital always felt stale. She worried that it clung to her – that she had a hospital smell that other people could detect, like some people smelt of their dogs. London air was never fresh but, in the cold, you could at least imagine it might be. It would be more pleasant to walk than get the bus, she decided. It might take forty minutes but it wasn't as if she was rushing home for anyone.

She lived in Kennington, in a street of rather twee Victorian terraced cottages, which did their best to ignore the roar of the traffic and the ugly jumble of the city that had grown up around them. It was pleasant and convenient and still more affordable than similar spots north of the river. The street housed young professionals and gay couples and a few older residents. The sort of people who bought these houses moved further out if they had children.

Except for the scattering of junk mail by the front door, everything in the house was as she had left it that morning. Eusebio was on an assignment and wouldn't be back for a week or two. There were some leftovers from a pasta she'd done last night. That would do, with a bit of chopped-up tomato and cucumber she could call a salad. She didn't like to open wine on a weeknight, but the conversation with the Durntons had taken its toll, so maybe tonight would be an exception.

An hour later she was sipping a pinot in front of a rolling news channel, the debris of her meal still littering her coffee table. It was all about the bombing, of course. There was a still photo of woman in a burn mask leaving the scene. Misty leant forward and squinted at the screen. They'd been using the image a lot, but this time, without her food to distract her, something else caught her eye. That woman in the background.

'Alex?'

The word escaped her lips even though there was no one to hear it. It was the first time she'd spoken that name aloud in years.

Her mind flashed back, suddenly flooded with images of glossy black curls, champagne, rebellion, extravagance and that million-dollar smile. Alex was the reason she was doing this job, the reason she was living this life. Every time she helped someone recover, it was a temporary salve on the unhealable wound that was Alex Penrith. Every time she lost a girl like Bella Durnton, it was like losing Alex all over again.

The woman fleeing the attack – the dust and filth-covered woman with her determined eyes, frozen in an instant as the backdrop to a horror story – was an uncanny fit with Misty's images of Alex fast-forwarded through three decades. This woman was older than the Alex she remembered – although the grime and dust that flattened her features made it impossible to tell how old. She shared Alex's distinctive curly hair, her elfin features and something about the way she held herself. The essence of Alex sang out from the screen. But despite the likeness, it couldn't be her.

Because Alex had been dead for almost thirty years.

Chapter 3

Misty
1987

Misty blinked and blinked again. She'd waited for this moment for two years, perhaps for her whole life. After pouring so much energy into hoping and fantasising and anticipating she was finally here. In her tiny bedroom at home, or out walking through the scrubby fields with Mack, her dog, there had been no space in her imaginings for even the slightest whisper of doubt. Only now, sitting on a narrow lumpy bed, next to the suitcase and two cardboard boxes that contained her possessions, did the doubt start to creep in.

Her mum, Elspeth, had driven her down in their battered Mini Metro; she didn't like to drive that sort of distance but Misty's dad couldn't get time off to come with them. They'd sucked Polos and alternated Ray Stevens and The Cure in the cassette player because the radio picked up nothing but static. Normally, she felt her irritation with her mum's jangly American country tapes was entirely justified. After all, she had Johnny Mathis to thank for her name, which had caused enough bother through high school. If there were any other girls christened Misty in Rochdale in

12

1968, she'd yet to meet one. Today, though, even the music couldn't spoil her good mood. Elspeth was in high spirits too – it felt like a holiday.

As they got closer to Cambridge, though, Elspeth's chatter had died away. Perhaps she was concentrating on the unfamiliar roads but Misty sensed it was more than that. Her mother, the most down-to-earth, suffer-no-fools person she knew, was daunted. Was it just that Misty was flying the nest? That tonight Elspeth would drive back by herself to a house from which her eldest child was missing? Or was it just the thought of Cambridge and everything that came with it?

Misty was excited, not daunted. When they arrived, she was the one who announced herself to the porters and collected her room key, whilst her mum waited in the car, fretting about a parking ticket and who knew what else. With a temporary college permit in the windscreen, Elspeth agreed to come inside for just long enough to see Misty's room and have a cup of tea. They'd picked up some supplies at a petrol station on the A14: milk, bread, teabags, a tub of margarine and two tins of ham. Misty put the kettle on and opened the cupboards. One had some breakfast cereal and a bottle of red wine in it but the others were empty. There was one carton of milk in the fridge. So, either Misty was the second to arrive, or else the others were even more cavalier about sustenance than Miss Muesli and herself.

She had the two mugs of tea in her hands when the kitchen door swung open towards her.

'Oh. Hello. I thought I heard someone else. I've been waiting all day. I'm Alexandra Penrith.'

The girl was half a head taller than Misty, slim, with lustrous dark curls and the poshest accent Misty had ever heard. She stuck out her hand in a rather formal way, but her smile was broad and genuine.

Misty shrugged, glancing down at the mugs she was holding and they both giggled. Alexandra dropped her hand and turned to hold the door open instead.

'I'm Misty Jardine. My mum's just leaving,' said Misty. 'I mean, once she's had this.' She nodded down at the tea. 'What room number are you?'

'Six. And you?'

'Two.'

'Great. Come and find me when you're ready. I'll be unpacking and accosting random strangers.'

You could arrive on Friday or Saturday. It turned out that only three girls from the corridor of eight were there the first night. The third looked around fourteen, whispered that she was called Emma and was studying maths and locked herself in her room. Misty and Alexandra – who said she preferred to be called Alex – chatted awkwardly in Alex's room. She'd brought actual furniture – a desk with elaborate carving that looked Indian to Misty's untrained eye and a pair of woven cane chairs, laden with sari-silk cushions. The bed itself looked the same as Misty's, but it was piled with more of the jewel-coloured cushions and swathed in an intricately embroidered throw.

'Wow, this is incredible,' said Misty, forgetting to try to be cool.

'Well, I just couldn't tolerate the awful stuff here, so Daddy arranged with the porters to stash it in storage. It's so important to be able to express yourself, isn't it? They don't know about the picture hooks yet –' she gestured towards a couple of frames hanging above the bed; Misty definitely remembered

14

there being something in the information leaflet about it being expressly forbidden to attach anything other than Blu-Tack to the wall '– but I'm sure I can talk them round.'

Misty thought of the two posters waiting to go up in her own room. One was Morrissey, the other a cute Labrador puppy. Both were a bit tatty having been up in her room at home. Would they count as self-expression in Alex's book?

They missed the canteen – which Alex informed her was called the buttery – which was on reduced opening hours because it wasn't yet officially term time.

'Well, we could get something in town?' suggested Alex, as they stood in a drizzly quad in front of the locked buttery door, clutching the mimeographed maps of college they had been given on arrival.

Misty had £22 in her purse. It had to last her until she sorted out a bank account and her grant came through. College food would go on a college bill that she could pay off at the end of term. She might not have got her head round the terminology but she was straight on that much. She thought of the tinned ham and loaf of bread in the cupboard. It wasn't appealing, but she wouldn't starve. Would Alex despise her if she suggested a ham sandwich?

'Are you okay?'

Before she could answer, they were interrupted by a cough behind them.

'Is the buttery closed, then?'

They turned to see another girl. Like Alex, she was wearing stonewashed jeans, pearl studs in her ears and a blazer-type jacket. Misty couldn't decide whether to feel insecure, but settled on mildly amused.

'I'm Karen Cooper. I just arrived today.'

'First year?' asked Alex, and, when Karen nodded, she added, 'Us too. We're just going to get something to eat, actually. There's a nice little bistro place not far away. I don't want to seem bossy, but my family live here, so I know my way around.'

'Sounds good.' Karen nodded. 'Let's go.'

They both turned to Misty, and she hesitated for a moment, thinking of the tinned ham and the £22. She'd have to go and see the grant office first thing tomorrow. She wasn't about to skulk back to her room with her tail between her legs.

'Okay,' she agreed, 'let's go.'

*

The skies were threatening rain and Alex led the way purposefully. Karen, who had long legs and a graceful stride, kept up easily, but Misty found herself distracted at every turn. There was so much to look at as they hurried through streets lined with medieval colleges that looked like castles, and passed rosy pub windows and clothes shops that Misty had heard of but never seen on any high street she visited.

'Your parents are academics then?' Karen addressed her question to Alex, but didn't wait for a response. 'Didn't you want to go away to university? Why not Oxford?'

Misty's ears pricked. Getting away had been her dream for as long as she could remember, but then she'd never really thought about people who lived in places like this already – who didn't need to escape to them.

Side-on, in the street light, she could see that Alex made a face, but wasn't sure exactly what her expression meant.

'It's a bit complicated,' she said, eventually. 'My mum would

16

say I need looking after. I would say she does.' She gave a hollow laugh. 'You two have waved your parents on their merry way, haven't you? I'd swap places with either of you if I could.'

Misty felt taken aback, as if Alex could read her mind. Only a moment ago she'd been thinking about how Alex's life seemed impossibly charmed. But it didn't appear that Alex felt that way.

'We're here anyway,' Alex announced. 'Not the best restaurant in Cambridge. But one of the closest. And just in time.' She stuck her hand out, and, sure enough, there were fat raindrops starting to plop from the sky. They hurried through the doorway.

Once they were seated at a generous table by the window, a waiter brought menus and Alex announced, 'We'll have a bottle of house champagne.' Panicked, Misty gave a small cough. Splashing out on a 'cheap' meal was one thing; this she hadn't bargained for.

'Please don't worry, darlings.' Alex lowered her voice. 'My dad's always in here; he's got an account. This is my treat – or should I say his.' There was a giggle and a glint in her eye, as if they were all up to mischief together.

That was the thing about Alex, as Misty would quickly come to learn. Although the way she acted and the things she said *should* have felt objectionable, or condescending – should have been, in fact, everything that Misty would have expected to despise – they somehow weren't. Alex had a wonderful warmth, a gift of drawing people in, of making them see the world from her perspective. Misty would soon discover that the world, from that vantage point was a much more colourful and exciting place than she'd previously imagined.

Chapter 4

Tasha
2019

Tasha knew that whoever invented Valentine's Day must have been a wanker. A sadistic wanker with a hatred of teenagers. It comes at the worst time of the year. When Christmas is over, but it still won't be warm for ages and the teachers are doling out crap results from crap mock GCSEs. It creeps up on you – you'd forget it was coming and then you'd be in town and see a card shop window stuffed with red heart-shaped balloons and your stomach would jump up and crash down again leaving you feeling queasy.

Tasha estimated that around two per cent of the girls in school actually liked Valentine's Day. They were the fit ones with boyfriends, or at least boys who would admit to liking them. If it wasn't for them, everyone else could just ignore it and forget about the whole thing. But they wouldn't let that happen. Girls like Lola Shirini and Nadya Bansal. They'd been going on about it for ages. The main WhatsApp group for the girls in Tasha's year was full of messages from them debating which boys were going to get them cards or presents and who else wasn't going to get anything.

Her friends Claire and Sonal felt exactly the same. The three of them were moaning about it at lunchtime, eating their packed lunches in the music quad. It was freezing, but still better than eating inside and contending with a zoo of screaming Year 7s and 8s and their stinky sandwiches. Sonal was in a bad mood to start with because she'd got a Grade 7 in her history mock. She was expecting an 8 and Tash knew she was hoping for a 9 in the real one, even though she wouldn't admit it. Tash had got an 8 so Sonal was being a bit pissy with her, even though Tash's actual mark was only three higher than Sonal's own.

Claire didn't do History and didn't get any marks back that day so she was keeping quiet, but then Claire was a real-life genius anyway and Tash just knew she was going to get a 9 in everything without even trying. Mr Taylor had already told her he thought she'd have a good shot at Oxford or Cambridge. Claire had been on at Tasha's mum to give her a practice interview, because she'd been to Cambridge herself. She apparently hadn't paused to think that it did a fat lot of good for Karen. But then perhaps geniuses weren't renowned for common sense.

Sonal was going on and on about Charles de Gaulle and how she'd been unfairly marked down because she'd forgotten when he died. Then Claire told her to shut up and said that when Sonal and Tash had been in History, she'd been in Geography and Lola had been nudging loads of the girls and getting them to look at something 'secret' in her bag. When the bag got passed to Claire, she saw a box of Lindt chocolates and a charm bracelet in a Pandora box. No wonder Lola was pleased with herself. Everyone knew that Pandora bracelets started at £100 or something and apparently this had three or four charms on it already.

After Sonal had whinged about her exam and Claire had told the others about Lola's bracelet, a Year 7 kid came up out of nowhere and said, 'Are you Tasha Neville?' She obviously didn't have a clue which one of them actually was Tasha, because she was talking more to Claire when she said it. So, Tasha butted in to say she was the girl was they were looking for and the Year 7 shoved this giant pink envelope at her and then ran off sniggering like a fruit loop.

'Well, open it then!' Claire and Sonal were all over her. So, she did, and it was a Valentine's card. It had a pair of those hideous grey teddies that are meant to be cute with massive hearts between them and part of her head was thinking about how it was possibly the worst card that had ever been printed and how she'd be embarrassed to buy it. But at the same time another part of her mind was thinking that this was the first Valentine's card she'd ever got. Claire and Sonal were obviously mad with jealousy and, after all, it wasn't like anyone would expect a boy to have good taste in greetings cards so they all decided they could probably overlook the bleurgh grey teddies. For Tash, the amazing thing was that someone actually liked her and wanted to tell her that on Valentine's Day with a big showy card at school.

She flicked the card open then shut it immediately. But not quick enough to stop the rush of blood in her cheeks. There had been some printed writing – she'd not had the card open for long enough to read it – then, at the bottom, just one word 'Stanno' and one crossed kiss.

Tasha had fancied him since Year 8. Thinking about it, she probably would have had more chance with him then, because ever since then he'd just got more fit and more popular whereas she'd, well, not. But they did still get on. He only lived a street away from her and sometimes they would walk home together off the bus. Maybe she'd made more of an impression than she'd thought.

'Oh my God.' She turned to her friends. 'It's Dylan Stanton. It's actually him. He *likes* me. OM-fucking-G. What the fuck am I going to do?'

And the girls were hyped, because they knew she liked Stanno, although she would never have told them quite how much. Claire's face lit with excitement and happiness for her, and then, just as suddenly, it crumpled.

Tash's stomach turned to ice. She turned, following Claire's gaze, to look over her shoulder. Lola Shirini swooped like a vampire bat, her glossy Kate Middleton hair swinging and her phone thrusting into Tash's face as her laughter ripped through the quad.

'She actually fell for it. Look at her! Little Miss Boffin-Head is in luurve with Dylan Stanton. Can you imagine it? Like he'd send a card to her – as if!'

The three or four worker bees she'd brought along for the ride swayed around laughing, making out like they were pissing themselves or unable to stay upright. The blood that had rushed to Tash's cheeks a few moments earlier was now joined by what felt like the rest of the blood in her entire body and an army of fire ants. Her face was blazing like an exploding oil tanker.

She stood up and shoved the card into Lola's free hand.

'Take it back then – it's not like I care.' She choked out the last couple of words in a sob, aware even as she said it that it was a pretty pathetic effort at a comeback.

Of course, when she was stewing at home that evening, she came up with about seventeen razor-sharp ripostes that would have left Lola for dead. But none of those were featured on the video that was instantly being shared all over WhatsApp and Snapchat. Tasha knew that even kids in other years who wouldn't have had a clue who she was that morning would be pointing and laughing when she went back into school the next day.

She wondered if it was true that Saint Valentine lived in Italy a zillion years ago and they made him a saint because he married couples so the husbands wouldn't have to go to war. Woot woot for them. She would bet he didn't realise the depths of misery he was storing up for generations of innocent schoolgirls, did he? Wanker.

Chapter 5

Karen
2019

They'd eaten the *Crespelle con Pollo* after all. She'd changed her clothes, cleared up the smashed mixing bowl, and mopped the gloopy batter from the floor tiles. There was plenty of flour and eggs in the house, so the whole episode only set her back twenty minutes or so. But the joy had gone out of it. The pancakes were greasy and slightly too thick. She burnt her hand being careless with the saucepan for the béchamel. Her mind was no longer on the food, but on the memory of the woman she'd once called her best friend.

When Tash came home with her friend Claire, they'd gone straight to the den. Barely a word, and they refused her offer of hot drinks and home-made flapjack. Callie had trooped through the door a few minutes later, proclaiming herself so exhausted that she needed to lie down before ballet. With the chicken in the oven, and an uneasy restlessness still troubling her, Karen picked up her phone and scrolled through reports about the bombing. There were plenty of pictures, but no more of the woman who looked like Alex.

Listlessly, she checked her email and immediately wished she hadn't bothered. More troubling news from her solicitor. She closed the email down; she wasn't in the mood to worry about money just now. In fact, all she wanted to do was tell someone what she'd seen. But who? *Jonathan*, said a voice in her head, and the familiar stab of pain twisted in her guts. Her husband had died in a boating accident in 2008. It did get easier, but it never got easy. She'd long got used to taking out the bins and making the big decisions about mortgages and schools on her own, but still the grief broke the surface from time to time, shattering her equilibrium, often when she least expected it.

Don't get maudlin, she told herself, sternly, and then another thought popped into her head. She could phone Andrew Dyer. With a renewed energy, she thumbed through her contacts.

'Hello, Karen? What's up?'

'Hi, Andrew. I ...' How to say it? She hadn't thought of this before picking up the phone. 'Um. I wanted to talk about Alex, actually, if you've got a few minutes.'

'Right.'

Even from that one word, she could tell he was taken aback, but there was something else there too.

'I'm actually wrapping up a meeting just now. Err ... do you want to meet up, maybe go for dinner? We've not caught up in a while.'

'Yes, okay. As long as Tash is in to keep an eye on Callie, I can do most nights. When were you thinking? Later this week works.'

*

He'd picked an upmarket Thai place, which boasted pale wood and expensive-looking art in place of the usual rhinestones and buddhas. The front of the restaurant was crowded and bustling, but a waitress had led her to one of the high-backed upholstered booths that lined the back wall. It had been a bit of a trek for Karen to come so far east, but it was near his offices. Andrew had set up an online furniture retail business years ago, and after steady initial growth it had exploded in the last couple of years. It seemed impolite to ask in anything but the vaguest terms but, given that the TV ad was now appearing all over the evening schedules, she could only assume that business was booming.

She saw him come through the door and took a moment to observe him whilst he waited to speak to a member of staff. There was a trace of the old jazzman cool about him. He had remained slim and a charcoal grey suit fell sleekly from his elegant frame. The silver showing in his dark hair did nothing to detract from his svelte good looks, but where she remembered a tanned complexion his face now carried the pallor of someone who spent little time outdoors.

When she'd seen enough, she waved him over, accepting his kiss on the cheek and his flustered apology for being five minutes late.

'Will you have a drink?' he said, pushing the wine list across the table. 'I always go for lager with anything spicy, so don't worry about me.'

'Actually, I think I'll join you. It's been ages since I had a nice cold beer.'

He ordered swiftly, checking quickly with her before telling the waitress they'd share a banquet for two.

'Saves picking,' he explained. 'So, tell me what's going on. Why on earth did you want to see me about Alex?'

His bonhomie had evaporated. He didn't add 'this had

better be good' but that was the clear message she took from his tone and the flint-hard look in his eyes. Suddenly the drive and decisiveness that he must possess to have become so successful was laid out on show. There was something vulpine about him.

She took a deep breath and pulled out her tablet. Wordlessly, she keyed in the passcode, tapped open the saved screenshot and slid it across the table to him.

He gazed at it, seemingly impassive, for a few seconds that seemed like an eternity.

'I think I need that beer.'

'You see it too then?'

By way of answer, his hand travelled up to his temples, mirroring the posture of the woman in the background of the picture. Karen didn't need to see the tablet – the arch of the woman's arm, half-raised, her fingers brushing her forehead as if to smooth away some stray, invisible hairs, was etched on her brain.

'She used to do that all the time. If she was anxious, or just uncertain. She was so polished, you know, always looking perfect, knowing exactly what to say, but when you got to know her there was so much vulnerability underneath.'

Andrew was right, now she came to think of it; she'd forgotten that tic of grazing her forehead with her fingertips, which had been one of Alex's characteristic gestures.

'Could it be her?' she asked, her voice a whisper. 'It's not a twenty-year-old who looks like she did then. This is the grown-up version, though it's hard to guess if the ages match because of all that dust. I just can't imagine anyone else being so like her, in so many ways. Right down to that gesture, like you say.'

Just then the waitress arrived with two frosted bottles of Singha. Andrew took his time – and a long draught of the lager – before he answered her.

'You know, there's nothing I'd like more than to believe it could be her.' He spoke to the bottle in his hand more than to Karen. 'I know we were only twenty-one, twenty-two, but she was the one for me. I've never had anything like that in my life since.'

'I do understand,' she said, softly. 'I know how it feels to lose a partner.'

'Of course you do, and I wouldn't for a moment take away from what happened to Jonathan. That was a tragedy and you had the girls' grief to deal with too. But ...' she watched his face crease with the effort of trying to express himself, '... I don't want you to take this the wrong way. I don't want you to feel like I'm diminishing your suffering or trying to be competitive.'

'No, no, of course not. I've known you long enough that I'd never think that of you.'

She reached out to place a reassuring hand on his forearm and was rewarded with a smile of relief. It struck her as the most heartfelt expression she'd seen on his face that evening.

'The thing is that when Jonathan died, everyone around you recognised your loss. That it was something horrendous, huge ... and that you needed and deserved every bit of support they could give you.'

She nodded, not entirely sure where he was going, but sensing that she couldn't hurry him, she just had to let him try to explain in his own way. He rubbed at his forehead and opened a button on his shirt. It was clearly difficult for him to talk about Alex's death, despite the length of time that had passed.

'Well ...' he continued, carefully, 'it wasn't like that for me when Alex died.'

His explanation was cut off by the waitress arriving laden with their starters. She fussed for a couple of minutes, clearing the table of its flower arrangement and candles and naming a variety of dishes as she set down the ornate little bowls. They waited in silence, save for the odd muttered 'thank you' and when the waitress was finally ready to depart, Karen found that she didn't want to be the one to break it. When Andrew spoke, his voice was strained with emotion, and his words were unexpected.

'There isn't a formula, you know, for losing the love of your life at twenty-one. I didn't know what was expected of me. I certainly didn't know what I should expect of them. Alex's family ... it felt like they closed round like ... I don't know ... like a flock of vultures or something. I was on the outside. All I got was sharp pecks to keep me away.'

He held up one hand and mimed a vicious avian attack, managing to laugh, in spite of himself. Karen wondered with a jolt whether he'd ever given himself the chance to talk about these painful memories before now and felt a weight of responsibility on her shoulders.

'What about your own family – surely they would have been there for you?'

He shook his head. 'They were living in Wales then. It was a long way to Cambridge. I spoke to my sisters about it a bit, but they were both a long way away too, and they had young families. Enough on their plates without a mourning younger brother to deal with.'

'So, there wasn't really anyone for you to talk to?'

'Nah. I mean, I had some mates who tried, but they were

twenty-year-old blokes, you know? Not exactly renowned for their emotional intelligence.' She acknowledged the comment with a grimace. 'Besides, I was so into Alex. I suppose I'd let other friendships wither a bit. I was happy to have a drink or a chat or whatever – I mean I knew you and Misty fairly well – but I didn't get beneath the surface with people, because I had Alex for that.'

'I don't know if it helps ...' she took a breath, trying to phrase what she wanted to say as carefully as possible, '... but I remember that she felt really deeply about you too. She used to joke that it was a shame she'd found "the one" at university, because you'd end up getting married and she'd never get to have a proper single life.'

He gave a sad smile and picked at some food.

'We did talk about the future,' he agreed. 'That's one reason why it's strange. She'd gone through a really bad phase, with the ... the weight thing.' Karen's stomach dropped at the reference. She didn't want to think about how Alex had died; she couldn't trust herself to go there. Andrew, though, was still talking.

'It had been over a year earlier, though, before we were going out – or at least going out seriously. I expect you remember?'

Karen nodded. She remembered only too well.

He shook his head. 'I really thought she was over it. We had all these plans – moving to London, getting a flat together. Then ... boom. It's all over.'

He gazed at her. His eyes were blue, intense – too needy to be the eyes of an entrepreneur. She felt a sweat break out on her palms and a lump rise in her throat. The last thing she wanted was to think back to that winter. She wouldn't. She couldn't.

'Okay ...' she said, trying to steady herself as much as anything else.

'It happened so suddenly ...' His voice had become a monotone. He was struggling to go on. 'I don't even know why she went home that night ... She should have been in college. And then ... and then she just didn't come back.'

His voice cracked then, and he rubbed at his face with the back of a hand, tears not quite coming but clearly not far away. Karen wanted to say something to make it easier, but nothing would come out. Mutely, she nodded.

'... I called the house. Her mum answered and it was clear something was very wrong. She couldn't tell me. She tried to get it out a couple of times, then she passed the phone to Alex's dad. He told me she was dead.'

'Her heart failed.' Karen's voice was a whisper. She felt her own eyes moisten as she remembered that horrible time.

'On the Sunday morning!' There was anger in Andrew's voice. It came suddenly, as if from nowhere. 'A day and a half and they hadn't told me. They hadn't even tried. If I'd not phoned the house, I'm not sure they'd ever have bothered.'

'They must have been in terrible shock ...'

'I know, I know. That's what everyone says, that's what was going around in my head at the time. But do you know what?'

'What?'

'He didn't sound shocked. Eric Penrith was as composed as a ... a traffic warden telling me he'd already written my ticket. I never saw him lose it. I never saw him well up, or struggle to keep it together. He certainly had the wherewithal to talk to me on the phone, even if his wife didn't.'

There wasn't much that Karen could say. It seemed likely that however much Alex Penrith and Andrew Dyer had loved each other, wherever the relationship might have gone, Alex's parents viewed it as little more than an inconsequential crush. Right or wrong, there wasn't much to be said about it all these years later.

'Do you know what? They never even let me see the body.' His face was twisted with torment as he spoke, the hurt and impotence of his younger self etched over the veneer of confidence and success. 'I pleaded – I fucking begged those people to let me say goodbye to her. I may as well have saved my breath. They were cold as stone, deaf as stone too.'

Instinctively, Karen reached out again. This time she took his hand, trying to offer a little bit of comfort where she knew that no words would assist.

'God ... I'm being ridiculous.' He took a shuddering breath. 'It's been years since I talked about this stuff – seeing that picture, out of the blue like that – it's just opened the wound again.'

'I'm sorry, I shouldn't have ...'

'No, no, it's not your fault. I'm glad you brought it.'

As she looked at his shaking shoulders and pained expression, she wondered if he'd done so well not in spite of that awful early experience, but rather because of it. Perhaps all of his life since that time had been about making sure he would never feel so desperately powerless again.

'I wish you hadn't had to go through all that, Andrew.'

'Well, it's in the past now, isn't it? But maybe it helps you to understand why I'd love to have hope. God, if you could bring Alex back to me, I'd give you the world on a plate. But no one can, Karen.'

She didn't try to contradict him; she didn't say anything at all. She just kept her hand on his arm whilst he stared ruefully down at the table. It was a moment of stillness, an accidental intimacy that would evaporate soon enough. Her thoughts, though, were anything but still. The image of the closed coffin, laden with white lilies, remained as crisp as the day she had first seen it. But if Andrew hadn't seen the body, then how did she know anyone else had? What if there was more to Alex's parents' mistreatment of him than an oversight on the part of a grieving couple who'd never thought that much of him anyway?

The waitress arrived to clear away the starters that they had barely touched and returned a minute or two later with steaming bowls of curry and rice. With a slight reluctance, Karen pulled her arm away. Andrew gave her an apologetic smile.

'We should talk about something else, probably?'

She nodded but busied herself with the food instead. Her mind was still whirling with possibilities. What if Alex's death had actually been some sort of staged disappearing act? Perhaps she'd been recruited into some shady branch of the secret service. Unlikely, perhaps, but not impossible; after all, it had been the height of the Cold War back then, and Cambridge was a prime recruiting ground for all that stuff, wasn't it? She glanced at Andrew, whose plate remained empty, his gaze heavy and settled in the middle distance. She had enough tact to realise that now was not the time to share her theories.

'Do you want some of this? It smells fantastic.'

'Yes, thanks, sorry, I think I drifted off a bit.'

'So, business good?'

'Busy, but good, yes. We're opening more bricks-and-mortar stores, and we've got a small operation setting up in Canada as a precursor to trying to get into the US market. Don't get me started though, we'll both end up bored witless. How's life with you?'

'Oh, same as ever. Evie's at university now – you probably knew that – she's doing law at Brighton and networking and CV-building like crazy. They don't just drink and piss about like we did, you know! Tash and Callie are fine, just glued to their phones all day like all teenagers.'

'And what about Karen?'

'Me? Well ...' For a moment she thought about telling the truth. That it scared her how quickly Evie had adjusted to life away from home, how little she seemed to need her mother and how soon Tash and Callie would be off down the same road. That she had money worries because the nice financial adviser she'd been paying to manage the payouts from prudent Jonathan's various insurance products and investments was turning out to be not so nice after all. That she was approaching fifty and contemplating the rest of her life on her own and finding it bothered her much more now than it had ten years ago. 'Well, I'm planning my fiftieth. I've decided to have a bit of a party.'

He smiled, his first genuine, untarnished smile of the evening. 'That's brave. I just had a skiing weekend with a couple of mates and we drank champagne and cognac in a bar where they played Edith Piaf on a loop.'

'Did it end in tears?'

'Absolutely. We got so emotional we slept in the next day and missed the surprise skidoo trip they'd booked for my birthday present.'

She had to laugh. 'Why don't you come to my party? I'm having it in the garden at home. I can't promise cognac, Edith Piaf or skidoos, but there will definitely be champagne.'

'Well, that would be nice, thank you.'

They checked the dates and he made a note in his calendar. It had been a spur-of-the-moment thought – the party guests were mainly local couples. With three kids and big age gaps she'd met a lot of school mums over the years. But there were a few friends she'd met as work colleagues in a previous life, some book club members and the odd neighbour.

'Feel free to bring someone; the more the merrier.'

'I'll have a think about that. I'm looking forward to it.'

They chatted easily as they finished the meal, staying away from the subject of Alex and university. After coffees, Andrew offered to call her a car, explaining that he was going back to the office to pick up a few things first. She was impressed by the sleek new Mercedes that turned up, and even more impressed when she got back to Twickenham and it transpired that the journey had been paid for on his company's account.

He'd said if someone could bring Alex back, he'd give them the world on a plate. What if Alex was out there somewhere? And what if Karen could be the one to find her?

Chapter 6

Misty
1987

Misty's little room faced east and had thin curtains. Every morning the sun woke her up slowly, and she basked in the joy of no longer sharing a room with a twelve-year-old boy who emitted constant noise whether awake or asleep. Those sleepy, early moments were her one oasis of calm and she treasured them.

The university didn't believe in easing you in. The work rate was punishing and the speed at which you were expected to grasp things dizzying. Thank God she'd found Alex. Alex was chilled about everything. She always knew how to get an extension or which lecturers would give her a bit more leeway. Not that that helped Misty directly, when she was studying medicine and her friend was studying English, but her calming influence was often enough. And when that didn't work, she'd just drag Misty out into town and ply her with booze.

There was a knock at the door.

'Come in! It's not locked.'

Alex's face tilted round the door, her curls falling over her shoulder and her make-up already perfectly applied.

35

'I knew it would be you. What are you doing looking so cheerful? And ... dressed?'

'It's ten past nine, you know.'

'Shit, it's not? Mullins will kill me if I miss another lecture.' Misty scrambled upright, feeling her head thump uncomfortably as she did so.

'Lectures? Pah. It's supervisions that count. As long as you're turning up to those and not talking nonsense, no one cares.'

'Yeah, maybe in English. Not in medicine. We can't get by on a thought-provoking interpretation you know; we've got to learn that shit. Actual facts – you know? Digestive system – facts about shit, in fact. Today.'

Alex was giggling and picked up a discarded T-shirt from the floor, throwing it at Misty. 'Go on, far be it from me to keep you away from the shit. Nine o'clock lecture? Well, you might make the last ten minutes. Good luck.'

Misty tossed the T-shirt back across the room and flopped back against her pillows, massaging her forehead. Alex had stepped fully into the room now and was followed by Karen. Misty's heart sank a little to see her looking, as ever, like a shadow that had gone a little awry. She wore a purple plaid skirt and matching top, which clashed with her coppery hair; Alex had been wearing the brown version the week before. Whereas Alex was bright and playful, despite their heavy night the night before, Karen looked dark-eyed and sulky. Probably, if Misty was honest, much closer to how she herself looked.

'Anyway, I've got something to tell you both,' announced Alex.

'Well, make it quick because I really do need to get to my ten o'clock. And I need a coffee.'

'Ooh. Good plan. We'll make one. That way you can jump

36

in the shower and then you can bring yourself to crack a smile when I tell you the good news. We'll see you in ten minutes, okay?'

'Why don't we take the coffee back to your room, Alex?' Karen's tone was helpful, but she gazed around with her nose wrinkled and Misty felt a flush of anger at Karen for making her feel ashamed about her messy room scattered with stuff that Karen wouldn't touch with a bargepole. At least Misty had her own taste, she thought hotly, and when she *could* afford to buy something, she didn't just copy the latest thing that Alex had got.

'Yeah, okay,' agreed Alex. 'Come and find us as soon as you're done, Misty. Yeah?'

'Yep.'

She gave it another couple of minutes before she forced herself out of bed, splashing some water on her face from the little sink the corner. Getting up was painful, but she was intrigued by what Alex's news could be, and it wasn't a lie that she needed to get to the ten o'clock lecture.

Ten minutes later she was nestled amongst the cushions of one of Alex's peacock chairs, damp-haired and clutching a bowl of Weetabix.

'Have you two had breakfast?'

Alex and Karen exchanged a glance.

'We're doing a forty-eight-hour challenge,' said Karen, failing to keep a boastful tone from her voice.

'A what challenge?'

'Forty-eight hours, you can't have anything other than chewing gum, black coffee or tea and water.'

Misty shrugged. 'Sounds grim. So, what's the news then, Alex?'

'Well, this weekend, my parents are having a party at the house. And you are both invited.'

Alex beamed around at them. Misty caught the quizzical look on Karen's face and they shared a rare moment of common purpose. Why on earth would Alex want them to go to a party thrown by her *parents*?

'Err, thanks,' said Karen. 'But we're meant to be going out with the boys from Selwyn College, remember? They've got that Entz thing on, with a proper DJ coming up from London. You wouldn't want to miss that?'

Misty wasn't part of the drinking society scene – the groups of male and female students that hosted each other at 'formal halls' across the colleges – but she had intended to go to the Entz at Selwyn. Karen and Alex had both been invited to go out with the college's girls' drinking society – the Valkyries. She knew Karen was desperate to become a full member and pulling out of something like this wasn't going to help her chances.

But Alex gave a dismissive snort. 'Well, Octavia Elsmore's coming to my house, so I hardly think the Valkyries can complain if the society president's hanging out with us.'

'*Octavia* is going to your parents' party?' Karen's mouth was still hanging open even after the words had left it.

Alex just nodded. 'She had my mum for supervisions in something or other. All my mum's students adore her. Octavia offered to help me with my history coursework when I was still in sixth form.'

Misty raised her coffee to her lips and a piece of the jigsaw fell into place. She'd always wondered how Alex had got to know people so quickly. They could never walk a hundred yards together without people nodding, waving or stopping to talk to her. But Alex must have known some of these people already. To Misty, Cambridge may as well have been an alien planet she'd been dropped onto from a passing spacecraft. She was as likely to run into someone she knew from before as she was to stroll past Isaac Newton. She flushed a little, feeling gauche not to have realised before.

'So, what's so great about your parents' parties then?' asked Misty.

'Music, alcohol, guys … same as any other party. But bigger and better. They don't do things by halves and they don't have that student obsession of worrying endlessly about how much it's all going to cost.'

*

When it came to it, Misty nearly didn't go. She had a dose of flu, which had left her hot and shivery in bed when the rest of them were at the buttery's Christmas dinner. Three days later, she was feeling much better but still weak and tired. She'd missed a supervision and had two essays to catch up on whilst everyone else had finished. A hot chocolate in the common room with some rubbish on the telly sounded like a more appealing way to end the day than trekking out to the suburbs for a party.

'Don't be pathetic, it'll cheer you up.'

Karen and Alex had come banging on her door, already doused in LouLou perfume and glittery eye shadow.

They were right – she was being pathetic and feeling sorry for herself. A little bit homesick too if she was honest. But she'd have all the time in the world to lie on the sofa and drink hot chocolate when she went home next week.

'All right, I'll get ready.' She eyed their miniskirts and shivered. 'I'm wearing my jeans, though.'

'Fine,' said Alex. 'Look what I've got.' There was a flat glass bottle tucked in her jacket. She unscrewed the cap and held it out to Karen to sniff.

'Eurgh.' Karen recoiled. 'Whisky?'

'Jack Daniel's. Get the party started. Just don't wave it about in the cab, yeah?'

Misty ducked behind her wardrobe door to pull on a blouse that might help disguise her as someone who'd vaguely made an effort. Her friends passed the bottle between them as she dragged a brush through her hair and stabbed her mascara brush up and down to try to pick up the last bits from the empty tube.

'I prefer it with cola,' Karen was saying, pulling a face.

'Gets us drunk faster this way *and* fewer calories,' replied Alex. 'Do you want some, Misty? I could put it in this mug, so we don't catch any of your germs!'

'You're so thoughtful. It's okay. I think if I had some now it might finish me off before we got there.'

'It's time we were going anyway,' said Karen.

'Just getting my shoes on.'

None of them bothered with coats just to walk across college to the front Lodge where the minicab would be waiting. But even in the quads there was a chill east wind and Misty shivered violently. The three girls clung together, a little knot of festive colour amidst the dun paths and darkened wintry gardens. Alex started a plaintive chorus of 'In the Bleak Midwinter' and Karen quickly joined in. Misty, without the benefit of the whisky, was too self-conscious to sing in public.

She was the one, though, who caught the moment in the shutter-click of her memory. Christmas, cold, the headiness of the perfume and the fever she hadn't quite shaken off. She felt a rush of love for Alex, exuberant enough to even take in Karen, and a sudden certainty that these friendships were true. That they would last and be important.

*

The house was a sprawling old villa on the edge of town, built of grey stone, rather than the typical Cambridge pale gold, which lent it an air of foreboding. Although the outside was austere, warmth and light seeped from the windows, shimmering like tinsel. When the door swung open a cacophony of sound tumbled out and the warm, fuggy air hit Misty like a solid object.

'Come on,' said Alex, grinning, 'let's go in.'

Misty was startled to be offered a glass of wine by a uniformed waitress in the large, wood-panelled hallway. The room was busy and full of festive welcome; a log fire blazed to the side, a glossy piano was garlanded with greenery, and the scent of pine and candles filled the air.

'Kitchen,' said Alex, pushing past the people standing around. Misty tried to guess who they were but there was such a mix of ages, of styles of dress, it was impossible to generalise.

There was definitely a younger vibe in the kitchen. Octavia was there and Karen, evidently half-thrilled and half-relieved, rushed over to speak to the popular older girl. Four young men, presumably students, were leaning against the kitchen table and drinking wine from plastic glasses. They were all in black tie, although three of them had lost their bow ties, and two clutched musical instruments.

'That's him,' Alex hissed nodding towards them.

'Who?'

'Andrew Dyer. He plays the saxophone.'

Misty focused in on the boy she was gesturing towards. He was half a head shorter than the others, but undeniably good-looking.

'And you like him?'

Alex rolled her eyes dramatically. 'I'd die for him. He's a second year. How can you have missed him at college? He's the most gorgeous boy we've got.' She made a determined move towards the band members, pulling Misty along by her wrist.

'Hi.'

The boys nodded and grunted hellos back at Alex.

'So, you're playing tonight then?'

One of the others looked down at the trumpet in his hand. 'Um, looks like it. Professor Penrith will be here in a minute, demanding we get onto the next set. She'll want her paid monkeys to be dancing.'

A third boy nudged the one who was speaking and nodded towards Alex. 'Shut up, you idiot. She's ...'

'It's all right. I know my mum's a slave driver. And I also know where they keep the good booze.' She raised an eyebrow. 'I'm Alex Penrith. And this is Misty Jardine. She's a first year at St Barts too, although she's a medic, so you've probably never seen her.'

'Misty, that's an unusual name.' The trumpeter was talking, and smirking. Misty sighed inwardly, cursing her mum and Johnny Mathis once again. But he let the point go and the boys introduced themselves properly. Alex produced some proper glasses and a bottle of Spanish brandy from one of the many kitchen cupboards.

'I can't believe she gave you plastic glasses,' she teased, 'it's like you're at the kids' table. All the adults out there have got the real ones.'

Octavia sailed over at that moment, bringing Karen and a couple of girls Misty didn't recognise with her.

'Alex, darling, amazing party. Do you know there are two members of the Royal Shakespeare Company here? And apparently a cabinet minister. Can't remember which one, granted, but then they're not very memorable, are they?'

One of the band boys put his arm around Octavia's shoulders, pulling her towards him. Another began to whisper to Karen. Misty caught something about going into the garden, but Andrew shook his head.

'We're on again in five minutes. You're not going anywhere, Eastley.'

As the boys collected themselves, Alex sloshed brandy and cola into glasses for the three of them and Octavia.

'No point in taking it easy when you're all staying the night anyway. Let's get wasted and shag some tottie,' Alex said, raising her glass.

Misty snorted her cola out through her nose, partly at the idea, but mostly at the word 'tottie'.

'In your parents' house?' said Karen, incredulously, having managed to hold it together enough to express the thought that was once again on the same lines as Misty's.

'You don't know my parents,' replied Alex, darkly, before decisively knocking back her own drink.

*

43

A few hours later – she was vague on exactly how many hours as she was on much else – Misty was sitting on the stairs, leaning against the wood panelling and looking through the railings at the comings and goings in the hall below. She felt like the little girl from *The Sound of Music*, except very drunk and slightly nauseous.

The quartet had long since finished their official set, and Andrew was conspicuously absent, as was Alex. The pianist hadn't got so lucky, or else preferred his music to the other pleasures on offer. He continued to jam with himself, his fingers chasing his scatting voice as he filled the hall with sound. Misty listened, watching groups and couples leave in the stream of taxis that pulled up outside. The crowds were thinning; it was much quieter. A fat, bearded man slept in a wingback armchair, his hairy stomach protruding from his shirt. The door opened once more and Misty shivered in the chill blast of outside air.

'I hope you've had a good evening?'

The question came from behind her, in a deep, calm voice that sounded much less drunk than most people now seemed to be.

'What? Oh, hi, I didn't notice you coming down the stairs.'

'I didn't mean to startle you.'

The man dropped down with graceful ease and sat next to her on the step. She guessed he was about the same age as the snoring man in the chair below – mid-forties, perhaps – but they couldn't have been more different. This man was slim and elegant, his hair was styled in the slick, dark waves of a Fifties leading man and there was a musky scent to him that made her want to fill her lungs. The deep inhalation turned into a yawn.

'You're tired.' There was a note of concern in his voice. 'Do you want me to call you a taxi? Where are you getting back to?'

'Oh, I'm not. I'm staying here. I came with Alex Penrith. You know? She lives here ...'

He nodded. 'I know.'

The pianist was enjoying himself, letting rip on a clutch of high notes and that made conversation momentarily impossible. The man turned away, rifling through his jacket pocket. Misty took the opportunity to stare, noting the plush velvet collar against the pale skin of his neck.

'Here,' he said, turning back suddenly. 'Want one?'

They were cocktail cigars, dinky and covetable. She'd never been tempted to smoke before, but she took one of these, wondering if her lack of experience would be obvious.

'Are you the cabinet minister, then?' she asked, emboldened by the alcohol. 'Apparently there's one here, but they all look the same to me on the news.'

'The vegetables, eh?' He laughed. 'No, he left quite early. Sorry to disappoint. I'm just a second-rate academic. But then I always preferred parties to work anyway.' He raised his cigar in a mock toast.

'You work at the university then?'

'Only when I really can't avoid it. But, yes, they've not managed to get rid of me yet.'

'I'm sure you're not anything like what you're making out. Is that how you know the Penriths, through work?'

'Oh, darling, you're exquisite.' He stuck out his hand. 'Eric Penrith. Delighted to meet you.'

She blushed beetroot up to her hairline and stammered some response, but he just shushed her embarrassment away.

'Now, clearly my daughter isn't being much of a hostess,

and you look ready to drop. Let's work out where she's put your stuff and I'll find you somewhere to sleep.' He glanced at his watch. 'If you can't sleep in daylight, you'd better take your chance now.'

Feeling even more tired, she got to her feet and followed him into the labyrinth of upstairs rooms, the sound of the piano fading behind them.

A few minutes later, after a couple of false starts, he had located both her belongings and an unoccupied room – a cramped attic with a single bed neatly made up.

'Servants' quarters, I'm afraid, we'll do better next time. Look, I don't expect anyone to bother you up here, but there's a latch on the door so use it, okay? Some people down there are rather blitzed. Better safe than sorry.'

She nodded. 'I understand.'

'Well, if I don't see you tomorrow it was nice to meet you. Hopefully we'll meet again. And merry Christmas!'

*

It was a merry Christmas, she supposed. At least it was the same as it always was, and it had never previously struck her as lacking in merriness. She enjoyed long mornings in bed, crispy winter walks with Mack, and her mother's home cooking in which pastry featured strongly. In a day or two she felt fully recovered from her flu and she spent the week or so before Christmas knocking around with her little brother, Martin, or old school friends, and making inroads into the reading lists for next term.

There was a feeling of restlessness, though, that she carried with her as she sipped half-pints of snakebite and fended off teasing about Cambridge. It carried on through Christmas morning when they tucked into their fry-up and she dutifully opened and praised the presents she'd been bought without really noticing them. It carried on through lunch with Granny Mavis who was deaf and batty, as well as Auntie Cathy, Uncle Derek and the three young cousins all squeezed into the steam-filled kitchen. It was there as she watched her dad heckle the Queen's speech and as they played gin rummy and as she drank a glass of advocaat with Granny Mavis and watched the creamy liquid coat the fine hairs of the old lady's moustache.

She imagined Christmas at the Penrith house. Exotic food, jazz, unctuous expensive cheese and cocktail cigars. When she was here, it seemed like a fairy tale or a film set, something she'd dreamt up. But that wasn't true; she might have got the details wrong in her daydreams, but the Penriths' Christmas was just as real as her dad sitting in front of the telly, mechanically lifting KP nuts into his gob. She tried to shake herself out of it, but she fell into the same reverie over and over again.

The thing was, it wasn't just the house and the party that had entranced her. Eric Penrith. She couldn't close her eyes without seeing his handsome, laughing face. She couldn't lie in bed without thinking about what it would feel like to have him lie next to her. A stupid schoolgirl-type crush – she didn't need anyone else to tell her that – but it didn't make it any easier to cope with. On Christmas night she drifted off to the sound of her brother's snoring and the Christmas number one leaking tinnily from the wireless. Pet Shop Boys. 'You Were Always on My Mind'.

Eric Penrith. She was desperate to get back to college in the hope she would see him. But she was equally desperate never to see him again.

Chapter 7

Karen
2019

The evening traffic was slow although rush hour should have ended several hours earlier. The cab crawled along, at a speed that gave her an intimate view of the endless front rooms and front doors of the south-west suburbs. Where curtains and shutters were still open, vignettes of life in all its variety were illuminated amidst the winter darkness. She watched her breath steam up the window and replayed the meeting with Andrew.

It was coincidence that they were still in contact, really. After university had ended so badly, Karen had fallen out of touch with almost everyone. She'd left with a poor degree and little motivation to start job hunting. She spent a couple of years doing bar work before eventually getting a junior role with a copywriting agency, coming up with campaign wording for drinks companies. Jonathan had been an up-and-coming solicitor at the law firm used by the agency. He was seconded to her office for a fortnight, going through some documents for a case. They got chatting in the canteen and three years later they were married. She'd been pleased enough to leave the work – which bored her and came with an unavoidable side order of lecherous lunches and drinks events – at his suggestion. She just regretted not having the foresight to think about what it could mean for her for the future.

Jonathan worked for a City law firm, and it turned out that one of the other junior associates was none other than Andrew Dyer. Andrew's brush with the law had been brief, but he and Jonathan had been room-mates for a while, and the two of them had hit it off. They'd kept in touch over the years, with the passage of time eventually eroding Karen's initial awkwardness. Andrew liked to reminisce about Alex, and he had few opportunities to spend time with people who actually knew her. Karen didn't share his enjoyment, but in tolerating it she'd been surprised to find some sense of satisfaction, almost as though it counted as penance.

As the years went on, life moved on and they'd talked about Alex less. Andrew had been supportive when Jonathan died. She felt he was one of the few people who could come close to appreciating what she was going through. Since then, though, they'd seen less and less of each other. Managing the girls on her own gave her little time for a social life, and he'd been growing the business.

All the same, her friendship with Andrew was the one fragile thread still connecting the woman she was now to the girl she'd been then. She blushed to think about that girl, and wouldn't normally linger, but seeing 'Alex' had jolted everything to the top of her mind again. Her friendship with Alex and Misty had always seemed unlikely, even though she and Alex were doing the same degree. The other two were both like magnets – they drew people to them. They had rooms on the same corridor in first year and struck up an alliance from day one. Karen's first-year room was stuck away in an annexe and she had bumped into them on the first day. Some instinct told her to cling on for all she was worth, and she spent every day waiting to be kicked out of the clique she'd never felt she belonged to in the first place.

*

The streets outside the taxi became more spacious, more suburban, and eventually turned into ones she knew well. It was not quite ten, so not a late evening. Callie should be in bed, although she'd probably be trailing her feet, unless Tash had decided that she was in the mood for playing the grown-up and nagging her sister along. It had always been Evie who had been left in charge before this year. Tash was still deciding how she felt about the responsibility. Karen smiled at the thought of it.

Remembering her own days at university naturally made her wonder how Evie's were comparing. She hoped that her oldest daughter was a little more streetwise, a bit more self-confident than she'd been as a wide-eyed grammar school girl desperate to fit in. She'd certainly seemed to be enthusiastic when she came home at Christmas, but then Karen felt sure she would have given the same impression to her own parents.

The driver pulled up across the driveway, following her directions. She fumbled for her keys and some cash to tip him with. She pulled out a tenner then pushed it back into her purse; she really did need to start trying to budget more carefully.

Once inside she called a soft 'hello', not wanting to wake Callie if, by some miracle, she had actually decided to go to sleep. Getting no response, she pulled off her heels and went to the kitchen to flick the kettle on before she investigated further. Upstairs, her younger daughter was reading in bed, her hair still slightly damp and smelling like fruity sweets.

'Mmm. You had a bath?'

'Yeah. Just a quiet night really. Tash was being grumpy so I thought I'd have a bath. I used that facemask I got for Christmas. Can you tell?'

'You look radiant!' She kissed her daughter's forehead. 'Tash sorted some food for you, though? I left some tagine out.'

'Yeah. We had that and I made some couscous but she didn't want it. You only have to pour the water on, though; it's not hard. I put in a bit of olive oil and raisins like you do.'

'That's right, well done, sweetheart. You should be putting your light out now, though.'

'I just ...' She started flicking forward in the novel.

'No, not at the end of the chapter. Now. I know what you're like. And you should be asleep already.'

'All right. Night, night. Oh, did you have a nice time?'

Karen found herself laughing. 'I'm not responding to the delaying tactics. You can ask me tomorrow. Night, night.'

Tash was in her bedroom too, still dressed and sitting cross-legged against the headboard. She had her phone in one hand and the other was raised to her chin, so she could chew the cuff of her sweatshirt, a childhood habit she'd never broken despite plenty of nagging. Karen's heart softened at the sight of her.

'Tash?'

'Hmm.' She looked up, slightly startled. 'Mum, hi, you're back.'

'Yep. Everything go okay here?'

Tash nodded. 'Yep, nothing to report. I suppose I should be getting to bed now. Time ran away with me a bit.'

'What are you up to on there?'

'Oh, nothing, internet rubbish.' She yawned. 'Was it nice to see Andrew?'

'Yes, he's doing well. I asked him to the party.'

Tash gave a mischievous grin. 'Maybe he'll bring someone.'

'Maybe, who knows? But I'm going to have a cuppa and stick the news on, then I'll be heading to bed. You should stop staring at that phone. Come down and tell me about your day?'

'Yeah, I've got to get my orchestra stuff together at the moment. I'll go over the fingering or Mrs Wilson will totally call me out – don't worry, I won't actually play. I know Callie should be sleeping. But could you do me a tea and I'll be down in ten minutes or so?'

'Course. Just a builder's?'

'Actually, could I have one of your jasmine-y ones? I like them.'

'Cheeky!'

'Cheers, Mum.'

While the tea brewed, she noticed the message light was flashing on the landline. An unease washed over her at the sight of it. Her mother used to use it, before a stroke immobilised her six months after Jonathan's death and then another finished her off six months later. After that, the only calls were from PPI and insurance claim scam merchants. Karen had thought about getting rid of it but never got around to it. The solicitor she was using to try to sort this financial mess had asked for a landline number and seemed determined to

52

continue using it no matter many times she politely suggested her mobile might be more convenient.

Sure enough, there was a terse message saying they had an update and asking her to get in touch as a matter of urgency.

'Who's that?' asked Tash, who had appeared silently, her flute still clutched in her hand.

'Oh, just a solicitor. I need to sort out some financial stuff. It's not a biggie but I suppose solicitors are the sort of people who like to sound important.'

Tash nodded, uninterested, then brightened.

'The post came late. There was a parcel from Auntie Manda,' she said. 'Callie and I opened it because we knew it was her writing, and it had the American stamps and everything.'

'And did she send you both something nice?' Karen handed her daughter the green tea, smiling indulgently.

'Yes. Some beauty stuff that you can't get over here. Primer and moisturiser and a few lip colours too. It's a new brand, I think. She sent enough for Evie but she's just going to have to have the last choice of colours for a change.' Her gleeful look fell away. 'She sent some random tablets for you, Mum. Don't know what that's about. Is Auntie Manda a drug pusher now, or something?'

Karen forced a tight smile. 'Well, possibly, you never know with Manda, do you? Look, I think I'm going to take that tea to bed after all. I'll bring yours up too and we'll have more of a chat in the morning, okay? I must be getting old when a trip up to town feels this tiring!'

'You're not old, Mum, you just need to do it more often.'

'Well, perhaps you're right. Don't stay up too late, okay?'

'I won't, love you.'

'Love you, darling. Night-night.'

Chapter 8

'*Full fathom five thy father lies.*'

Tash thought she could probably have got some sort of compassionate exemption from having *The Tempest* as a set text, but nobody had thought to ask if she was bothered by it. Least of all her mum, who just giggled when she told her, and then went on about how she'd seen it in Stratford on a school trip in the early 1980s when Ariel's tights had caused collective hysteria amongst the Sevenoaks Grammar School girls.

Instead of studying, Tash was wedged in her window seat looking down over the back garden where Karen stood, like a suburban Prospero, waving her mobile phone around at a couple of bewildered Eastern Europeans trying to erect the marquee. It was obvious that she loved this house. She couldn't resist taking every opportunity to show it off, like she was the chatelaine of fucking Chatsworth or something. They used to live in a little Victorian terrace close to the station until they got this with Jonathan's life insurance money and the inheritance from Tasha's gran. Tash knew in her heart that her mother had been devastated when her dad died, but his careful investments had undoubtedly provided a silver lining. When she was feeling uncharitable, Tash occasionally wondered if, given the choice, Karen would have picked the house and the money over having her husband back.

That was what the party was about – Karen's chance to show off her gorgeous house, her charming daughters, her wonderful charity work. Tash wasn't sure quite what it was that her mother felt she had to prove, but it was bloody exhausting watching her doing it. Callie said she wanted a party – what twelve-year-old wouldn't? But this was Karen's own vanity project, make no mistake.

Still, at least Stanno was coming.

He'd heard about the Valentine's card. Of course, he had; the video got something like seventeen hundred hits. But he'd come up to Tash a few days afterwards to tell her that he'd had a word with Lola. Apparently, he let her know that he and Tash had been mates for years and she should lay off. All of which would have had zero impact other than making him feel like he'd earned some brownie points ... except that two days after that he actually asked her to go out with him.

It wasn't like when they were in first or second year and (after lots of pushing from the girls) a boy would say 'will you go out with me?' to one of the girls and if she said yes everyone would start saying that they were boyfriend and girlfriend. So, he didn't ask her out to be his girlfriend, but he did ask her out to an actual thing. It was a band showcase. One of the local pubs was putting it on and it was open to sixteens and up so the door policy wasn't as strict as it usually would be.

She had a bit of a panic in case they asked for ID, because she wasn't going to be sixteen until July. But the doorman wasn't really fussed. Stanno got one of his mates to get her a vodka and lemonade, but she wasn't really that keen on it, plus she'd just started the dieting thing so she only sipped it and stirred the ice around until it melted. They stood around in a group, unable to chat much because of the noise of the bands. But Stanno had his arms around her shoulders the whole time and Lola and her mates were shooting her these looks like they couldn't decide whether they hated her or suddenly wanted to be besties with her.

Then, at the end, Stanno walked her home and they had a quick kiss in the street. It wasn't like it was her first kiss or anything, but it felt more grown-up than anything she'd done before. His lips were soft and dry and he smelt of stale lager. When Tash got home her phone pinged with an invitation from Lola to join the Panda Eyes WhatsApp group, which, for some unknown reason, is what Lola had called the group that only had about twenty of the most popular girls in it.

Best of all, Stanno and Tash had become a thing. They went out most weekends on their own or with friends, and hung around together at school when he wasn't playing football. Tash was working on her history teacher to let her sit next to him. It was just a shame he wasn't in Maths too. They were getting better at kissing – well, it felt that way to Tash anyway. Stanno was an only child with a room in the attic, so they could mess around a bit when she went over to his house. It wasn't like at home where there was always someone around just waiting for a chance to catch you out.

The party would be the first time he'd really spent any time at her house. The first time he'd met her sisters, or her mum (not that Tash was bothered what her mum made of him). So maybe the party wouldn't be totally hideous after all.

Chapter 9

Misty
2019

The call from Andrew Dyer had been a shock, but not a huge one. They'd kept in touch a little over the years, mainly through mutual college friends from the old music crowd. He had been asking her to come to Karen Neville's fiftieth.

'I don't think so, Andrew, I've not spoken to Karen since we were at Cambridge.'

'Exactly, it would be nice for you to see each other again.'

'Or maybe not.'

'Well, you might both get a pleasant surprise. And if it doesn't work out, we can just leave and go to the pub. Is Eusebio around? What else would you be doing?'

Knowingly or not, he'd hit on her weak spot. Her Costa Rican partner, Eusebio, was due to return from one of his lengthy photographic expeditions into the Amazonian jungle. While he was away, she could expect nothing more than a couple of ten-minute sat-phone calls a week. Now he would be ensconced in front of his computer, sorting and editing the images, fulfilling his various commissions and hustling for sales. The low-maintenance relationship suited her because it didn't interfere with her drive to devote herself to the clinic.

As friends had settled, had families and moved to the suburbs or away from London altogether, both the pressure and opportunity to engage in much of a social life had declined. The chances of her being busy on any given Saturday with anything other than a weekend on-call duty were minimal. Even if she had been on call, she'd taken on so many extra shifts from junior colleagues over the years, she wouldn't have struggled to find someone who owed her a swap.

'Eusebio's due back that week, but we don't have any plans yet ...'

'Exactly. Bring him along then. It starts at half two. Meet me at Twickenham station around three, there's a good coffee place – I'll send you a link – and the three of us can walk over to Karen's together.'

Now it was only a couple of hours before Andrew would be waiting for them at the café. She sighed, wafting two dresses on coat hangers in front of the mirror. It was impossible to summon the enthusiasm to actually try them on. The bedroom door creaked open and Eusebio slunk in, unshaven and still in the joggers and T-shirt he had pulled on when he got out of bed.

'Well, what do you think?'

'The red one. The colour suits you more, and the dress give you more ... oomph.' He mimed uplift in his chest region, and she couldn't help but smile. That was one benefit of living with a Costa Rican – in her experience there were few British men who would commit to an opinion on an outfit, even fewer with the frankness and (she had to admit) accuracy that Eusebio generally managed.

'You'll have to get a move on.' She nodded towards the linen suit that was hanging on the wardrobe door. 'We should be leaving in half an hour.'

His shifty look told her what he was going to say before he opened his mouth.

'I'm not so sure, *cariña*. I'm already late getting the proof shots back to Marco and the jet lag is really killing me at the moment.'

'But you said you'd come. That's part of the reason you flew back yesterday.'

He shrugged. 'You go. There is no reason for you not to have fun with your friends because I am a miserable old grump-head. Wear the red dress. Have some fun.'

'But they're not my friends, that's the point. I'm hardly going to know anyone.' She could hear the irritation creep into her voice, and knew he must hear it too. But Eusebio was an expert at refusing to take the bait. He simply shrugged again, more cheerfully this time, and flopped down to sit on the bed.

'Then where is the problem? If they are not your friends, don't go see them! I'm going to email Marco and go back to bed.' He stroked the duvet cover and put on an exaggerated smoulder. 'Would be better with you here too.'

She shut her eyes briefly and then turned back to the mirror. He'd promised to come. There was no point in rising to it, though, she'd simply get more and more wound up whilst he could keep up his 'what's the problem?' insouciance indefinitely. Sometimes it was like living with a fourteen-year-old.

Still, it wasn't like she hadn't dealt with all of this for years. He put up with her erratic hours, her obsessing over patients and her stress. She put up with his ... well, let's say *individu-*

59

alism, even if it did drive her bloody mental at times. And of course, he was right about the dress. She dug out a bra that would give her enough support to allow the dress to pull off its magic and wriggled into her outfit before getting started on some make-up. Tempting though it might be to use Eusebio as an excuse to give the whole thing a miss, she'd promised Andrew she would come and she hated the thought of being flaky. She squirted some perfume then went downstairs to pull on her heels and pick up the bouquet that she'd bought that morning.

'See you later!'

'Have fun!'

Normal couples probably shared more affectionate good-byes. But then normal couples would be going to the sodding party together.

*

The house was almost exactly as she'd imagined. A Victorian villa, high walls and an immaculate gravel drive giving little away to the outside world. Today, though, the large wooden gates were open and a posy of balloons above an artfully makeshift wooden arrow sign directed guests down the side of the house to the party in the back garden.

'Sounds busy,' observed Andrew.

Misty nodded her agreement. A hubbub of noise was already bubbling down the side passageway, and the street had been jam-packed with parked cars.

A substantial-looking marquee loomed at the far end of the garden, which presumably explained why Karen had felt able to risk organising a garden party for the first weekend of April. As it turned out, the gamble had paid off. After a week of fine weather, the garden was dry and the carefully tended beds brimming with spring bulbs. Guests milled around, visibly thrilled to be outside in the first really decent weather of the year. The sides of the marquee itself were rolled up and Misty could make out the shadowy shape of tables and what appeared to be a bar. Beyond a handful of people waiting for drinks, though, the interior was deserted.

A young girl who looked moody and overheated in black jeans and Doc Martens offered her a glass of something fizzy. Andrew had filled her in on the basic details of Karen's children. The daughters were presumably being pressed into waitress service. He also reminded her about the death of her husband. Misty remembered being told something of it at the time, although she couldn't say by whom. Sipping the drink, she smiled despite herself; you couldn't get away from the fact there was something utterly glorious about a sunny spring afternoon in well-tended garden.

She moved out of the shadows of the side passage. As she walked forward, she scanned the scene for Karen, or for anyone else who might be here from college. It was a very big garden, and there must have been at least eighty people milling around – if not a hundred. She hadn't expected anything on such a grand scale.

'There's Karen,' said Andrew, pointing off to the left, and Misty was grateful to have a moment or two to take in her former friend unobserved. She looked move confident now. Misty remembered Karen hanging back on the edges of conversations; now she stood assertively, feet planted apart, her red hair mellower but still striking, swinging out over her shoulders. She was holding court amongst five or six others, entertaining them with a story by the looks of it. But then it was her birthday party, it was hardly a surprise that she should be in her element here.

Andrew began walking towards her and gave a wave. The movement must have caught Karen's eye, because she swung round and called, 'Andrew!', her voice cutting through the hubbub like crystal. She'd always had that knack, and the sound of it brought back the old Karen more than anything Misty had seen so far. Immediately leaving the group she was with, Karen crossed the lawn towards them. Misty watched her look grow quizzical, and then astonished.

'Misty Jardine?'

Misty nodded confirmation.

Karen was with them now. She grasped Misty by both forearms and kissed her cheeks.

'My God, my God, I don't believe it! How long has it been?' She turned quickly to Andrew. 'You didn't say anything!'

He shrugged. 'You brought me a ghost, so I thought I'd bring you one. Seriously, I hope you don't mind. When we spoke the other week, you seemed ... maybe in a difficult place. I thought perhaps it would do you good to rekindle some links with the past. If I got it wrong, blame me.' He turned to include Misty. 'Both of you, blame me, not each other.'

Since breaking off their initial embrace, Misty and Karen had circled each other cautiously like a pair of fighting cats.

'Well, I can't think of a better birthday surprise,' said Karen, breaking the silence. 'Come on, let me get you both some champagne, then we can have a proper catch-up.' She kept up the chatter as they crossed the lawn. 'I'm trying to think of the last time we saw each other. Would it have been Benjy

62

and Kirsten's wedding? Evie was a flower girl and I'm sure I remember seeing you.'

'Yes, we were there. I remember Evie looking cute as a button. I suppose she's practically an adult now?'

'Yes, twenty – I can't believe it. She's here somewhere. As are Benjy and Kirsten, actually. I suppose the weddings have rather dried up since then, haven't they? I shudder to think of the number of people I've not seen since Jonathan's funeral.'

Misty murmured an apology. She would have gone to the funeral, but she and Eusebio were in Chile at the time. Karen brushed off her condolences but the word 'funeral' jarred Misty back to a sleety April day. A flat fenland churchyard and a gaggle of college friends in black, their heels sinking into the mud. She shivered, wondering if Karen was also thinking of the last funeral they *did* both attend together. Hoping to banish that from her mind, she asked tentatively how Karen had coped in the years since Jonathan's death.

'God, I've missed him every day. I mean, not like he ever *did* anything.' She gave a brittle laugh. 'He was a City dad, you know, expected a pat on the back if he was home for bath time once a week. Took them to the park at weekends and they'd come back missing a glove – or even a bike!'

Misty smiled. The set-up was familiar enough even if she'd never experienced it herself. 'But they adored him, and he adored them. I had adult company when they went to bed and the chance to read a novel while he taught them to swim on holiday. Luckily, we'd made some investments and he had great life insurance cover – he was always very nerdy and cautious about that sort of stuff, which turned out to be a great blessing. So, I've had it easy compared to a lot of people.'

'I bet it doesn't always feel that way, though.'

'No. It doesn't.' Karen's deep inhalation signalled the end of that part of the conversation. 'But what about you, Misty? Are you still with ... Estabio?'

'Eusebio. Yes. He's just got back from a trip or he would have come along. I'm afraid Andrew was rather free with his invitations.'

'And now he's disappeared. It's almost like he's trying to be a very unsubtle matchmaker. So, are you married?'

'No. I used to say "not yet", but I think I'm probably safe to stick with "no".' She struggled to find a label for Eusebio. They were too old to be boyfriend and girlfriend, and she disliked the word 'partner'. They had no children and his work took him back to South America for weeks on end. Most of her friends struggled a little to compute their relationship. In the scheme of things, Karen's reasonable attempt at his name counted as a good effort. Her distraction had caused a pause in the conversation, which threatened to become awkward. Casting her mind about, she recalled the strange comment Andrew had made introducing them.

'What did Andrew mean, about bringing you a ghost?'

'Oh.' Karen paused, flagging down a waitress to offer Misty some canapés. 'You remember there was that terrorist incident on the tube a few weeks ago, the bomb that didn't go off properly?'

'Yes.'

'Well, there was a picture they were using in the news footage ...'

Misty knew exactly what she was going to say next. 'The woman behind the girl in the burn mask ...'

Karen nodded, and there was a glow in her eyes that looked almost fevered. 'You saw it too?'

'Yes, I mean I saw the news report. I saw the resemblance.'

Karen lowered her voice and grabbed Misty's arm. 'But what if it wasn't just a resemblance? What if it actually *was* her? I mean, she could have chosen to disappear, couldn't she? Even Andrew didn't see the body.'

There was something surreal about it. Karen was a woman of substance, able to gather all these people about her, in the beautiful gardens of her enviable villa. In the blink of eye, she'd changed entirely. Misty shifted uncomfortably.

'Whoever was in that picture, it definitely wasn't Alex.'

The change that had fallen over Karen disappeared as though a veil had been lifted.

'Of course, you're right. My imagination is running away with me. You were always the practical one.'

Misty let the remark pass, neither confirming or challenging it but choosing to take another canapé from a timely passing teenager instead.

'So,' continued Karen, apparently trying to steer the conversation back to something less controversial, 'did you continue with medicine then?'

'Yes, yes, I did.'

'And do you still do it now?'

'Yes. I'm a consultant. I run a clinic attached to a teaching hospital. It's busy but rewarding. I can't imagine doing anything else to be honest.'

'That's fantastic. Good for you. What sort of clinic is it? What do you specialise in?'

'Eating disorders.'

The colour drained from Karen's face. 'Is that meant to be some sort of joke?'

'No, no. I ... well, after what happened to Alex ... I got

interested, then I got involved. I wanted to make a difference. It's not that surprising, is it?'

Karen's hostess smile had returned, more brittle than before. Misty sensed that it had taken her an effort to pull herself together. It seemed odd that she should be so shaken by Misty's career choice, especially after all these years.

'No ... no, I suppose not. I guess I've just always tried to avoid the topic. I ... I found it hard.'

'I'm sure we both did. But people cope in different ways. And it's not the best subject to be dwelling on when it's your birthday. In fact, you don't want to spend all your time stuck with me ... Go on, I'll find out where Andrew's wandered off to. You should be chatting to all these people who have come to celebrate with you. I can tell you for free there wouldn't be anything like this number turn up for me.'

Karen muttered some pleasantry and then took Misty's suggestion and walked away. Misty was startled by how dazed she seemed, almost shell-shocked. But then it was no light endeavour to organise this sort of extravaganza, never mind the shock of having Misty turn up unannounced.

Chapter 10

Karen did not feel well.

When she'd opened her eyes and squinted at the clock it had said 09:13. She'd pushed herself up and surprised herself with the ease of the movement. Apart from a slight headache she felt pretty good, even sprightly. She crossed the room and poured a glass of water at the sink in the corner. Catching sight of her reflection she grimaced – her eye make-up hadn't survived as well as she had. As she sipped the water and set about repairing the damage, a sort of pride swelled inside her. Maybe she had a knack for this drinking thing. She'd matched Octavia drink for drink and here she was – practically good as new. It had been her and Alex's last session drinking with the Valkyries as invited guests. In the next day or two they would find out whether they were going to be invited to initiation or told to sod off. Alex was a shoo-in, of course, but after last night, Karen had felt quietly confident.

Except that had been four hours ago, and she was beginning to realise that she must still have been drunk. It had all unravelled when she'd gone to the buttery for a late breakfast and the sight of congealed fried eggs on the hotplate had prompted a green-gilled dash to the ladies. She had emerged to a posse of 'concerned' students waving toothpaste in her face and making barfing noises that emphatically failed to match the horrific sounds she'd been producing in the toilets minutes earlier.

Hoping that some fresh air might help, she'd decided to leave college and found herself wandering along the Backs. An autumn mist hung heavy over the meadows, pierced by the stately gothic rooflines of the oldest and most prestigious colleges, as well as by the looming trees burnished with their autumn colours. Unfortunately, as she walked the hangover set in with increasing vengeance. She found a bench and slumped down, staring into the water and trying to work out whether she was hoping to be sick again or hoping not to.

It would have been nice, she considered, with more than a touch of self-pity, to have a friend with her now. Before going down to the buttery, she'd tried Alex's room and then, more reluctantly, gone to knock on Misty's door too, but there was no answer from either of them. It was always possible that Alex was still comatose, but generally she was an early riser, even after a night on the tiles. Karen thought it was more likely that she and Misty were off doing something together. The uncomfortable twisting in her stomach intensified at the thought.

Envy shot through Karen's friendships like the streamers of green weed fluttering in the water at her feet. It had always been that way. It wasn't edifying, but she couldn't help it. She couldn't shake a profound dissatisfaction with her life that seemed so predictable and pedestrian. She envied Misty's authenticity: the way she could speak about music or politics and everyone would listen and nod appreciatively, because she came from the north and her dad worked in a factory and had even been the dole. On top of that, Misty was attractive, in that sort of disarming way that people didn't notice at first, and then couldn't help noticing. And there was an easy inclusivity about her company; without trying, she would draw a crowd around her in the college bar or in the buttery. Compared to Alex, though, even Misty seemed dull and pedestrian.

Karen and Misty revolved around Alex like two planets around a dazzling sun. While Karen's attitude to Misty veered between envy, annoyance and vague tolerance, she adored Alex and would spend every minute in her company if she could. She was never happier than when they strolled along to lectures, arms linked, heads bent together in giggling confidence, Misty safely packed off for a day in the lab. But even underlying the adoration, there was jealousy.

Because she and Alex read the same subject, Karen saw first-hand how clever Alex was. She grasped ideas instantly – and had the deftness to play and juggle with them – whilst for Karen they remained slippery and difficult to keep hold of, or else altogether out of reach. This wouldn't be so bad, if Alex was just a brain on legs, but she was anything but. She was beautiful too – much more obviously than Misty. She had the assurance and polish of a privileged upbringing, but one that shared none of the staidness of Karen's.

Everyone adored Alex's bohemian academic parents – rumour had it her dad had inherited a fortune, along with a title he disdained using. Her mum was a refugee from Franco's regime in Spain. Their party last term had been the talk of the whole university. In the future, Alex and Misty would be people who mattered. Karen would just be someone who'd gone to university with them. Probably an admissions mistake.

It wasn't hard to imagine that more than one Karen Cooper might have applied.

'There you are!'

Alex's voice jolted her out of her reverie.

'Alex. Misty. How did you know where to find me?'

'Sara Neves told us about you puking in the buttery. She said you'd headed out in this direction.'

'I didn't actually puke in the buttery, you know.'

'Yeah, details, details ... I hope you're looking forward to your meeting with the dean when he finds out.'

Karen felt her stomach lurch again.

'God, she looks like she's about to puke again,' put in Misty. 'Karen? Just do it into the stream, yeah?'

'There's no need for you to laugh, Misty, just because you aren't on probation with the Valkyries.'

'No. And I wouldn't want to be either. But I did go out to get you Alka-Seltzer, Coca-Cola and bacon for superior quality, non-buttery bacon butties.' She waved a carrier bag in the air. 'I woke Alex up and spent ten minutes banging on your door before I realised you'd actually got yourself out.'

'Oh.' Karen felt momentarily taken aback, but then told herself that Misty had probably only included her in her hangover-relief efforts to impress Alex. In fact, Alex had probably given her the money and the shopping list. 'Well, thanks. I suppose we should go back then.'

'Finally,' said Alex, tossing her hair. 'I feel like death warmed up too. At least it's a Saturday.'

Karen picked herself up and they began to meander back to towards college, the three of them spread out across the width of the footpath, Alex, inevitably, in the centre.

'Maybe we should head over to your place later?' ventured

Karen, feeling buoyed by the fact they had come to find her. 'We could rent a video and crash on the sofas and go to bed at about eight.'

But Alex's face darkened. 'Not this weekend.'

'Why? What's up?'

'Things just aren't great at home.'

'What can be not great? Your home's basically paradise. You should try coming to Kent and hanging out with my parents sometime. It's practically a vicarage.'

'Just leave off her, Karen.' Misty's voice was sharp.

Karen's cheeks burned like a scolded child. She wished she didn't feel so crap with this hangover. She'd obviously blundered into something, but it was just like Misty to try to take the moral high ground. Looking up, she spotted the wrought iron of the college gates materialising in the mist. They walked the last couple of minutes back to Alex's room in silence.

*

'Maybe I should have said something before,' said Alex, picking up their conversation as they sat around with mugs of tea and bacon butties. 'My mum's, well ... I suppose a bit mentally unstable ...' She was looking down, picking at a sequin on one of her Indian cushion covers. 'Sometimes she's up and fabulous and inspirational, but then other times all the stuff that she went through when she was younger sort of comes back to haunt her. She gets very controlling – Dad and I aren't allowed to do stuff.'

A look of confusion crossed Misty's face. 'But what do you mean? She can't stop your dad, surely? And you're an adult too now ...'

Alex grimaced. 'It's hard to explain, it's sort of emotional – she can rant and rave and argue and cry. From the outside it sounds bizarre, but you don't know what it's like until you're in it.' She looked around at her friends, catching eyes with each of them in turn. 'I know you both think I have this charmed life. And I know in lots of ways I do, and that other people go through much tougher stuff – more obviously tough stuff.'

Neither replied. Karen felt awkward and she guessed that Misty did too. She couldn't deny that she thought Alex had things pretty cushy, and that she didn't quite get what Alex was trying to tell them.

'That's why I'm still here and not at Oxford or somewhere else,' Alex continued.

'Because she needs you, like, like she might if she was ill or something?' Misty offered.

'She *is* ill,' Alex corrected her quickly. 'You're the one who wants to be doctor. If you don't get it, how is anyone else meant to?'

'Okay, sorry. I'm just trying to understand.'

'Yeah, well, it's partly that she needs me, but also that all this weird family dynamic had an effect on me too. You know how I took a year out, yeah?'

'Yeah, when you were travelling,' said Karen.

But Alex shook her head. 'I wasn't actually travelling. I mean, I've been to all those places, but just on family holidays and things. I've never done the proper backpacker thing.'

'Right ...'

'Have you heard of anorexia?' Alex's voice was almost a mumble, her gaze fixed on the plate in her hand, with its virtually untouched bacon sandwich.

'Like Karen Carpenter?' Karen added, perhaps more eagerly than was appropriate.

'Yeah, but without the shit, whingeing songs.' The familiar Alex was back with a wicked smile that lit up her face with mischief.

'You were too ill to start university last year?' said Misty.

Alex nodded. 'I was an inpatient for a bit in this private clinic stuck out in the countryside. It was voluntary; I never got sectioned. It was full of boarding-school girls – we did the full Enid Blyton, everything except the midnight feasts. Anyway, I'm better now, but it's given Mum an excuse not to let me out of her sight. And the crazy thing about that is that I'd probably have been fine if it wasn't for her in the first place. It's a control thing, and there was only space for one person to have control in our family.'

Karen's mind was spinning. She naturally ran on the plump side and had had more than one conversation with Alex about dieting. She'd also noticed Alex sometimes got very enthusiastic about food, especially when they were eating out, only to leave most of it on her plate. But if she'd thought about that at all she'd have put it down to her friend's magpie-like excitability. Despite those small clues, Alex had never hinted at any of this before. This wasn't casual stuff, this was a shining jewel of a confidence she could hug to herself, using it to ward off doubts about whether Alex really saw her as a friend, or just put up with her hanging around. The germ of a different thought was forming at the back of her mind too, as she quickly tried to recalibrate her assumptions about Alex's charmed life. Knowledge was power, and Alex's brief revelations were packed with the explosive potential of a bomb.

Misty looked thoughtful. Clearly the information was as unexpected for her as it had been for Karen. Finally, she spoke.

'You still need to be careful, though, I suppose? Do you still see anyone – a doctor I mean – to keep an eye on it?'

But Alex brushed her question aside, putting on a haughty, matronly voice she often used jokingly.

'My darlings, never fear, I am in the best of health save for this *appalling* hangover.'

Karen raised her mug in a mock toast.

'But seriously,' said Alex, returning to her normal voice. 'You two are my best friends. I don't mind courting insane levels of jealousy in every other saddo in this parochial city, but I think it's only fair for both of you to know that anyone wishing to step into my shoes ought to be very careful what they wish for.'

Chapter 11

Misty
2019

What was she doing here? Eusebio had had the right idea all along. She and Karen had never really got along that well. The thing they'd had in common was Alex, and after she died, they'd quickly gone off in different directions, as disconnected as two wheels if you whipped away the bike bit in the middle. Andrew was happily talking with some guys who worked in banking – she wasn't surprised to see that he was a consummate networker. She'd be perfectly happy to catch up with him over a pint in the pub, but didn't see any attraction in hanging around at his shoulder and nodding along with chat about the AIM market and investment rounds.

She thought she might just slip off when, slightly mortifyingly, Karen homed in on her in one of her hostess rounds.

'It's my fault,' she said. 'You floored me a bit when we were talking about your work. But I should be finding someone fun for you to talk to.' She lowered her voice. 'Believe me, there are a lot of very *not* fun people you could end up stuck with a long time if you leave it to chance. Wait, just let me get rid of this.'

She waved an arm and shouted, 'Tasha,' and after a moment or two the girl in the Doc Martens emerged from a huddle of teenagers lounging at the far end of the decking.

'This is my middle one,' said Karen, as the girl made their way over to them. 'Evie's over there. I can't see Callie now but you'll spot her. She'd with her bestie, Bea, and they're the only two around that aren't fully grown. Although she's twelve going on twenty-five, of course. They have to go through that diva phase before they turn into rational human beings.' Karen broke off her pen portraits as Tasha arrived at her side. 'Go and hand these out, will you?' she instructed, passing over the canapé tray. 'And I mean to the actual guests, not just to you and Evie's mates. Okay?'

Tasha shrugged, but she started off towards the main lawn where more of the 'actual' guests were gathered. 'There's another two in the kitchen, and the trays need to go back in there when you're done,' Karen called after her.

There was an awkward, coltish grace to Tasha's walk and Misty felt a flicker of intrigue despite – or perhaps because of – the fact that the girl had shown zero interest in her. Karen and Jonathan had had too little time together, yet they'd still managed to create Tash, who was now poised on the brink of a whole new life of her own, and two other girls, all of them individuals, all of them complete new lives. The sight of them rekindled the old ache Misty had felt as, one after another, her friends had started having babies. It took her by surprise. She'd long since accepted that she wasn't going to be a mother. But here was a novel loss, unexamined until now. Not of the children she would never have, but of the nascent adults they would never become. She hugged her wrap closer in spite of the heat, and thought of Eusebio sprawled on the sofa at home, engrossed in his laptop and mainlining coffee. They weren't children people; they had careers, interests, conversation. They'd made their choices, as, indeed, had Karen.

Following Karen, she allowed herself to be led onto the gravel path that circled the garden in order for her hostess to find someone to palm her off on so that she herself could get back to whatever urgent party duty might present itself next. She would chat for half an hour or so to whomever Karen thought she might get on with then make a discreet exit, she resolved. The party was clearly a rolling success – she didn't need to stick around.

'Kirsten!' Karen's voice broke through Misty's thoughts. 'Where's Benjy? Oh, he's gone to the bar. Right, well, this is Misty Jardine. Remember – she was at college with Benjy and me? Misty, you'll have met Kirsten at the wedding, of course, but nobody gets to talk to the bride at those things.'

Misty remembered the dark-haired, slightly sallow sort of boy, who had hung around with the sports club/drinking society crowd despite seeming neither very sporty nor particularly obnoxious. They'd vaguely kept in touch over the years, including that slightly unexpected invitation to his wedding.

Karen continued, 'Benjy met Kirsten when he was working in Hong Kong. She's far too good for him. Anyway, I think the pair of you will get on. Kirsten, are you still working with teenagers? Misty's a doctor. She deals with eating disorders, so you both know how difficult teenagers can be, even without the joys of having them living in your house.'

As Karen concluded her little introduction, she waved a hand towards Tasha, who chose that moment to glower in their direction in an aptly stereotypical way. Rolling her eyes, Karen told Misty and Kirsten that she'd leave them to it.

'Well, nice to see you again,' Kirsten ventured, sticking out a hand. She had a soft American accent.

'You too. So, well, Karen wasn't exactly clear about what you do?'

Kirsten giggled. 'That's probably because she doesn't really know. I'm a glorified careers officer really. I go into a lot of the South London colleges and try to help kids work out what they might do next. We try to raise aspirations – make the clever ones realise that they could go to uni, or could go to a better uni. We can signpost them in the direction of mentoring programmes and things like that. It's not all that interesting ...'

'Not at all, it sounds fantastic. And Karen has a point about the crossover – so many of my patients are in that age range. It's such a time of transition for them. It's hardly surprising that some of them struggle.'

Kirsten nodded enthusiastically. 'Yes, although my impression was always that anorexia sufferers were unlikely to be the ones lacking in ambition or aspiration. Isn't it the high achievers, who put too much stress on themselves?'

'Well, I could talk to you for hours about the causes of the disease, and there's actually still a lot that we don't know for sure.' Misty always found it tricky to talk about her work in social situations. Eating disorders – especially anorexia – was a subject that everyone had an opinion on. She felt an obligation to engage with that and try to gently educate people without coming across as lecturing, or even just downright rude. It could be a fine line to tread at times.

But Kirsten wasn't waiting for Misty to elaborate. Her eyes were elsewhere, gazing across the lawn, and she nodded towards Tasha, who had passed them a moment ago. Now the girl was talking to Karen – or rather being talked at by Karen – judging from the body language of the pair of them.

'Now there's one that you should have your eye on.' Kirsten lowered her voice even further, taking pains not to be overheard by Karen. 'Tasha, their middle daughter. Karen's always on about Evie, because she's had a few wild moments. Tasha gets great grades and has nice friends and keeps her nose out of trouble.'

'And that's all to the good, surely?' Misty felt slightly uncomfortable at the way this woman was whispering gossip about Karen's family. Misty might have been out of touch with Karen for a while, but she still considered Karen an old friend and she had been, at one point, a close one.

'Well, yes, of course, but I just get this sense that she's been unhappy recently. Benjy and I were round for Sunday lunch last week and she seemed positively miserable.'

'She is a teenager.'

'I know, that's what Karen says.' They both looked again towards the mother and daughter. Karen had cut off her lecture in order to greet some new arrivals, but Misty sensed that whatever gripe she was taking up with Tasha had been put on hold rather than finished with. Tasha was standing sheepishly where her mother had left her, pushing bits of gravel around with her toe and looking as if she'd rather be anywhere than this idyllic garden. Kirsten was still talking: '... so she barely touched her food on Sunday. I mean, literally, almost nothing. You could tell that Karen was mortified although we all just kept talking about other things. And I'm convinced that she's lost weight. They go up and down teenage girls, don't they? But the last few times I've seen Tash she's been wearing really baggy stuff. I mean look at her, who would wear a jumper like that on a day like today?'

As far as Misty was concerned, the oversized sweatshirt above skinny jeans looked quite normal. Tasha was hardly the only teenager here who was reluctant to show off her body. But it was equally possible that Kirsten was right. The sweatshirt could be hiding weight loss – it was a common enough tactic for the girls who came to the clinic. Often, they would layer up other clothes under a baggy top, not just to obscure their body shape, but also to add extra ounces for the weigh-in. She knew girls who would cut their toenails before weighing themselves at home, but would attend a weigh-in at the clinic with coins or even cutlery hidden in their clothes to try to deceive the medics.

'So, do you know the girls well then?' She kept her question to Kirsten neutral, broadening the focus to include Tasha's sisters.

The other woman shrugged. 'We see Karen quite a bit. Sometimes the girls are around, more often not. But you get to know them over the years.'

'And are you worried about Tasha?'

It was clear that Kirsten was uncomfortable to be put on the spot. She glanced past Misty towards the tent, obviously hoping for her husband to turn up with the drinks and put an end to the awkward conversation. There was a moment's pause, and then a smile broke across her face. Misty turned to see a short man, swarthy and now slightly overweight, but definitely Benjy from college, striding towards them with a tray of what looked like G&Ts. Kirsten gave him a quick wave, making sure that he'd spotted her, but then reached out and touched Misty's arm, pulling her closer.

'If Karen asks, then you didn't hear it from me. But, yes, I think Tasha needs help. I've tried to chat to her, but she shuts me out. She's a nice kid. I've known her since she was born. And I'm worried.'

Benjy's arrival at Kirsten's elbow meant that Misty didn't have to reply. More than that – the other woman's warning look told her she'd better not.

'Misty Jardine! It *is* you, isn't it? God, it's been about a million years.'

'Yep, pretty much that.' She held out her hand and Benjy kissed both cheeks instead. He smelt of alcohol and sweat masked by some sort of peppery shower gel.

'You've met my wife, Kirsten, our two not-so-little horrors are around somewhere too. How about you, who are you here with?'

'Oh, I came alone. My partner picked today to come down with a bug. I should probably be getting back actually. He'll be expecting the Florence Nightingale routine.'

She fended off his attempts to press one of the spare G&Ts on her, and managed to extract herself after only a few minutes of college anecdotes and career résumé high points. She swapped numbers with Kirsten, but doing it was easier than finding a way to refuse politely, and Benjy showed no shame in boasting that she organised their social lives and whilst it would be lovely to catch up again it would only happen if Kirsten put the effort in.

*

Hopefully her second attempt at leaving the party would be more successful, but she did need to go to the loo first. Having practically downed that glass of wine, the last thing she wanted was to end up dancing around and desperate before she got back home. The bi-fold doors led onto a kitchen where regimented platters of canapés were set out, awaiting their turn for delivery to the guests. The sink was piled up with the returnees, smeared with sauces and lumps of food that no one had had chance to scrape yet. A sign, obviously put up for the party, directed her to the downstairs cloakroom. It was occupied and two other women, who seemed to know each other already, chatted whilst waiting their turn.

'There's another one on the upstairs landing,' one of them told Misty. 'You go – Karen won't mind. Don't wait for us. We'd stand and chatter all day given the chance.'

She got the distinct impression that she was intruding on some gossip the two of them were keen to have aired in private. Because of that, rather than any particular urgency to find the toilet, she took the woman's advice and set off up the stairs.

She paused at the top, getting her bearings, when she heard a muffled sobbing sound coming from a room to her left. The door was ajar, and decorated letters, clearly many years old, spelt out the word 'Natasha'. Well, if there was reason to be worried about Tasha, then she'd never have a better chance to find out. She turned back, knocked softly, and then pushed the door forward.

The girl was sitting cross-legged at the head of the bed, which faced towards the door. The first thing Misty noticed was that she still had her Doc Martens on. Seeing the shoes on the bedspread, she tried not to wince. The girl stared up at her, red-eyed, but belligerent.

'Tasha?'

No response.

'I'm Misty. I went to uni with your Mum. You sound upset. What can I do to help?'

The best way to talk to the girl came instinctively from her years of clinical experience. Her tone was gentle but firm – the sort of tone you would use with a frightened animal. Don't ask if she's okay when she's obviously not; ask what you can do to help. And smile.

'Nothing.' A muttered response and a shrug of the shoulders. It was a more positive start than Misty had expected. She smiled again, encouraging Tasha to engage with her. Don't offer to leave – if that's what the girl wants, she'll have to ask for it.

For a few heartbeats they sized each other up. Then a flounce and a dramatic sigh from the bed.

'This party's so fucking stupid. I just want it to end.'

'Well, your mum seems to be enjoying it, and it is her birthday after all.'

She snorted. 'It was a month ago, actually; she just wanted to make the party later to show off her precious garden.'

'Well, she got lucky with that then, everyone is enjoying being out in the sunshine.'

'I bet they're all as fake as she is.' The last word was almost spat out. 'She's out there smiling and chatting away when she hates most of the people here. She'll be slagging them all off when they're gone.'

Misty had a sudden, unformed memory of lurking scornfully in the background at her own parents' parties. Surely there was no judgement more harsh than that of a teenager on their elders. She bit back a smile. As far as Misty could see, there didn't seem anything particularly out of the ordinary or unhealthy in Tasha's venom. The girl was undeniably thin, though. Twig-like arms emerged from the baggy sweater. The bone structure in her wringing hands and delicate jawline was sharper and more obvious than it should be. Was she dangerously underweight? It was impossible to tell without a proper examination, taking a full history. The elder sister seemed to be slim too, but not worryingly so.

'Well, sorry for intruding on you,' Misty said, flashing a warm smile towards Tasha. 'I was actually just leaving, but I suspect it may be quite a while before you get your house back.'

'Probably,' said Tasha, picking up a magazine from the bed. Misty turned to go, but something made her turn back from the doorway. She opened the clutch bag she'd brought with her and fished around at the bottom. Surely there would be a business card in there – the hospital had had hundreds printed up and she'd stashed them in every handbag rather than bin them.

'Here ...' She held the white slip of card out to Tasha. 'My number's on it. If you ever want a friendly ear to talk about stuff, give me a call. I've not really seen your mum in years, so I'm a neutral. And I talk with a lot of young people about the challenges they're facing.'

Tasha rolled her eyes. 'You mean like Kirsten "Puh-lease, I just wanna be your friend" Adams.' She made a puking gesture and Misty laughed because her impression of Kirsten actually had something to it.

'Well, hopefully not like that. I don't mind if you call or not. But you've got the number if you want to.'

'Yep. Bye then.' Tasha held Misty's gaze as she lifted the card and dropped it, letting it flutter into what looked like a pile of underwear on the floor beside the bed. Well, that was her call; Misty wasn't going to rise to it. She was going to get herself out of here and back to Kennington for a relaxed glass of sauvignon blanc and Netflix.

Chapter 12

Tasha
2019

It had gone one o'clock in the morning and her mum's friends were still infesting the back garden, drinking gin like there was going to be a shortage, ranting loudly about Brexit and generally embarrassing themselves. Joy.

Why would anyone even want to celebrate turning fifty, she wondered. You may as well celebrate being dead.

Evie, typically, was all over it. Handing round trays of party food and remembering people's names and stuff. Like it might help her get an internship or something. Or maybe she was looking for a rich banker wanting a second wife. Even Uncle Stu had noticed she was overdoing it earlier on and had to take her aside for 'a word', much to Tasha's amusement.

Still, it made a change for them to notice *something*. She might have guessed it would be Evie. Never mind the fact that she'd lost nine pounds in the last six weeks and nobody had bothered to say a single word of congratulations.

The losing weight bit was turning out to be easier than she'd imagined it would be. Although there had been times when the hanger had got pretty extreme. Tash certainly hadn't appreciated having to hand out those stupid canapés that afternoon. If people ever stopped to think about how many calories you get in a tempura prawn, then the Thai oceans would be safer places for the little creatures by far.

She reckoned it was because she had GCSEs coming up – everyone was just expecting her to be grumpsville anyway. In this world you had to be mad if you thought there was anything to be cheerful about. Between Trump and global warming, Tash knew that it would be a miracle if the human race was still running by the time she was old enough to be having a fiftieth birthday party.

The trick to dieting was willpower, and that was something Tash had always been good at. The first few pounds came off really easily, but then it started to slow up. Apparently, that's what happened – your body adjusted to taking in fewer calories. She had been reading some stuff on the internet to explain it, and she'd found some sites with really good tips on how to feel full and take your mind off eating and stuff. Some of the girls posting on there had gone waaaaay too far, though. They posted these pictures of themselves where they looked like freaky marble-heads on sticks and all the regular posters were like, 'babe, you look amaaazing' and Tash really felt like typing, 'whoa, girl, eat some chips'. But still, the tips were good.

She'd been all set to enjoy the party. She'd planned to have such a good time with Stanno that she wouldn't even be thinking about stuffing her face with mini-cheesecakes. But Lola and a couple of others let her down at the last minute, so there was no one really there to show him off too. Stanno seemed surprised that she'd not asked Claire and Sonal. It would be pointless to try to explain to him. Boys never really got all the school friendship politics stuff. It was too complicated for their little brains.

She really hadn't wanted to be awful to Sonal or to Claire. (Well, to Claire at least – Sonal sort of had it coming). But she was always going to be a target for people like Lola as long as she was hanging around with them. She could have pissed off Sonal and Claire and then found that Lola's crew still didn't want to know her either. And then where would she be? Loserville. It was a gamble and Tasha had taken it.

So, she'd dropped the two of them. Let them down gently as far as she could. One day she just quietly went to sit with Lola for lunch and that was that. She'd not really spoken much to Claire or Sonal since, though she was still sitting next to Sonal in Maths and History, which was awkwardsville. But she resolved that she couldn't let other people hold her back. Plus, on Lola's table they all had Diet Coke for lunch, which made the whole diet thing much easier than sitting next to those two pigging down canteen chips and chocolate muffins.

She could hardly undo all that careful work by inviting Claire and Sonal round to her mum's bash, could she? But then she and Stanno just didn't seem to have as much to say to each other as she'd imagined they would.

Eventually, when they'd both got a bit bored, they started to niggle at each other and he ended up trying to bully her into eating a cocktail sausage. He pretended not to understand what a big deal it was, but she wasn't sure she believed him. A bit like when he pretended to be surprised when she said it would be awkward to invite the girls she'd been best mates with from Year 7. But then maybe it was real. Everyone knew boys were simple creatures, right?

Maybe it was just easier for them. Lucky boys. Life certainly didn't feel particularly easy for Tasha at the moment.

Chapter 13

Karen
1988

Things were gearing up now. They'd break up for Easter in a couple of weeks and then once they got back the few short weeks before exams would drain away, quick as water. Karen and Alex, along with the other first-year English students, had picked up their lecture attendance and were trying to read about ten books' worth of stuff a week. It made A levels seem like a picnic.

Karen was on her way back to college after another incomprehensible lecture on Ben Jonson. She'd wanted to read English because she loved Laurie Lee and D. H. Lawrence, but found herself endlessly mired in the sixteenth century. To her mind, they barely wrote English in the sixteenth century, although she could barely imagine what the consequences would be of voicing such a heresy – possibly burning at the stake. She'd waited for Alex at the end of the lecture, but her friend had waved her on, saying she had to have a word with someone and would catch up. That, along with the complexities of *The Alchemist*, was what had kicked off her gloomy rumination. However much she told herself that Misty and

Alex didn't *have* to be friends with her, that they wouldn't stick around if they didn't like her, there was always the small undermining voice insisting otherwise. The voice that thrived on scraps like this.

She was nearly at Silver Street, where she would leave the watery peace of the Backs for the hubbub of town, when she heard footsteps behind her and Alex called her name.

'Wait up!'

She turned. Alex was about ten paces behind, doing a little jog that made her glossy curls swing and gave her the air of a well-groomed pony.

'Aaaaa-eeeeee.' She grabbed Karen's arm as she reached her and emitted an odd sort of shriek.

'Andrew Dyer! He's asked me out. Cinema and a drink. Tonight!'

'Oh. What are you going to see?' Before the words had left her lips, Karen was kicking herself for the inanity of her question. What did it matter? Her best friend finally had a date with the boy she was obsessed with and Karen should be thrilled.

'Um ...' A quizzical look crossed Alex's face. 'We'll just see what's on. Or go for a walk or something if there's nothing that looks good.'

'Yeah, course. Stupid question.' Karen forced herself to laugh. 'That's great news.'

She'd been fairly sure that it had been Andrew that Alex had slipped off to speak to after the lecture – that was probably another reason she'd felt out of sorts as she walked back alone. She hadn't told Alex or Misty how much she liked him. You couldn't just start fancying the guy your best friend had been after all year. It wouldn't be cricket. But then if you *did* inconveniently find that you had this ginormous crush on him it wasn't exactly like you could switch it off, was it?

Anyway, there was nothing to be done about it. There was no way Andrew would choose her if he could have Alex. End of story.

Alex was still yapping on about what films might be out at the moment and what she should wear. They were crushed close together on the narrow Silver Street pavement, the glowing lights from the buildings making it seem darker here than it had a moment ago on the Backs.

'Why don't you ask Jessica to borrow that River Island top she got last week?'

'What, that black velvet one?'

'Yeah, it's really clingy. You've got boobs now, you should flaunt them!'

The sentence was guileless and innocent as it formed in her mind, but before even quite leaving her lips the words acquired a sheen of guilt and goading. Alex said nothing, but her lily skin turned a shade paler and she briefly pursed her lips together. Karen knew instinctively that the comment had cut Alex to the quick, that she would have no choice but to react to the perceived criticism. She should feel bad; she should be looking for a way to put it right. But she didn't. Instead, she felt power ... and she liked it.

Anyway, if Alex was going to over-react to the tiniest, most well-meaning little comment, well, that wasn't her fault. It wasn't fair, she thought, how boys always went for beauty and wit and not basic good sense and emotional stability.

They entered the main gates of college, leaving behind the bustle of the darkening streets for the winter stillness of the quads, where the lack of conversation between them became harder to avoid.

'I'll come over later,' said Karen, with sudden effusiveness, when it was time to part ways. 'Help you get ready.' Alex looked doubtful but then nodded. 'Okay, thanks.'

A dark thought had seeded in Karen's mind. She retreated into her little study/bedroom, flicking on the kettle and the plug-in heater and delaying taking her gloves off. There had been a chink in Alex's armour all along. What did Karen gain by exploiting it? She wasn't entirely sure. It seemed unlikely that Andrew Dyer was suddenly going to fall for her – although it wouldn't hurt if Alex looked a little bit less perfect than she did now, could it?

There was more to it than that, though: Karen was fed up being the one tagging along. Alex always decided where they were going, what they were doing, who came along with them. It was the Alex Penrith show with Karen, and even Misty, as little more than the biddable sidekicks. But with that one simple comment about Alex's shape, the power balance had shifted. And the idea of having even just a little bit of power over perfect Alex was appealing, almost intoxicating. How would she use it? She could worry about that later. Karen sighed and pointedly switched her thoughts to the essay she had to write for tomorrow's supervision.

Chapter 14

Karen
2019

With a deep sigh, Karen surveyed the mess in the kitchen. A mixture of the usual breakfast clutter on top of two-day-old party debris that hadn't been dealt with in phase one of the clean-up operation yesterday. The party had been entirely civilised. Despite the presence of the girls and their friends, there were no vomiting episodes or dubious stains, but seventy people still made an awful of a lot of mess.

She'd actually turned fifty a few weeks earlier, but decided to have the party to coincide with the Easter long weekend. Now, with the party and bank holiday over, the girls back at school and Evie vanished to spend the last week of her holidays with a new boy friend (though avowedly not a boyfriend) in Norfolk, Karen had a million cleaning jobs still to be done and felt every day of her fifty-and-a-bit years. Oh, well, nothing for it but to roll up her sleeves.

Easter was late this year – often it fell close to her birthday, or even before it. This time the schools had set their holidays to end on the long weekend, and May was just a blink away. That meant only four more months until the money ran out. By then, Evie would be into her third year and Tasha would have taken her GCSEs. Poor Callie would just be going into Year 8. There was roughly a four-year gap between each of the girls. It wasn't that they'd planned things that way, that was just how it had turned out. For Karen, the recollection of the baby years had never had that intense, panicked, time-slip quality that her friends who had had two or more close together talked about. Karen's experience had been relatively easy, but at the same time it had seemed *endless*. Just as pull-ups for one girl faded into memory, she would find herself right back at the start with a newborn in nappies. She'd ended up as longest-serving mum at the girls' primary school – the other parents of children in Callie's class regarded her as a battle-scarred veteran, and were constantly trying to involve her in PTA projects or disputes over school policy.

Now she was at the point where she could reasonably anticipate some self-sufficiency from her eldest, but that didn't lessen the reality of years of providing for Callie yet to come. Poor Callie, who lost a father before she had chance to remember him. Who would always be in the shadow of her sisters. Who was going to have to bear the brunt of their straitened circumstances.

Over the last few months the bad news from the solicitor and financial advisers had continued to roll in. It was hard to think herself back ten years; to the months when she was coping with Jonathan's accident, and then her mother's decline into dementia and death from stroke, in quick succession. When she had three bereaved and confused children between eighteen months and nine years old to comfort and manage.

There were random gaps, both large and small, in her

recollection – it was almost as if her brain had been so traumatised at the time, it lost the ability to properly lay down her memories. She did remember that with her half-share of the inheritance of the Sevenoaks house (or that part of it not eroded by care home fees) on top of the bounty provided by Jonathan's life insurance products, she'd unexpectedly found herself a wealthy woman. She'd been more than happy to delegate the management of her finances to the financial adviser who had sold Jonathan those serendipitous insurance policies.

Unfortunately, although the investment vehicles he'd recommended had initially seemed sound, they were now turning out to be a much poorer bet. There had been around one and a half million put into a tax evasion vehicle that had been subject to an HMRC crackdown. The excess tax and fines, along with the poor performance of the underlying investment, had halved the value of the pot.

Even that wouldn't have been critical, but two months ago she'd discovered that the adviser himself had transferred two hundred and fifty thousand that was meant to be invested for the girls' future into his own companies. When greed or circumstance had started to drain them, he'd been dipping his fingers into the main investment to try to balance the books, as well as to make the drawdown payments that he had to keep up to avoid alerting Karen to the problem. She'd been blindly burning capital for the last five years or more, with no idea – before the start of this year – that her money was dwindling away.

They weren't the only victims. The guy was now facing trial and expected to go down for a number of years. But even once they sold his flash cars and ski lodge, the share she would get back by way of compensation was going to be woefully small.

The party had gone ahead because she'd booked the marquee and sent the invitations with her Christmas cards, but she hadn't imagined at that point that she'd be doing all the cleaning up single-handedly in the interests of costs-saving. She needed to find a job. A proper one. One that paid enough to cover two sets of school fees and the cost of keeping the house running. It was a big ask. She hadn't enjoyed advertising work, but she had been *good* at it. Once she'd got a foot on the ladder and her track record began to speak loud enough to drown out doubts over her lacklustre qualifications, she'd secured a few quick promotions and got used to speculative calls from recruiters. Until she happily walked down the aisle with Jonathan and off into the sunset as far as the advertising world was concerned.

Benjy had been mouthing off at the party about how with all this gender pay gap stuff and political correctness everyone was desperate to hire female return-to-workers. But she was hardly the savvy thirty-four-year-old who had just waved her kids off on primary school. She'd been out of the workforce for two decades – she *was* the generation gap.

So here she was on Tuesday morning, surrounded by the dirty cereal bowls and orange juice glasses that everyone else in the family had carelessly clattered down onto the breakfast bar. Even Tasha, who this term was at home on Tuesday and Thursday mornings on some kind of independent study programme that Karen felt demonstrated a woeful lack of understanding of teenage study habits on the part of her school, had simply abandoned her breakfast stuff and gone back to bed.

Karen planned to put a load in the dishwasher, including some of the party backlog, then hoover the stairs and upstairs landing (which might encourage Tasha downstairs to engage in some revision), and then she had to get ready for a trip into town. She had coffee with a 'contact' – so she'd blow £12 on the train and then probably £5 or £6 on the coffee, with every possibility that nothing would come of it.

That was another reason she'd gone ahead with the party. She was waiting for fate to send a rescue line but she knew that she had to give it the opportunity to arrive. It had also been a bit of a two-fingered gesture to the bad luck that seemed to be piling up on her, as well as the school mums who had started to gossip when she'd belatedly withdrawn Callie from the ski trip. For all his opining on the subject of female returners, Benjy hadn't come up with any opportunities for her. Nor had anyone else she'd subtly broached the subject with that afternoon. Since February, she'd applied for over twenty roles, got four interviews. No offers. It was a far cry from what she'd imagined for her fifties – seeing the world and maybe dipping a pedicured toe in the middle-aged dating game. She'd put all that to one side whilst she brought the girls up on her own. Now it felt as if the reward she'd earned fair and square was being snatched away just as it came within sight.

She placed a tablet in the dishwasher and closed the door with a clunk. The floor she'd swept and mopped first thing yesterday needed another clean too. She could see cake crumbs scattered under the windowsill and a stray tissue lurking in the dusty corner by the radiator. Ugh.

Her mind drifted back to Andrew Dyer again. His company was big enough to have some meaty marketing roles, but she'd always worked in ad agencies and it would be a big step to go in-house. She'd asked a couple of questions about his marketing set-up and his responses had been professional, almost banal. She wasn't sure if her hints had been too subtle or if he was deliberately failing to take her up on them. Either way, she had her dignity, and she had no intention of straight-out asking him for a job when that would put both of them in an awkward position.

The one thing she had done that had unquestionably got his attention was showing him that picture of Alex. She'd known that he'd never married of course, but he had turned up with various women at different events they'd been to together. It had never occurred to her before now how badly he had lost his way all those years ago.

There was a synergy of sorts, she mused, filling the mop bucket and slopping soapsuds across the floor: she'd missed out on a career; he'd missed out on a relationship and family. They were like two broken halves. What if they were meant to fit together? That could answer a lot of problems. After another hour or so of cleaning, she hammered on Tasha's door. She'd got used to the fact that even if she couldn't actually hear music, the girls would inevitably be plugged into something.

'You up, Tash?' she shouted.

'Yes! Revising.'

Pushing the door open, she could see the papers and text-books spread out on the desk, but Tasha was sitting on the floor, her forehead glistening and her feet jammed under the edge of her bed. Karen motioned for her to remove her head-phones.

'Revising?'

'Movement break. Good for the body, good for the mind.'

'Maybe some fresh air would be better than sit-ups?'

She had to get going to make that coffee meeting. Now wasn't the moment to chat revision technique with Tasha.

'I'm heading into town for the afternoon. Can you make sure you're around when Callie gets in? I'm not sure if she's got a key with her.'

'No problem, Mum.' Tash nodded, less resistant than Karen had expected.

'Good girl, I'll see you later.'

*

Her phone went as the train was approaching Waterloo. It was Evie.

'Hi, darling, are you having a nice time?'

'Yes, Mum, it's all good. Tom's gone out to pick something up. I just wanted to take the chance to give you a buzz when Tash wasn't around.'

'Hmm. What about?' It wasn't the time to explain that Tash actually was around due to her study leave, but that Karen herself was away from the house. It didn't seem to have occurred to her elder daughter that she might not be perfectly placed to have a cosy chat.

'She seemed really thin compared to when I was at home at Christmas. And grumpy. I just wondered if everything was okay with her?'

Karen's brow creased. 'Yes, darling, everything's fine as far as I'm aware. More than fine. She's got this boyfriend, he seems nice, and she's been happy about that. Maybe she wanted to lose a few pounds.' Her mind flicked to the image of Tash exercising in her room when she was meant to be revising. 'I think she's looking really healthy at the moment. Has she said to you that something's wrong?'

'No. Not at all. I'd be less worried if she had, but we've not had a proper conversation in ages. But if you think she's fine ...'

The train was slowing up. She didn't want to navigate the exit and the ticket barriers whilst carrying on a call.

'I'm sure she is. Look, I'm actually on my way somewhere and I've got to go. Have fun with Tom, darling. We'll speak soon, okay?'

She cut off Evie's reply, not that she meant to, but the train was jerking to a stop and she fumbled the phone. Poor Evie, she'd gone a bit mother hen for a couple of years after Jonathan died, taking it upon herself to look after the younger two and try to make things easier for her mother. Perhaps being away at university was bringing it out in her again. Karen would give her a call tomorrow, talk properly, and check in with Tasha too. She smiled to herself. They might think they were independent but that was only half the story.

Chapter 15

Misty
1988

'I like wiiiii-iiine!' They sang together at the tops of their voices, immediately collapsing into giggles. It was one of the many good things about coming to Alex's house: you didn't have the college porters, or some fun-sucking PhD student coming round to tell you to shut up at the slightest bit of noise.

The Elkie Brooks cassette was Alex's. Her taste was idiosyncratic, and Misty secretly liked the fact that her friend didn't give a damn whether her music was cool or not. The mistake, on the other hand, was Misty's own. She'd misheard the chorus of 'Lilac Wine' as 'I like wine' and they all agreed it made for a much better version. Karen made a show of disdaining Elkie, although her mum was fan and had a copy of *Pearls* taped from friends, so she knew the words as well as either of the others. And even she was happy to sing along to the new version.

It was always a stark contrast, catapulting themselves out of the rather austere life of college and into the seductive luxury of the Penriths' home. On previous visits, Misty felt that she had to be careful to remember that she had essays due, or chapters to read for supervisions. The day-to-day pressure she felt in college melted away here, as if she was a character in a fairy story, who wandered into an enchanted kingdom and risked forgetting the responsibilities of their real life.

Now though, for once, she could allow herself to forget all about epidemiology, histology, the structure of the cardiovascular system and even John Noakes (the cadaver she and her lab partner had christened thanks to a passing resemblance to the former *Blue Peter* presenter). The exams were over and it was the best feeling in the world.

Since the pre-Christmas party, they'd spent a few weekends at the house, generally on quite short notice when Alex deemed that her mother was 'holding it together' as she put it. Tonight, though, they were only here for a few hours, getting ready for the May Ball at Trinity College. It was the hottest ticket in town, and difficult to get hold of for those not at Trinity itself, but Alex, naturally, had known someone. She had also refused to take any payment from Misty, who was not entirely comfortable about being indebted to her friend, but was *definitely* not willing to miss out on the chance of experiencing the ball.

From Alex's dark mutterings, Misty had pictured Mrs Penrith as a severe foreigner, swathed in black and staring disapprovingly, but at her first encounter with Catarina Penrith, a few weeks after the party, she had proved quite the opposite, welcoming both Misty and Karen with smiles, hugs and kisses. She was Spanish, and more demonstrative than either Misty or Karen was entirely at ease with. Here, she insisted, they would have a proper meal, not the rubbish in college. They were too thin, they needed to eat! The embrace she had given her daughter seemed to morph into a shake, and her frustration was palpable. Misty and Karen had waited awkwardly in the hallway, shifting the weight of their overnight bags and trying to think of something to say to Catarina that might change the subject.

Alex had got thinner through the year, especially over the exam period, when she consumed mostly laxatives (which her mother didn't know about) and cigarettes (which she did). But odd or obsessive behaviour during the exam period was hardly unusual. Misty hoped that Alex would get back to normal again now the pressure of exams was out of the way. She had, after all, been the one who was insistent that she was cured.

Misty had done a bit of reading on eating disorders. It hadn't been touched on in their syllabus so far, and she doubted there would be more than a ten-minute mention unless she chose a psychiatric specialism later on. Medicine was such a vast subject, most of the first three years seemed dedicated to giving them a grasp of exactly how much they *didn't* yet understand, presumably on the sound principle that it might lessen the chances of them going blundering in as junior doctors and accidently killing someone with a misdiagnosis or an ignorant oversight. So instead she'd found herself flicking to the relevant pages in her introductory psychology and neurology textbook and using the references there as a jumping-off point to find more information in the library.

There had been an explosion in awareness of anorexia when Karen Carpenter died in 1983. Misty had been fourteen and already set on studying medicine, but it was the first time she'd encountered the idea of an illness that caused someone to starve themselves to death. She'd read the coverage in her father's tabloids with surreptitious fascination.

'What's the plan, then?' asked Karen, once they'd cheesed their way through 'Pearl's a Singer' and Elkie had moved on to more downbeat numbers.

'Dinner at seven, as usual,' said Alex, making a face. 'And then taxi at half eight to make sure we get there for nine. Believe me, I was there last year and you do not want to miss a minute of this ball. But first we've got the small matter of Misty's makeover to sort out.' She winked and waggled a small cardboard box towards Misty. Somehow, she had agreed to go blonde for the ball. It had seemed like a good idea after a few glasses of wine in the college bar.

Misty looked at her watch. 'It's five o'clock already. Maybe we don't have time to do it. I don't want to mess it up.'

'You could leave it in over dinner,' suggested Karen. 'I mean, if Alex's mum wouldn't mind you sitting at the table with a towel round your head. That way we'd have plenty of time.'

Alex shrugged. 'I don't think Mum and Dad would notice. They'll be too busy counting the grains of rice on my plate.'

'Yeah, thanks for the suggestion, but I think I'd rather get it washed out before sitting down with your parents. Let's get on with it.'

'And if it turns green then I'll just have to style it out. Because there is no way I'm staying at home tonight!'

*

It didn't turn green. Misty's scientific rigour, Alex's methodical application and the fact that she already had relatively pale hair combined to make the home-peroxide job startlingly effective. The hanging sweep of mousy-brown nothing that she'd worn every day since starting college (and long before) was now transformed into a vivid white-blonde choppy bob.

'You look like Meg Ryan,' Karen said, gleefully.

'Are you sure you don't mean Glenis the Guinea Pig from *Roland Rat*?' Misty's mascara had run as Alex washed the dye off over the bath. The stark whiteness of her hair accentuated the smudgy black around her eyes. She prodded her hair. It was dramatic, but, tentatively, she thought she liked it.

'Not Glenis,' said Alex, firmly. 'It looks amazing. Now let's try our dresses on before dinner.'

Alex and Karen had both had dress-shopping trips to London with their mothers, Karen returning with a floor-length, floral Laura Ashley evening dress which, along with her hair, gave her more than a hint of the Duchess of York. Misty was wearing a new black maxi-skirt from Etam with a black knitted top threaded with metallic strands and a wide kimono belt. It looked like a dress when you put it all together and, whilst it would have been nice to have spare cash for a ballgown, she was honestly more comfortable in her outfit than she would have been dressed up like some sort of debutant. It was hard to blend in at five foot ten.

Although Karen had waved her dress around on the hanger, neither of them had seen Alex's. They'd been told that Catarina had gone full-on designer and that it came from Calvin Klein, but beyond that it was a mystery.

Misty had pulled on her clothes in seconds and was already experimenting with dark eye make-up, admiring the effect of her new blonde crop against the dramatic outfit, when she heard Alex call out, 'I'm ready!'

Karen joined Misty on the half landing that served the three guest rooms and they looked at the staircase expectantly. They heard the rustle of the skirts before they saw her, then suddenly she was there, like something from the Oscars. The dress was astonishing – a hot pink Calvin Klein number, with full ballgown skirts and a ruffled neckline. The colour popped against her black hair, piled on top of her head with a few ringlets spiralling down, and her snow-white pale skin. She was grinning with delight, and the whole thing should have looked fabulous.

It almost did, but there was something just slightly off-key. The hollowness around her collarbone, the slight gapes where the dress should sit on her shoulders. She must have lost weight since she bought it because somehow, despite Alex's vibrant personality, the dress was wearing her.

'It's amazing,' said Misty and Karen at once, because there really was no other word for it. Alex descended the last couple of steps and they crowded her, touching the silk, admiring the ruffles, gasping at the volume of the skirt.

'You both look fantastic.' Alex laughed, trying to deflect some of the attention, but it was clear who the star of the evening would be.

As Alex turned backwards and forwards for them, a frown crossed Karen's face. 'Is it … no, no, it's just the way the light caught on the silk for a moment.'

'What?' asked Alex. 'What's wrong?'

'Nothing. I thought for a moment, it seemed stretched.' She gestured across her own stomach, whilst frowning at Alex's. 'But it was the light, like I said.' She flashed a broad smile. 'My mistake!'

But the glee that had filled Alex's face moments earlier had drained away. Misty wondered what Karen thought she was playing at.

'Well, we should take these off anyway,' Alex said, her voice tight. 'Mum will want us down for dinner soon.'

*

'My gracious!' exclaimed Catarina when the girls bustled into the kitchen. 'Your hair, Misty, what a change! I like it!' Mrs Penrith was a neat woman, conservative in her appearance. Her pale skin and blonde hair worn in a neat chignon at her neck meant that her strong Spanish accent tended to come as a bit of a surprise, no matter how many times Misty heard her talk. According to Alex, her mother's parents had been socialists. She'd been removed as a child by the Franco regime, but despite her upbringing in a 'respectable' bourgeois Catholic family she developed views on feminism and reproductive medicine which, as an academic, had brought her into conflict with the state. Her marriage to Eric in 1963 had been part-elopement, part-defection and Alex boasted that MI6 still bugged the family's phone line.

None of this could have been guessed at from Catarina's neat twinsets and low-heeled shoes, but perhaps it nevertheless explained a tolerant view of peroxide. Misty took her place at the kitchen table with some embarrassment at the fuss being made over her, and busied herself with complimenting the dishes on the table. She stuttered to silence when Eric entered the room. Every time she visited it was the same – half of her praying he wouldn't be there at all, and the other half gleeful to see him and crushed by disappointment if he wasn't.

He greeted them all effusively, uncorking a bottle of wine and leaning over the table to pour. With a waft of spice and tannins, he leant over her and his arm brushed her shoulder, she felt her skin prickle and she blushed furiously. Her discomfort lifted slightly when he moved round to the other side of the table, only to flame up as strongly as ever when he sat down and winked at her.

'I like it too,' he said quietly. 'I hope you're prepared for the attention.'

'Oh, I'm sure everyone will get used to it really quickly.'

'Perhaps.'

The table was laden with baskets of bread, different salads in mismatched ceramic bowls, squat glass tumblers were used for water, for wine and some scattered with a couple of flowers snipped from the garden in them. Taking centre stage was Catarina's huge iron paella dish, gleaming yellow with the steaming seafood stew. It felt a million miles from the routine of dinners at home – cottage pie, shepherd's pie, bolognese, chilli. Mince and carrots whichever way you cut it. Misty adored Catarina's food, although she couldn't always say the same about the atmosphere.

'Eat! Eat!' commanded Catarina and Misty loaded her plate obligingly. She tried not to look at what Alex was taking, although she knew that the showdown would come later. The mussels – which neither she nor Karen had ever eaten before – were plump and sweet. The rice, so tasteless at home, exploded with saffron and aniseed and a savoury fatty richness that made her want to lick her lips. Alex ate the salad, ignoring the dressing in its cute jug, and pushed a few grains of rice around on her plate, whilst talking brightly about the rumours of who might be playing at the ball.

'That was delicious, Mrs Penrith. Would you like me and Misty to take these plates through and make a start on the dishes?' Karen's offer to help was so natural and cheery that no one could refuse her.

'What were you thinking of?' Misty hissed at her when they reached the kitchen. 'Telling Alex she looks fat in that dress. It was practically hanging off her.'

Karen shrugged. 'I didn't say anything of the sort. I said it looked stretched over her stomach – which it did – and then I realised it was just the light catching on the silk. Like I also said. The dress is amazing, of course it is.' Without another word she got stuck into the task – rooting around under the sink until she found the Fairy Liquid and some rubber gloves, then grabbing a dish towel from the radiator and tossing it towards Misty. Misty would never dream of making herself so at home in a stranger's house. Her own mother would throw a fit at the thought of someone else elbow-deep in her Marigolds.

Misty dried half-heartedly, listening to Karen's chatter about the ball, and how often she'd have to redo her hair dye if she wanted to stay blonde, but still wondering about Karen's bizarre comments. Tentatively, she looked for obvious homes for the items as she finished them, before resorting, in most cases, to stacking them up on a bit of clear worktop space by the back door. She mused on how different Alex's home was from her own – this kitchen was bigger than the whole of their downstairs and filled with more *stuff* than they had in the entire house. There were patterned plates on the walls, displays of glasses and books, vibrant artwork and, at the far end, two sofas piled with blankets and cushions. You could live in here, and given the bright, relative homeliness of the décor compared to the grand entertaining spaces upstairs, she suspected they pretty much did.

'I'm done.' With a flick of her wrist Karen wiped round the washing-up bowl and turned it upside down to allow any last drops to drain down in a practised gesture that wouldn't have occurred to Misty in a hundred years. 'Listen, will you finish up whilst I nip out for a pack of ciggies? I forgot to grab some earlier and if I wait till they're done in there we'll end up running late.'

'Fine.' Misty picked up the next glass from the draining board. There was still a stack of stuff left to dry.

'They go over there – look.' Karen nodded towards a glass-fronted cupboard, and sure enough, there were even more of the little tumblers stacked behind the glass.

'Good spot, thanks,' Misty called, but the back door was already shutting.

She dried a few more tumblers, stacking them in twos before putting them in the cupboard. There were voices coming from the dining room, Catarina's mainly. The tone was urgent but Misty couldn't make out the words. She wasn't sure if Catarina was raising her voice to Alex, or if it was just audible now that Karen had gone, and the noise of the washing up had subsided.

The kitchen door clicked open. She turned to see Eric leaning against the larder door, eyes clasped shut. One hand still held his wine glass but the other was cradled to his forehead. He let out a slow breath.

'I'm sorry …' she stuttered, when he opened his eyes and caught her staring.

'No, no, I forgot you were in here. Look, I'll help you with those.'

He crossed the space between them in a few quick footsteps, picking up another dishtowel draped over a wooden chair. Suddenly he was close enough for her to see shadow of the stubble he would shave off in the morning. She smelt his scent again: warm and aromatic, conjuring nutmeg, brandy and newspapers.

He must be worried about his daughter, even if he left it to his wife to do the talking. She wanted to say something that would show she recognised that, to express some sympathy. It was tempting to apologise for being there at all; no one liked a witness to their family's darker moments. But expressing such complicated sympathy was seemingly beyond her.

'It's brave, the hairstyle,' he said, nodding towards the window, where the darkening evening and kitchen lights were bringing out her reflection.

'Yes.' She touched her hair. 'That's a nice way of saying you don't like it, isn't it?'

He laughed, and the laugh seemed to take him by surprise and she found herself laughing back.

'No. Not at all. It's fun and ... chic ... and, well, it's perfect for you.' He paused a moment. 'I, on the other hand, might struggle to carry it off.'

They laughed again and Misty leant a hand back against the counter, pushing her body towards him, enjoying her own reflection with its shock of blonde hair, and her wine-flushed laughter, and feeling for a moment a heady rush of glee at the *chic* woman she suddenly felt she could be on this warm evening, in this bohemian kitchen. She'd felt something between them when she'd visited before, even on that first night at the party. She'd convinced herself she was imagining it, but perhaps she'd been wrong. His eyes held hers, unflinching, his gaze as tangible as a physical touch. Misty Jardine was a different girl to the one who had turned up in Cambridge eight short months ago. She felt her own power, and she liked it. Returning his look just as steadily, she reached out for the wine glass he still held in his hand, took a sip and let her lips curl up into a lazy smile.

He slowly set down the towel he was holding and took a step towards her. The laughter dropped away between them. There was a heartbeat of nothing, then she leant forward, closing her eyes just before her lips met his.

Chapter 16

Karen
2019

Andrew Dyer. A. Dyer. A. D. Holdings.

She pored over every reference she could find, googling articles in the financial press, calling up official company records and picking over his (very limited) social media presence. There was a period at university where she'd fancied him a little; but her memory of that, as with her actual pre-Jonathan relationships, had more of the quality of a film or TV programme that she had once watched, rather than feeling like part of her lived experience.

In the years since, she'd had an awareness of him, rather than much direct contact. Occasionally they'd see each other at social events, but more often he'd be the person others were talking about. Plenty of her contemporaries had done well for themselves, but Andrew's success was exceptional. Plus, it was more obvious. You weren't reminded of peers who had become professors or judges in the ad breaks on Saturday night TV.

Not that she'd previously given it all that much thought. She was absorbed in her own life, with the girls, the house, the PTA, the gym and a couple of local charities she helped a bit with marketing.

But now that contented, small life was feeling much less secure. There was a persistent little voice in her head about Andrew Dyer. They were two sides of the same coin, weren't they? He had the career and the success. She had the home and the family. None of her research gave any hint of his personal life. She was confident that he'd never married or had children. She'd have heard about it if he had. Maybe he was missing what she had; maybe they could be the answer for each other.

'What are you looking at?'

She slammed the laptop shut. 'My God, Tasha, you made me jump!'

Her daughter shrugged. 'Sorry, just came down for a glass of water. Didn't mean to interrupt your online dating!'

'I am *not* online dating.'

'Well, you shut that down quickly. And you've been on it a lot recently.' She paused to fill a glass from the filter then, quietly, still with her back turned. 'I wouldn't mind, you know, none of us would.'

Karen had opened her mouth to speak, but the words caught in her throat. She closed it, and then started again.

'I've not seen Claire or Sonal for a while. You've not had anyone over recently. We've got a quiet weekend, do you want to get them round for a film night or something?'

'No, thanks.'

'Have you fallen out? You can tell me, you know.'

'Nah. We're all just a bit stressed with the revision and everything.'

Tash turned back towards her mother. She did look peaky,

with slightly greasy roots and dark smudges under her eyes. Karen wondered if she should make her sit down, try to have a bit of a heart-to-heart, but she wasn't sure she could cope with coaxing a truculent teenager. The solicitor was due to call again, and she had the beginnings of a headache kindling behind her eyes.

'You're sure everything's okay?'

'*Yes*. Except I should be doing some revision.'

'Go on then. I'll bring you up some toast, shall I?' But Tash shook her head and waved the water. 'Fine with this, Mum, thanks.'

After she'd left, Karen poured herself a glass of water and opened the odds and ends drawer, where she kept plasters and painkillers. Her fingers brushed the paracetamol pack but then she reached instead for the little pack of pills her sister had sent. She'd tried them a couple of times and they definitely had more kick than paracetamol. Hopefully she could kill off this headache before it got going.

Chapter 17

'*Nothing tastes as good as skinny feels.*'

That was how Tasha got to know Alesha Berry. The words were handwritten, swooping, pretty letters penned in biro on a rough canvas fabric. It must have taken some effort. She'd been sitting next to Alesha, one of the quieter girls on the fringes of Lola's gang. Alesha's school bag was slouched between the two of them, gaping open, and the motto had slipped out from under the flap. Alesha wasn't the sort of girl to write on her hand, particularly, or to doodle on her books. The rest of the creamy canvas with its leather and brass fastenings was pristine. Tash knew she was proud of that bag. It was some label or other. From Italy.

Tash looked at her again. Alesha was an inch or so taller than she was, at a guess. Tash thought she was about five foot four, so that would make Alesha five foot five. She didn't know her height for sure because the measuring chart in Callie's room stopped at five foot and she wasn't about to ask anyone at home to stand there with a ruler over the top. Alesha had a flat stomach, long swishy hair and, probably, a

115

thigh gap. Tash couldn't quite tell with her school skirt but she made a mental note to check on Thursday when they both had PE.

Alesha was picking some lettuce out of a sandwich whilst Tash was sipping fizzy water and staring at the apple and crackers in front of her. Her stomach was growling inside and she quickly gulped some water to stop it from making a noise. Alesha noticed her looking at the bag and snatched it onto her lap so that the writing was hidden under the flap again. But then she sort of looked at Tash, and half smiled, then picked up her phone and said she had a Spanish revision session to go to.

That night Alesha sent her a link to a members-only chatroom.

I think you might be interested, she said. *I'm trusting you. Don't tell anyone. Don't dare dox me. Don't talk to me about it.*

She didn't check it out straight away. She had revision to do, but she was also holding back a little bit, like the link was a temptingly gift-wrapped present she didn't want to open too soon.

That evening, Tash said she was feeling tired and went to bed early. Once she'd tidied her room, had a quick shower and cleaned her teeth she was ready to look at the website. She sat up in bed with her phone and clicked through to the chatroom and logged in with the guest details Alesha had given her. She called herself Bellatrix on the basis that anyone who knew enough about Harry Potter to know that Bellatrix was a Harry Potter character wasn't going to be taking the piss out of her for being a HP fangirl.

For a few minutes she just scrolled through. There wasn't anything earth-shattering – a lot of the chat and the tips were similar to what she'd seen on other thinspiration sites. But then a message popped up, from someone called ScallyCat.

Hello, Bellatrix, are you new?

Yes. Who are you?

I'm one of the regulars. I see Attagirl13 sent you. Wanna chat?

That's right. I know her IRL. Ok.

Great. What's your goal?

I want to be thin.

What are your stats?

??

Height, weight, waist, hips etc etc??

Tash typed in her weight and her best guess at her height, feeling a little odd about it. She didn't know any other measurements, and said so.

I measure EVERYTHING.

ScallyCat followed up with a detailed list of dates and measurements. The numbers swam, but they sounded pretty crazy. Tash racked her brain to think what she could ask to keep the conversation going, to look like she knew what she was doing. This felt a little risky. She wasn't sure that she wanted someone like ScallyCat in her life. But she wasn't ready to walk away either.

What's your goal then? she typed. *To be thinner?*

TO BE THE THINNEST.

*

They chatted for almost two hours. A few more people popped in and out. Everyone seemed to know ScallyCat. Attagirl13 – Alesha – didn't show up. Tasha drifted off to sleep dreaming about measuring tapes. She remembered that her mum used to have a box of sewing things. Not that Karen was much of a sewer – it only came out when one of the girls had swimming or gymnastics badges to sew onto things. And for the dreaded name tags at the end of the summer holidays. Callie still went to Guides, Tash reasoned, so it should still be around somewhere. But she had no idea where to find it, nor what excuse to give if Karen found her rummaging about in it. Easier to buy one. The big Asda near school would have them, she reckoned.

The next day she avoided Alesha, determined to show that she was chilled. It was sunny and she persuaded Stanno to eat lunch on the field rather than in the canteen with the gang.

'You fancy doing something at the weekend?'

He shrugged, non-committal. 'Got to do some revision, haven't I?'

'You could come over?'

'Maybs.' He chewed a bit of sandwich, for a long time, like it was filled with leather or he'd forgotten was he was meant to do next. Then he nodded at the crackers in her lunch box.

'You not having them?'

She looked at them too. Dry and cardboardy. Eighty-nine kilocalories each.

'You want them?' She held the box out and a little gremlin in her stomach did a silent screech of protest.

'You should eat them.'

'Not in the mood for crackers.'

'Why fucking bring them, then? Jesus, Tash, you need to eat something. Have you looked in a mirror recently?'

Tasha had never seen him like that. The flash of anger just burst out of him from nowhere. She opened her mouth to speak but the words wouldn't come. There was a lump forming in her throat instead and she felt the heat rush to her face. She couldn't be humiliated like this; she couldn't let him see her cry. She stood up, grabbing the lunch box and shoving it into her bag, turning away so Stanno wouldn't see the tears pooling in her eyes.

She must have stood up too quickly. The grassy field seemed to lurch away from her and for an awful moment she thought she was going to faint. With sheer effort, she put one foot in front of the other and walked back towards the school building. Her head was thumping and she was gasping in air like she'd been underwater.

Luckily, there were some girls' toilets in the English block, which was the nearest one to the field. In there, she was able to sit down and let the tears come. She'd thought that Stanno had understood her, that they were great for each other. After all, he was the one who was doing a sodding PE GCSE and was all into his nutrition and everything. He was the first to take the piss out the fat kids – she'd heard him enough times. Maybe he was jealous because it turned out she'd got more willpower than he had. Maybe he just wasn't the right person for her, anyway. He'd seemed to be, when she was on the outside looking in, but now she'd got to know the real Stanno. And she didn't like what she saw.

Hell. She was five minutes late for History already. And she would have to sit next to Sonal who was blanking her because she was still pissed off about Tash 'defecting' to Lola. Tash wasn't sure if he could cope with this. Her stomach growled. The black grout lines on the floor tiles jumped around like the bars of a prison. Fuck this. She wasn't a kid. She wasn't going to go to History.

It was easy enough. She took some time to wash her face properly. Then she strolled through the main entrance, head high, calling out, 'Dentist,' to the two old biddies who sat behind the front desk. They just nodded back. It's not like she was a Year 7 and they had to worry about her getting lost or abducted or something. She was a prefect; not the sort of kid who skives off.

As she walked down the driveway the gremlins in her stomach turned to butterflies, in a good way. *They're not the boss of me,* she told herself. They just wanted to keep her fat and ugly and everyone's good little girl. Even Stanno. But she was smarter than them. She decided to buy some fizzy water and go to the park. Luckily, she'd charged her phone that morning. It should have plenty of juice. Maybe ScallyCat would be online.

Chapter 18

Karen
2019

Tonight was their fourth date. Admittedly, she recognised that Andrew might not perceive it that way, but then men could be very dense about these things. Karen thought there was at least a fifty per cent chance that it was going to turn into the first time that she had had sex since Jonathan's death. The thought was terrifying, but with an edge of top-of-the-roller-coaster excitement to it as well. This was out of character: Karen didn't do dating; she didn't do risks or letting go at all. She definitely didn't do roller-coasters. It was natural, she told herself, after what had happened with Jonathan, never mind the business with Alex all those years ago. Nobody could blame her for wanting to keep things safe.

But things weren't safe. The news from the solicitor had been gloomy. There was virtually no prospect of recovering the investments. He was apparently having to work to keep HMRC from launching an investigation into her – they seemed determined to view her as the villain rather than the victim. The girls were tense and glum. After making an excuse about Callie's skiing trip she'd had to tell the truth when she'd cancelled the cleaner and their planned spring family holiday to Italy. Tasha, in particular, seemed worried about it, although Karen had reassured her over and over again that the money from her own mother could cover her school fees. There was no way she was moving Tash before A levels; she just dreaded the moment when Callie would ask about hers.

She took one of Manda's pills as she examined her face in the mirror.

She'd just about held it together during the four-hour waxing and tanning session that morning. Parting with the money for that had been painful, but not as painful as the thought of exposing her ravaged flesh to a near-stranger. Now, with her new underwear on under her most flattering dress, and her re-heeled Louboutins waiting by the bed, she was on her own with the primer and the highlighter, trying to turn back the clock on the familiar landscape in the mirror, trying to make autumn mimic spring.

They were having dinner at Céleste at the Lanesborough. There had been a review of it in a supplement she'd been browsing through when he turned up for their theatre trip a couple of weeks earlier. Perhaps it had just been something to break the ice, but he'd pounced on it, asking if the review was good and immediately deciding they should try it out. He'd texted a couple of days later to say that as he had an early meeting out west he'd decided to book a room in the hotel as well, and that he'd booked one for her too, in case she'd enjoy a night up town. *My treat, but no problems if you need to get back*, the message continued. *I can cancel it on the day.*

It was direct, but discreet. She liked the fact he'd not tried to put her on the spot after a bottle of wine but had given her time to mull it over and come prepared.

Not wanting to look like she was turning up for a holiday, she'd decided against any sort of extra baggage. Instead, the largest of her smart handbags, a big Mulberry shoulder tote she'd bought herself for her fortieth and never really got on with, was gaping open on the bed. Her flattering dress could be dressed down with sandals and a cardigan for the next day, and they'd be easy enough to fit into the bag. Her toothbrush, deodorant and travel skincare stuff was simple enough too. And there was no need to worry about shampoo or shower gel going somewhere like the Lanesborough.

But then it got tough. Should she take nightwear? The loungy pyjamas she lived in at home hardly fit the bill; they were the opposite of seductive as well as being too bulky for her handbag. Jonathan had liked sheer, lacy things, and the bed was strewn with the negligee ghosts of Christmases past. But although she couldn't bring herself to get rid of them, she knew in her heart she was never going to wear them again either. So, she'd decided on nothing. It went with the illusion of non-pre-meditation. Plus, the hotel would have dressing gowns. It wasn't like she'd have to jiggle to the bathroom naked.

Then ... condoms ... she had none. Did she need them? Her memory took an unwelcome detour back to 1991 and a barman she'd had a one-night stand with a few months before she and Jonathan started dating. Turns out condoms don't protect you from pubic lice.

She'd bought some nicely packaged lubricant at the chemist's, which she tucked into a zip pocket in her handbag. It might give her a confidence boost, just in case. Christ, what was she doing carrying on like this? She should be worrying about propagating dahlias or finishing that worthy novel for book club. Evie was the one who should be premeditating sex because she'd got to date four; Karen's job was to gently chide her about chlamydia testing and try not to think about it in too much detail.

Fuck. What was she doing? Did she even want to? God, she really didn't know. The tablets were making her brain a bit fuzzy, but then without the fuzziness she'd probably be completely unable to cope.

At seventeen she'd been dying to shag someone – anyone pretty much. There had definitely been times since Jonathan had gone when she'd felt a similar sort of ache – less urgent, but deeper, and more yearning. But fantasy and reality were different things. The thought of being with someone – naked, intimate, *judged*. If she thought about it too hard, she'd be sick. But if she didn't go for it now then there was no reason to think she ever would. And the thought of giving up on that for the rest of her life was profoundly saddening, in a way that took her by surprise.

She glanced at her watch. Whatever it was she was doing it now because the dinner booking was for half past seven and she was already cutting it fine given the vagaries of South West trains. She'd told Tasha that she was going to visit a friend who was recovering from minor surgery and that she might stay overnight. Her daughter hadn't questioned the story – hadn't even asked which friend it was.

She swept the jumble of nightwear and toiletries off the bed and into a drawer; she'd sort it out another time. Then she slipped her feet into the waiting heels, picked up the tote and took a last look in the full-length mirror. It was now or never. She walked out of the empty house with her heart hammering. Even the ping of her phone as she walked down the road made her start. It was a reminder to go to her Pilates class; she allowed herself a sly smile.

'Mum!'

She jumped at the sound of her name, although she recognised Evie's voice immediately. As she got closer to the station, she'd begun to pass commuters coming from the opposite direction. The streets here were busier, and it took a moment to pick her daughter out amongst the rumpled crowds spilling out from the station.

'Over here!'

Her waving arm finally caught Karen's eye. She was on the other side of the street, poised on the kerb, waiting for a chance to cross over. Karen halted, watching Evie as she scanned the traffic with her customary impatience. She had a rucksack – quite small but bulging – slung over one shoulder. The plan for her to come home for the weekend was a long-standing one – she had a school friend's birthday on Saturday night. But she was meant to be arriving tomorrow. Karen could even picture the scrawl on the calendar because she'd checked the date so many times when she was gearing up for her rendez-vous with Andrew.

'Hello, darling. I thought you were back tomorrow?'

'No lectures tomorrow so I decided I'd come tonight. Glad I spotted you, though. Where are you off to?'

'I'm going to see Belinda. I think I mentioned to you – she had an op a couple of days ago.'

'Oh. Right. I don't remember you saying. Everything okay with her?'

Karen nodded, perhaps too enthusiastically. 'Yes, all fine. I just said I'd keep her company for the evening. You'll be okay? You've got your key? Well, Tash is in anyway so ...'

Evie took half a step back, looking at her quizzically. 'You look ... nice. That dress suits you.'

'Thanks. So ... I'd better get to the train, then.'

'Look, I came home early because I wanted to talk to you about something.'

'Well, I'm sorry, darling, really but you should have told me if that was the plan. We can talk tomorrow, can't we?'

'Yes, I suppose so. I just ... well ... I wanted to talk about Tasha. It's been on my mind – that's why I wanted to come down. I'm worried about her.'

That threw her for a moment. She flinched and took an involuntary step back, wobbling on her heels.

'What about her? What's wrong with her?'

Evie glanced from side to side. 'I'm not going to talk about it in the street, Mum.'

Karen sighed with impatience. She'd given years of her life to the girls' dramas, and now it seemed that she couldn't have so much as single evening to herself. Plus, if there really was anything to worry about regarding Tash, Karen knew she'd be the first to know. Evie was living fifty miles away.

'Look,' she said, smiling sweetly. 'I've promised Belinda I'd be with her tonight, and I've really got to get this train. You and I can talk tomorrow when Tash is at school, okay? That'll be easier than whispering tonight when she's at home.'

'Okay. I suppose. I'll see you later then?'

'I might stay the night. But if I know you, I'll probably be back before you've surfaced from your bedroom!'

She pulled her eldest daughter into a quick embrace, breathing in the smell of her.

'Gosh. I love having you back.'

'Well, go on then, run away!'

*

On the train, she replayed the conversation, worried that it would cast a shadow over the evening, however much she tried to brush it off. Could there really be something wrong with Tash? The kids all got stressed about exams. The whole social media thing made it much worse than it had been in her day. But Evie herself had got through okay, and she was much more anxious than her younger sister. Tash was smart; she had sensible friends. Of course she was okay. It was some kind of sibling drama – hardly unfamiliar territory.

She treated herself to a cab for the journey between Waterloo and Belgravia. It was a sunny evening and the streets were full – tourists, commuters, young couples in love enjoying the sunshine. The traffic was slow but not gridlocked, and she took pleasure in watching the postcard London – the one she so rarely visited – unfold in front of her. The Lanesborough was a stucco wedding cake of a hotel and as the taxi pulled into its forecourt her pleasure evaporated and the earlier panic returned.

She fumbled her purse and managed to scatter change on the pristine paving, prompting a white-gloved doorman to scuffle around recovering her coins. She blushed and muttered an apology. He brushed himself off with an air that was unctuous but somehow less than gracious.

At least Andrew was waiting for her – although that was hardly a surprise given she was late. Her apology was just as flustered as the one she'd given to the doorman and the cab driver, but Andrew's smile put her at ease immediately.

'Don't worry. The truth is I like to look at the menu for far longer than is socially appropriate. I could tell you the provenance of every ingredient in the kitchen tonight. You want to know the middle name of the pig responsible for the rillettes? Go on, test me!'

He laughed and she laughed with him. There was nothing of the endearing geeky awkwardness she remembered from when he had been Alex's boyfriend. She guessed the polish been hard won over the intervening years.

They opted for the tasting menu and the meal was a procession of delicate, delectable concoctions. Karen had never been much of a foodie, and she'd still tend to go for something simple and pronounceable over this kind of titivated haute cuisine, but it did make for a sense of occasion, as well as a talking point. And it certainly wasn't a case of style over substance – she couldn't deny that the taste of every plate was sensational.

From the start, their conversation had ranged both wide and deep. When they first met for a coffee close to Andrew's offices, she'd ended up telling him about the surreal situation between her and Jonathan. It put a very different spin on their subsequent meetings, but it also set a precedent of frank disclosure. She knew that Andrew had suffered deeply after Alex's death – still suffered to be truthful – that he blamed that for the fact he'd not had any serious relationships in his twenties. Later, as other people were settling down, he'd gambled everything on his growing enterprise. At one point he'd been living in a friend's garage, and then there was a stint on the office floor. Every penny and every minute had gone into the business.

He seemed genuinely interested in hearing about the girls. On his urging, she'd flicked through photos on her phone. His wistful look as he took in their pictures was heartbreaking.

'It might still happen,' she said, gently. 'You could meet someone. If she was a bit younger ...'

'Then I'd still be old. I know the biological clock isn't half as vicious to us men, and I've no reason to think I couldn't father a child, but that doesn't mean it would be a good idea. I'm fifty already; realistically that might be closer to fifty-five by the time I got there. I wouldn't want to be the one hobbling at the back of the dads' race at sports day. I don't believe twenty-year-olds should be spending their time picking out nursing homes.'

'I think you'd be a really good dad,' she said gently. 'Running around after them – or in the dads' race – is a tiny part. There are loads of fifty-something dads out there, and the fact that you're thinking about it from the point of view of a child, and looking at the downsides, I bet that already puts you streets ahead of most of them.'

He smiled, but shook his head. 'You've got me on the back foot now. I'll just have to come clean and admit I'm too fond of whiling away an evening with good food and great company to let that all vanish in a haze of nappies and vomit.'

He swiped the last piece of langoustine from the dish in front of him and gave a wolfish grin.

'Well, it certainly is pleasant. And I wouldn't be rushing to go back to the nappy and vomit stage. But then I've done my time.'

'My sister has three,' he said. 'Two boys, one girl. They're younger than yours. I think childless friends can have a lot to give. I might not know one end of a Pokémon from the other but I can give her a break. The kids enjoy putting me right on the stuff I get wrong, and they know they're not competing with any of my own. I like to think that when they're older they might talk to me about stuff they don't want to say to their parents. Especially the boys.'

'There's a lot of sense in that,' she admitted. 'I'd like to think my girls will have people to turn to when they hit a rocky patch. God knows we all need that.'

'And do they have people?'

Unexpectedly, she found herself giggling. 'Well we have one friend who works as a counsellor in the local sixth-form colleges. She's a bit needy. She may as well wear a T-shirt saying: "Tell me your problems – pretty, pretty please".'

'So, the girls aren't impressed then?'

'You could say that. But, look, I feel like I've just gone on about my kids all evening.'

'I've enjoyed it!'

'We should talk about something else. We should talk about you – what's new in the business, or where you're going on holiday or –' she broke off and glanced down at the latest plates to materialise in front of them '– or exactly which part of a pigeon you think is lurking in those panko breadcrumbs?'

'Confit heart – I told you I'd memorised the menu.'

'Definitely not what I was thinking of – look at the shape of them.'

'Pigeon balls? Maybe they're an aphrodisiac.' He smiled.

'Three hearts on one tiny plate, though. That's a lot of dead pigeons.'

'You brought that up just in case I was feeling amorous?'

'No! I mean, no one likes pigeons, do they?'

'Mary Poppins?'

'Are you trying to get this back to what turns you on?'

'Chim-chimeree.' He winked.

Fortunately, she'd ventured to put one of the mysterious balls in her mouth and it was chewy enough to mean that she wouldn't have been able to voice a reply even if she'd been able to come up with one. Once upon a time she remembered putting men who wink at the top of a dating 'red lines' list. Perhaps fifty-year-olds winked differently to twenty-year-olds.

'So,' he said a few minutes later, as she cleared her plate, pushing the last of the red wine jus onto her fork with a buttery chanterelle. 'I think we're on the home straight of the tasting menu.'

'Just as well, I've probably only got room for one bag of chips,' she joked.

'Well, we still have pre-dessert, dessert and coffee.'

'Let me guess, memories of elderflower, suet-roasted strawberries and a Nescafé chaser?'

'Undoubtedly. And I can barely contain my anticipation.'

Karen gulped, her savoir-faire evaporating as quickly as the steam from the lapsang-scented broth the stern-faced waitress had poured over the langoustines earlier in the evening. She was finally here – teetering at the very top of the roller-coaster. This was the moment.

'Actually, Andrew, I was wondering if you might like to have it sent up to the room?'

He looked at her, his expression unreadable, then he blinked once or twice and the movement seemed to bring him back to life.

'Yes, yes, I suppose we could. Your place or mine?' Without

waiting for an answer, he flagged over their waitress, gave his room number, and then pulled her chair aside as she stood up.

*

The room was generous, more like a suite. Whilst he poured coffee she sat on the elegant sofa and immediately stood up again, playing with the buckles on her bag and gabbling about the food. She thought wistfully of the pill packet tucked away in the bag, but told herself not now, she needed to be thinking clearly.

He handed her the coffee and she leant in, muttering what she hoped was an alluring 'thank you' into his neck. He took a fraction of a step backwards and they both sat on the sofa.

'So, do you often stay here if you have meetings at this end of town?'

He shrugged. 'I often stay close by. I work well in hotel rooms – fewer distractions – and learning to always prioritise my own time and effectiveness was a big lesson for me when I started out. It used to be hard to justify the cost of a really nice hotel until I worked that out. Of course, it makes a difference that I'm not going home to anyone; that would change everything.'

Her heart leapt. That comment couldn't have come from nowhere. He *was* thinking along the same lines as her – they had everything each other needed. She nodded slowly and smiled at him. Playing it cool.

'I got you the room just across the corridor,' he said. 'I'll have time for breakfast if you don't mind an early start.'

She put her coffee down, and leant towards him, placing

a hand gently on his thigh. 'It's all very gallant of you, but I really don't think two rooms are necessary, do you?'

For a moment, nothing happened. Then: 'Oh. Shit, Karen, you've really got the wrong idea here. It's probably my fault – it was a stupid idea to suggest the room. I thought it might be a treat for you but that was patronising and silly ...' He rubbed his face with his hands. She jumped back from him as though burnt, her heart immediately racing. Oh God, how could she have been so mortifyingly stupid. It was a small grace that he was still talking, which saved her from having to try to say something.

'I've had a lovely evening. Really. I enjoy your company. It's been really nice to reconnect. But I'm just not, you know, looking for that. I thought ... after Jonathan ... well, it probably doesn't help what I thought.'

He gave another deep sigh and then unexpectedly pulled her into a bear hug.

'You're a wonderful, wonderful person, Karen. Let's not make this awkward. We're both too grown-up for that. Let's finish this coffee and forget the last five minutes.'

She nodded, dumbly, her cheeks flaring far hotter than the rapidly cooling drink.

Chapter 19

Tasha
2019

Tasha heard her mum leave and it was only a few minutes before the door opened again. She thought Karen must have forgotten something, but then came the thud of a bag being dropped on the hall floor and footsteps on the flagstones that were very different to Karen's going-out heels.

'Callie, Tash, you in?'

Evie. For a moment, Tash had panicked that someone was breaking into the house, but not being a burglar was pretty much the only good thing she could say about her older sister turning up. She heard Callie call, 'Ye-es,' from opposite end of the house, but stayed silent.

Tash waited for the sound of Evie coming up the stairs, her finger poised over the log-off button on the touchscreen. Luckily, her sister went into the kitchen instead and, even more luckily, Tash heard Callie's patter as she raced down to go and tell her about some party she'd been invited to and how they were going to ride in a pink limo. Tash had already had twenty minutes of Callie showing her Insta pics of it and debating whether their mum would pay for her to get her nails done. She reckoned Callie would keep Evie occupied for a while.

Cautiously, she turned her attention back to the chatroom. Tash and Alesha were hanging out at school now, and they liked to be on the forum at the same time although they kept low-key about the fact that they knew each other offline. Today, Alesha had posted a pic in teenie denim cut-offs and a bikini top and asked people to guess her weight. Tash knew what she was down to because they told each other every morning and they'd sworn not to lie about it. Grinning, she added two kilos and posted a response on the forum. Alesha would be furious.

Alesha was ahead of Tash but Alesha's mum was really getting flapped about it. She was taking her to see the doctor next week and stopping her from doing any exercise. Tash was about four hundred grams heavier at the moment, but hopefully she'd get that off in the next week or so and maybe even start to beat her, especially if Alesha's mum got her way.

Tash would post a pic when she got to her next big milestone. She'd already planned it in her head. She was going to put her hair up in a beehive and do eyeliner flicks like Amy Winehouse. Even though she was from ages ago, Tash and Alesha both loved her. Modern singers were all fake, reality-TV Insta-Barbies. They made her want to vom. She'd do her Amy Winehouse look, with cut-offs like Alesha's and this frilled gingham bandeau top that she'd found online. She knew it was going to look awesome. People were commenting on Alesha's picture already with #thinspiration #thinspo and #collarbones. She'd cut the picture off below her eyes so it was deniable. Maybe Tash should do that, or blur her face or something. But then nobody would see her eyeliner flicks. It was a tough choice.

Evie had started cooking curry, and the smell of the spices toasting in the pan hit her like a punch to the stomach. That's what her dad used to do – curry and barbecues. It was a huge stereotype, but no less true for that. Tash knew that Evie didn't believe she could remember properly, but she could. His curries were legend, and Evie's were pretty good too, to be fair. Tash's stomach was growling now and she focused on persuading herself that she wasn't really hungry, just thirsty, and that a nice glass of water would sort it all out.

'Tasha!'

She ignored Evie's shouts a couple of times but then she began to sound pissed off.

'Coming!' God, that smell. It was torture. She looked one last time at Alesha's picture and then locked down her phone. Her lock screen was a drawing of a skeleton crowning a girl with a tiara made of bones. It was a pro-ana thing, but subtle enough for others not to pick it up. She needed to focus on that, instead of on wanting the curry. Willpower, that's all it came down to. And she'd be damned if she was letting Alesha win.

*

Dinner didn't go well. Evie loaded the curry sauce with cream even though she should have known that Tash wouldn't eat it like that. If she came home early to pick a fight then she got what she was after. Stupid Callie ended up bursting into tears and then Evie was down Tash's throat about how she was trying to upset Callie and couldn't she see the damage she was doing?

Tash just looked at her, keeping her eyes locked on her sister's the whole time. Then she picked up the pasta bowl she was eating from and moved her arm out to the side. She stretched as far as she could and then calmly dropped the whole lot on the floor. They had slate flagstones in the kitchen so it was only going to end one way. With the sound of smashing china still ringing in the air, Tash smiled at Evie, really sweetly, like Callie might.

She felt giddy. She'd never done anything like that in her life. It felt scary but kind of powerful too. She got sort of a rush from it. Afterwards, she imagined that Evie would go full-on mental. The eldest Neville sister had always been the goody-two-shoes one, but she had a proper temper on her. Not that night, though – she didn't say a single thing.

There were pieces of the bowl and rice and curry everywhere. Tash looked down and saw that her ankle was splattered with some of the famous curry sauce. She pictured herself licking it off. Sixteen calories? Eighteen calories? Would she use up more trying to reach it than she'd get back? She realised Evie's hands were shaking. She looked back up at her sister's face, and saw an expression she'd never seen on it before, sort of crumpled. Raging and defeated at the same time. It all felt too big then. Not safe. It tipped over suddenly, like when you light a campfire with your mates and then someone gets out an aerosol and it takes just a second to slip from being in control to being out of control but that second may as well be a lifetime because you can never get back to the other side of it.

Tash stood up and walked out of the kitchen, back to her

bedroom. She took the stairs very slowly, holding on to the handrail. She couldn't tell if the dizziness came from hunger or from what she'd done. She could hear Callie sobbing and Evie shushing her and saying it was going to be all right.

*

She fell asleep. It was hard to imagine how; after all that had kicked off. But she found she was very good at sleeping these days. It was her stupid body's way of trying to trick her and stay fat.

When she woke up, she tried to guess what time it was before looking at her phone. Was there a glimmer of light outside? Could she hear anyone up in the house? The pain in her stomach was intense. The catastrophic dinner meant that she'd actually eaten even less than she normally would. She might have to allow herself an apple or a cracker. Given the choice, she'd prefer to eat on her own. That way she could take it as slowly as she wanted to, and give up when she decided it was the right time. But normally she made a point of eating only in front of others and lying about what she ate the rest of the time. That way they were less likely to think there was something going on.

Just now, though, she'd take having the apple on her own.

She got up tentatively. She still had the giddy, spinning sensation in her head, but it was starting to feel more normal. She smiled to herself. If this was something she could live with and manage then that was a big step forward. Perhaps she could be strong enough to do without the apple and just go back to bed. She checked the time on the wall clock. It wasn't actually that late, just getting on for midnight. It was too much of a risk to eat nothing before morning, she decided. The most important thing, above everything else, was that she had to remain in control.

As she slipped along the landing, she thought she heard the sound of her dad's voice coming from the study. The sound was so real, she couldn't have made it up. She didn't remember it well enough to make it up (though she'd die before admitting that to Evie). The study was up a few steps, off a little half landing. She hesitated at the foot of the stairs, listening, but everything was silent. Of course it was. He was *dead*; he wasn't going to be chatting on the phone in the middle of the night.

She carried on to the kitchen. There was only one apple left in the bowl. That never used to happen – her mum was always too on top of things. It was a bit wizened but she took it anyway and then made her way back to bed. It was only moments before she heard footsteps outside her door. Damn. Evie must have been listening.

But it wasn't Evie; it was ... her dad. He came in and sat down on the edge of the bed – heavily. She opened her eyes and looked at him. He looked grey and weary even in the half-light. But he was there – the weight of him and the smell of him – it catapulted her back instantly.

'It's really tough for you just now, isn't it Tish-Tash?'

That was his baby name for her. She nodded. She couldn't trust herself to do anything else.

He nodded at the apple. 'Hope it's a red one?'

Tash and Jonathan liked red ones. Karen and Evie liked green ones, and Callie had been too young to eat them. So they always used to buy both. It was Tash's thing with her dad, at one point, the Red Apple Crew. They had a handshake.

Usual sort of dumb four-year-old stuff. She looked at the apple; she hadn't even checked what colour it was. Red and green. Like it couldn't make up its mind.

'You're not alone, you know, Tish-Tash. There's friends around if you look for them.' He glanced towards the old dining chair in the corner of the room. She mainly used it for stashing clothes that she couldn't be bothered to put away. She followed his gaze and jumped, startled. There was a girl sitting in the chair. She was chewing the end of a curly, dark-coloured bob, and grinning at Tash.

Tash stared at her. She was familiar, but she couldn't immediately think from where. The girl lifted a hand in an affected sort of wave.

'I'm Alex.'

Then Tash remembered. There was a photo on the wall of the study – her mum had put up a group of different pictures of herself when she was young – she must have been having a moment. There were three of them in that photo, the best friends she made in her first year at Cambridge. Karen, Misty and Alex. The girl sitting on the chair was the girl from the photo – same hair, same stripy black and white dress, same ana figure.

Alex had died from anorexia while they were all still in uni. Karen hadn't tried to hide that from her daughters, but she'd not told them much more. Occasionally a reminiscence or a story would come up about her uni days, and sometimes Alex would be mentioned. Karen still seemed a bit in awe of her, but she'd clam up if any of them asked her questions.

Tash glanced back to her dad, but he'd gone. Instinctively, she reached out a hand to touch the place where he'd been sitting. There was nothing, but perhaps a faint hint of his aftershave hung in the air. A piece of apple lodged in her throat. There was so much she wanted to tell him, to ask him. So much she would give just to have him sitting beside her on the bed for a moment longer, even if she could tell him nothing at all.

Eventually, she looked back, but the mysterious Alex had disappeared just as silently as Jonathan had.

*

She wasn't sure how long she had lain there before finally falling asleep. The two slices of apple that she had eaten felt like rocks lodged in her gullet.

For some reason, she kept replaying Callie's chatter from earlier on. Tash had ridden in a pink limo once herself. It was Sonal's birthday, her thirteenth. Five of them went to the West End to see *Les Misérables*: Sonal, her mum, her sister, Tash and Claire. They had stuffed themselves with ice cream and sung songs from the show with the windows down. Tash still had some photos printed somewhere of the three of them with the biggest grins on their faces. How could that have been less than three years ago?

She must have fallen sleep eventually because the next thing she knew the sun was up and Evie was shouting at her to come down for breakfast. She felt even more ravenous than usual, and didn't have the energy to fight with her sister again. The funny thing was, as she chewed on some cereal, she found herself staring at the one red-green apple lying neglected in the bottom of the fruit bowl. The one she could have sworn she'd eaten the night before.

Chapter 20

Misty
2019

'I want to get better, Dr Jardine. Straight up, I'll admit it – I don't want to eat, I know it's going to be tough. But I totally get that that's what I'm going to need to do. It's going to be different this time.'

Misty looked at the young woman on the bed, saying nothing, letting her speak. Jodi MacFarlane's foster carer sat on the other side, stroking her bony hand. The elderly, plump white woman couldn't have looked more different from Jodi, whose height and striking mixed-race looks had won her interest from a couple of modelling agencies before the disease really took hold.

Was it the truth? There was no way of knowing. The older woman looked to Misty with fear and trepidation in her eyes.

Jodi's BMI meant she was medically starving. Her body was consuming its own organs to meet the calorie requirements it needed to keep going. Including her brain.

She was saying all the right things about wanting to get better, demonstrating that she knew what it would take. She was saying all the things that patients said when they had made a turnaround and were genuinely on the road to recovery. The problem was that it was what the other patients said too.

Anorexia wasn't a parasite or a virus; it wasn't an organism at all. As far as Misty could tell there was no evolutionary explanation for it, yet she couldn't help but attribute it with a level of cunning that any blind watchmaker would have been proud of encoding. Just as cancer turned the body's own cells into the enemy, anorexia turned its victim's minds into the enemy. It reversed a sufferer's natural will to fight and survive. As the illness progressed, the brain, along with the rest of the organs, became starved and depleted. The ability to make rational decisions decreased dramatically. There were delusions – the skeletal teens who genuinely looked in the mirror and saw mountains of flab; there were hallucinations – the patients who heard voices commanding them to refuse sustenance. The disease was in control and its grip was unrelenting. It was the disease doing the talking now. She pictured it as a vulture, claws sunk into Jodi, shrouding her jealously with ugly, tattered wings. In Jodi's eyes Misty saw the yellow, jealous eyes of the raptor; she saw its wish to drag the girl away, out of sight, away from scrutiny. Where it could drink in peace until her lifeblood was gone.

Misty picked up a chart. 'You've managed to put on some weight since you were admitted.'

Jodi nodded eagerly. 'I know.'

'But not as much as we'd aimed for in the treatment plan.'

'I'm very close. I'll do even better when I'm out. I know how important it is.'

'You're not actually close,' Misty kept her voice as gentle as possible. 'Your BMI is still dangerously low. The longer it stays at this level the more significant the risk of long-term serious health implications.'

'But it doesn't mean anything! Because I'm tall, my BMI always looks worse. I'm getting better, and Linda can look after me. Can't you? Tell her they can't keep me here.'

Her foster carer's eyes welled up at the panic in Jodi's voice. Misty knew that Jodi had lived with Linda Sillitoe since she was seven and a half. Although she'd known the pair of them for only a couple of months, she could see that Linda felt just as confused, as guilty and as devastated as any of the biological mothers who had passed through this ward.

'If it comes to it, Jodi, we *can* keep you here.' Misty paused for a breath, to let her words sink in with both of the women. 'Your food is your treatment. Everyone has the right to refuse medical treatment, as long as you have the capacity to make an informed decision and understand the consequences. Do you understand what I'm saying?'

'You can't *make* me eat.' There was a glint of victory in the girl's eye, in the vulture's eye. Misty's confidence in her instinct grew.

'We can't make you eat. *Unless* the disease has impaired your brain functioning to the extent that we believe you no longer have capacity to make rational decisions. Your BMI is far too low. As we said, the human brain can't function at that level. I can show you the science if you like.'

'So, what, I can decide not to eat and be sane and then I get down to a random number and I'm suddenly insane? And what then? You're going to force-feed me?'

'Well, firstly I can keep you here without your consent. There's a legal process for that – I'll explain more to you both later. We don't use the term "force-feeding" but, as you know, tube feeding is pretty common on the ward. If a patient needs it and won't give their consent then we can get a court order to use a feeding tube against their will. But I don't want to let it get there, or even close. And neither do you, particularly given everything you've just been telling us.'

The only response was a hollow laugh from Jodi. Linda looked stricken. Misty would never lie to a patient, but the reality was that judges did not hand out orders over-riding the lack of consent of adults or near-adults very lightly. By the time a case got to that point it might still be possible to save a patient's life, but the likelihood was that they were facing the rest of that life with a ruined body that would never again function as it should, as well as permanent psychological scarring. She needed Jodi to do this for herself, and if it took the threat of an extended stay in hospital and a court-ordered hook-up to a nasogastric tube, then she was more than prepared to dangle that possibility.

'Now, time to eat. I want to see you getting up to 2,500 calories consistently over the next three days. Otherwise we need to talk again about that tube.'

As if on cue a porter opened the door of the four-bed ward and clanked an unwieldy trolley into the room.

Jodi's spiky composure finally wavered.

'You're torturing me. I fucking hate this place. You're a bitch. You both are. Why can't you just leave me the fuck alone? I hate you.'

Misty let the tirade flow over her, turning instead to Linda and taking the older woman's hand in her own. Linda's cheeks were wet, and she looked as if she was trying to speak but not managing to get the words out. She must be in her late sixties, Misty reckoned, if not older. How tragic that she should have this to go through. Misty squeezed her hand, her heart heavy. They were saving lives here, she knew they were, but very often it felt like the opposite.

The next destination on her ward round was Silver Birch. The inpatient unit was made up of eight main rooms with four beds in each, as well as two critical care rooms and two additional individuals rooms, normally used for private patients. Silver Birch was the four-bedder reserved for the unit's male patients. There were rarely more than four male inpatients at any one time, but the room was never empty. As with the women, some of the boys and men had waited weeks or even months before they finally got admitted.

Misty spent plenty of time that she could have used to care for patients fighting for ever-diminishing resources instead. There were many occasions she'd been enraged, setting out on the frantic mission to pull someone back from the brink, knowing full well that they'd been lined up for admission weeks earlier but there were too few beds in the unit and no space for those who weren't desperately ill.

She consulted her notes on Silver Birch. Three patients today. The fourth bed was on a turnaround. Matt Isherwood had been discharged yesterday. She smiled at the thought of the twenty-year-old's cheeky grin and sardonic sense of humour. He'd responded really well to the regime, a model patient. She had high hopes of never seeing him again.

'Dr Jardine!'

Her smile flickered at the sight of Liz McNeal, the unit's admin coordinator, clacking towards her in heels that, strictly, had no place in a hospital corridor. There was an unmistakable look of concern on her colleague's face.

'Liz, what's the problem?'

'The desk have taken a call for you. Someone called ...' She paused to look down at a Post-it in her hand. 'Evie Neville?'

It took a moment to come to her – Karen's daughter. The older one.

'Right?'

'She said you were a friend of her mum, and that her sister was ill, and needed help. I was going to page, but I knew I'd find you just as quickly if I came up here. Are you their emergency contact or something?'

Karen shook her head. 'No. I know her mother – a little. I don't know the girls at all.' Her mind flickered back to that day at the party, Tasha's jutting collarbone and her dark sunken eyes looking up at Misty from her cocoon at the end of the bed. The eyes that said she needed help even as her lips were saying something else. Misty handing over her card – the card with the phone number of this unit on it. She began to put the pieces together.

'They took a number from Evie, did they?'

Liz nodded.

'It won't be ambulance territory, don't worry. Her sister's having a tough time and I told the girls they could contact me if they wanted to. I think they probably only had the number for here. I'll do Silver Birch – it's my last room anyway – and then I'll ring her back.'

Liz nodded and turned to go. She wouldn't be pleased about being dragged away from her emails but there was little she could do about it. With no children and a partner who was away more often than he was around, nobody could accuse Misty of being the type of doctor who brought her home life into work.

The ward round in Silver Birch was routine. All three of

147

the remaining patients were following established treatment programmes, which seemed to be going to plan. She'd been a little concerned about one of them, a talented gymnast called Ben, who'd only turned thirteen a few weeks earlier. It was hard to be in hospital so young, and even in her experience of troubled, struggling adolescents, the boys somehow seemed less mature than the girls. But a couple of the nurses had taken a shine to him, and Hywel, the older lad in the next bed, was a gregarious sort who was tolerant enough of Ben's chatter. Maybe it helped that they were both Liverpool fans. Whatever the reason, Ben was coping better with it all than she might have expected.

As she ran through the boys' latest weigh-ins, adjusted their intake levels and answered a couple of questions about Hywel's psychotherapy sessions, her mind was only half on the job. She hoped she'd made the right decision in prioritising finishing this work over returning Evie's call. The bit she was struggling with, was why it had been Evie who had got in touch. It was all too easy to imagine that whatever 'diet' Tasha had put herself on had spiralled into something more sinister.

Doing her job, it was an obvious trap to assume that was where every teenager on a diet ended up. She had to consciously remind herself sometimes that for some young people losing weight was an entirely healthy endeavour, and that even for the ones who took it a bit far, it was often no more than a phase, easily resolved and with no real danger. That was the approach she'd taken when she saw Tash at the party. Don't make assumptions. Don't jump to conclusions. Surely the more likely reason for the phone call was that, unfortunately for her, Tash had not had such a lucky escape.

But on the other hand, if that was the case, wouldn't it be

Karen calling her? The best scenario would be Tash herself recognising there was a problem, but experience said that was unlikely. Almost invariably, certainly with the teenagers, the people who raised the alarm were the parents.

The unit occupied the seventh and eight floors of the main block of a large teaching hospital. Misty made her way down from the inpatient area on the eighth floor to her office on the level below, filing the boys' notes and taking a couple of mouthfuls of water before she sat down to call the number on the Post-it that Liz had left stuck to the edge of her screen.

'Yes?'

The voice on the other end was young, but more abrupt than Misty had expected. She sounded as if she had better things to do with her time.

'This is Misty Jardine. Is that Evie Neville?'

'Yes, yes, thanks for calling back. Give me a second.'

Misty listened patiently to the dislocated noises of Evie moving through a building. Doors opening and closing, footsteps going upstairs and indecipherable words hissed away from the phone.

'Sorry. Just needed to go somewhere private. I'm in my room now.'

'So, what can I do for you?'

'You left your card with my sister at the party.'

'You're right, that's me.'

'And you're an anorexia doctor.'

'You could say that.'

'Well, my sister's got it. I'm sure, and it's bad. I'm worried about her.'

'I'm really sorry to hear that, Evie. Does Tash know you're calling?'

Misty knew she had to tread carefully. There was always patient confidentiality. Always consent and privacy to think about. It was tempting to brush them aside when a medical threat seemed so much more tangible. But she recognised that following that path devalued the very lives they were trying to save, not to mention potentially leading her to an awkward run-in with the GMC. But Tash wasn't her patient – not yet at any rate. She had a little bit of leeway.

Evie didn't answer immediately. A muffled sound carried down the phone line and Misty pictured her shaking her head. 'No. I've been trying to get her to do something for weeks. She said she would go to the GP. Then she said she'd been but I'm convinced she was lying. I came back from uni for the weekend and made a meal, which she threw on the floor. She won't talk to me about it – she just shuts down.'

'And what about your mum?' *I'm asking as a friend*, Misty told herself. *I'm not crossing any lines.*

'I ... Mum ...' For the first time Evie seemed unsure of herself, unable to understand, or to articulate, whatever force was dismantling the family that had been her bedrock for her entire life. 'She's not acting like herself either. She's out a lot, but not so much that she can't have seen what's happening to Tash. It's like ...' Misty's own throat caught as she heard the raw emotion in Evie's words '... it's like she can't see it. Or she won't see it. She keeps insisting that Tash is fine.'

Misty's brow creased. Maybe this was good news. Perhaps Evie was a little prone to over-dramatisation. But she still sensed something odd about the whole situation.

'But you don't think so?'

'She looks like a skeleton.' The girl was sniffing now, and

150

there was a note of hysteria in her voice. 'She's skipping school. She's sleeping half the day. She's not ... she's not my sister anymore and I don't know what I can do about it. Even our little sister Callie can see that there's something wrong, but Mum just keeps saying it's a phase and she'll eat a bit more when she's ready.'

Misty's mind was racing through the options. She was used to dealing with patients themselves denying there was a problem, resisting intervention. But this was something different. Parents could be doubting, could be difficult; there were some clinicians who stuck to the old theories that parents were largely responsible for causing anorexia, albeit inadvertently. But she had no precedent for dealing with a parent who was actively enabling that behaviour of a child who – if what Evie said was right – was clearly very ill.

'Do you think you could get Tash to meet me, Evie?'

By now, the girl on the other end of the phone was openly sobbing. 'She wouldn't even call you. I've begging her to call for days.'

'I don't mean coming to the clinic. Just informally, in a park, or a café or something like that?'

'I don't think so.'

She took another gulp of water, hoping she wouldn't come to regret what she was about to say. 'Can I come to the house? Perhaps when your mum isn't around. We can say that I'm coming to talk to you about something – careers advice? When Tash would be in and I could see her?'

'Sure. Tash never goes anywhere. It won't be a problem. Mum's going out tomorrow night. When could you come?'

She did a quick calculation, thinking back to the journey times on the day of the party. 'I've got an early shift tomorrow.

If I came straight from work, I could be with you by five. Is that too early?'

'Maybe a little. Mum will definitely be out by six. Tash is normally awake in the early evening too, wandering around glued to her phone and looking like some Halloween joke.'

Misty winced, not so much at the words, but at the stark contempt in her voice. Sisters, eh? Evie's affection for Tash was definitely of the 'tough love' variety.

'Okay, Evie. I'll see you then. I've got your mobile. I'll send you my number, and text me if there's any problem. Otherwise I'll see you shortly after six tomorrow.'

'Okay, thanks, bye.'

Evie was gone, ending the call as abruptly as she'd started it. Leaving Misty staring at the plastic receiver in her hand and wondering what the hell she was doing. Hopefully, hopefully, it was something and nothing. Evie didn't know Tasha's weight – everything she'd said was a subjective view. Perhaps the worst that would happen was that Misty would end up embarrassing herself by charging across London on a cloak-and-dagger visit to a couple of kids who were just a bit spoilt and self-obsessed. She hoped that was the case.

Slowly, she replaced the landline receiver and reached her pocket for her mobile. Taking care not to switch any of the digits, she typed in Evie's number from the Post-it and composed a short message.

This is Misty Jardine. See you tomorrow evening. Let me know if there's a problem.

She wasn't sure if Evie would reply. She double-checked the number she'd texted and then crumpled up the Post-it and dropped it into the bin near her desk.

The ping of her phone made her jump, even though she

was half expecting it. When she swiped the screen, she gasped. It was a picture. The girl looked to be sleeping; her head lolled back and her mouth was slightly open. Her skin was so shadowed it could almost be bruised, and the bones showed so sharply it appeared they could pierce through her skin at any moment. The stark globe of her skull conjured up famine, concentration camps. It was an echo that Misty had never quite rid herself of, however often she saw patients whose condition had become desperate. Below the picture, a message from Evie: *Tasha now. She needs u. CU tmrrw.*

She glanced at the clock on the wall. Philippa from Oak Ward would be down any moment for her psychotherapy appointment. She had two more patients – including Hywel from Silver Birch – back to back after her. That was her lunch hour gone. Maybe she could carve out a five-minute cheese sandwich break between Philippa and the next session. Some psychologists probably got to put biscuits out for their consultations and could sneak a couple of those in if they missed lunch. Not here, though.

Chapter 21

Misty
1988

Second years moved out of college, although for the most part they moved into college-owned houses in residential streets a few minutes' walk away. They still generally ate in the buttery and the college cleaners still came round to make the beds. Although there was a little hysteria around the idea of living out, it was pretty obvious that Crocodile Dundee-level survival skills were not going to be required of them.

Misty, Alex and Karen had arranged to share a six-bed house with three other girls in their year. It seemed promising, but over the summer Alex had written to say she'd been readmitted to hospital. She'd blamed the stress of exams, and then not being able to get herself back on track afterwards. Her weight loss had dipped into the 'danger zone', she wrote, but her tone was as effusive as ever and she was insistent that she would be coming back and was looking forward to sharing the house.

Misty hoped she was right. She'd been shocked by the way Alex had tumbled back into her illness. However long she spent thinking about it, she found it impossible to understand

154

her friend's thought processes and motivations. Misty recognised that comments from other people could be unhelpful (and she was dismayed at the way Karen seemed to continually want to undermine Alex) but fundamentally Alex was the one who wasn't eating: she was desperate to fix things, yet she couldn't bring herself to do the tiny, simple thing that would fix everything.

But Alex had made it back. In her usual dramatic style, she'd arrived at the house four days after term had started. Eric Penrith blocked the road with an antique black Bentley that shone like a black beetle. His daughter emerged from the passenger side into the brittle October sunshine as a tiny black-clad frame topped with sunglasses and a billowing-bright silk scarf. When a driver stuck behind the Bentley honked his horn, she simply waved.

Following a deal struck with her director of studies, Alex was spending a long weekend at home at least twice during each eight-week term. She seemed to be managing, and had put on a bit of weight, although Misty wouldn't dream of asking her how much. Now it was November and Alex was due back from a weekend at home. Misty was sitting at her desk with her textbooks spread out on the desk in front of her, staring out the window looking for a Bentley.

The first time, Alex invited Misty and Karen to go home with her. Although she'd gone alone this time, there was still the prospect of seeing Eric when he collected Alex or dropped her off. The thought of it made it difficult to concentrate.

'They're coming!' Karen's voice sang down from her attic room. Misty heard her rushing down the two flights of stairs. Five minutes later her red hair was mingled with Alex's curls as the pair of them huddled together on the sofa giggling at a magazine article that Karen had saved to show Alex. Unseen, Misty sidled past them, to where Eric was waiting in the car, engine idling and cigarette in hand.

She bent down, resting her forearms on the doorframe, breathing his smoke through the open window.

'Hello, gorgeous,' he muttered. 'What can I do for you, then?'

'Kiss me?'

They'd kissed once more since that day in the Penriths' kitchen, a slightly drunken encounter in one of the labyrinthine corridors of the house. She'd replayed the moment so often it felt as if the tape was running thin. She was hungry to supplement that memory with something else – something more.

He laughed. Not the snort or splutter of an embarrassed student, but a lazy, melodic rumble.

'Not likely.'

'Your loss.' She shrugged, attempting to imitate his nonchalance.

'Come and find me in the faculty,' he said, keeping his eyes fixed on the rear-view mirror. 'I'm there most days.'

The engine purred to life and she jumped back from the window as he dropped the cigarette end on the road. Without waiting for a reply, he was gone. Slowly, she walked back towards the house.

*

It wasn't hard for a medical student to find an excuse to go to the chemistry department, and it wasn't hard to find Eric when she got there. The visits became frequent. They snogged and fumbled after-hours in Eric's tiny office. If her hand knocked a stack of journals as he pushed her against the desk, he was never too caught up in the moment to fail to pause and straighten them.

He bought her lunch, twice, in a place that was little more than a sandwich bar. Somehow, he managed to make that feel more furtive than the snatched moments in the office. She wasn't proud of what they were doing, but her body was hungry for him, in spite of herself. The shadowy darkness of his chest, the swarthy width of his shoulders and the curve of his jaw. Those images swam in her mind as she lay in bed, as she washed the dishes, the second her attention wandered in a lecture. She dreamt of possessing him, of sinking her teeth in.

The reality was less satisfactory. Her dreams were all passion and mastery. The reality was the rasp of stubble on sunburn and awkward buttons and the smell of stale cigarettes on his breath. Her hunger never lifted; she always felt that she was in touching distance of something, but never quite there.

Their most peaceful times were when they sat in the office during the day. They couldn't do more than talk, Eric said, because of the risk of a colleague or a student coming in. No one ever did.

Instead, they smoked and chatted about nothing much. Science sometimes, articles in *Nature* or in one of the medical journals. Eric was interested in immunology. He thought she could keep up when he enthused about the latest advances, but she was mainly pretending. She liked the fact he gave her credit, but sometimes it felt more like a supervision than anything else. Otherwise he talked about other people in the department or at his college. He felt overlooked. His position was still that of a junior academic. He didn't need the money – the little he said about his family confirmed what she'd already heard about his wealth and aristocratic pedigree. What he was desperate for was for his work to be taken seriously, but he wanted his pampered lifestyle too. Misty had no idea how talented he might be as a scientist, but she couldn't imagine him devoting himself to the lab for days on end.

'What about Catarina? Do you love her?'

She wasn't exactly sure why she asked these things. Partly she craved the reassurance that was never forthcoming, she wanted him to tell her that he loved her more, that she was important to him. Partly it made her feel grown-up. Partly, truth be told, she needed something to distract him when he launched into one of his incomprehensible monologues about departmental politics.

For whatever reason, she needled endlessly about Catarina.

Eric explained how he'd met her at an academic conference in Spain. He'd never met someone so luminescent, so intense – she made him come alive. He was drawn to her and then singed by her brilliance, like a blundering moth. Misty never got the sense that she was any sort of lantern in his eyes. She yearned for him; he tolerated her. How was she supposed to compare to the memory of Catarina?

Spain in the Sixties was an odd place, he informed her. New jets belched out thousands of tourists, the Costas threw up their concrete towers and a money-making jamboree of fun, sun and flamenco cranked up a gear with each passing year. Away from the beaches, though, Franco's authoritarian grip on power seemed secure. Political prisoners languished in the notorious Carabanchel and social conservatism was rigidly enforced.

'I booked package tours twice to go and see her. I even bought a sombrero.' The scorn on his face indicated that the tacky souvenir was the last sort of thing a man like him would choose to spend his money on. Misty pictured him wearing it, riding a donkey, and supressed a smile. Whilst his fellow tourists had toasted themselves red and necked sangria, he had picked up a few words of Spanish to enable him to catch trains to Madrid, where he met Catarina in dank and fuggy bars and stayed in back rooms belonging to friends of hers who declined to meet his eye.

'At the end of the second visit, two airport guards pulled me into a side room to question me about what I'd been doing during my stay. I missed the flight and they had to find me a space on another one. The holiday reps from the travel company looked at me like I was a leper. A couple of weeks later, Catarina was arrested. When they let her go after three months, I knew I had to get her out.'

'So, you got married?'

'There was another conference. This time in London. I managed to get her an extended visa and then we tied the knot at a registry office in Islington. I thought I was blooming Humphrey Bogart in *Casablanca* or something.'

'Fairy-tale ending,' said Misty, lighting a cigarette. Eric raised an eyebrow, and beckoned for the packet.

'I assumed I could rescue her and she could leave it behind. That's where I went wrong. If I told you some of the ways my wife struggles with life, you might think she was weak. It wouldn't be true. She was stronger than most people could ever be. But it would finish her off if she found out about ... this,' he'd added, drawing deeply on one of Misty's Marlboro Lights and gazing stonily out of the window.

And so it continued, sporadic and partially satisfying, for the rest of the autumn term and into the new year. At Christmas, she saved and bought him a silk tie. He sent her truffles and champagne and designer underwear through the college post, never putting his name on anything. She loved getting those gifts, the clandestine feel of the anonymous brown paper, the luxury of the contents. Unfortunately, the underwear was two sizes too big. She was too embarrassed to try to return it. When it became clear that he was never going to ask to see her wearing it, she couldn't decide if she was relieved or disappointed.

One late afternoon in February, Karen knocked on her door.

'It's pancake day. For once, Alex isn't off with Andrew, nor is he hanging around here. Debbie, Jenna and Harriet are going to a meeting in college, so it's just the three of us. So – cunning plan alert – I'm going to make pancakes! You in?'

'Yeah, why not – sounds good. When are you starting?'

'I'm going out for some lemons. We've got everything else. Say half an hour?'

'Sure. Thanks.'

It was fun. Karen was right about Andrew hanging around a lot. He and Alex were getting quite serious. It was nice to have Alex to themselves, and Karen was on good form, enjoying showing off her pancake-making skills.

'I'll soon be the only single one,' said Karen, 'between you and Andrew, and you and your secret lover.' As she said the last part, she waved a spatula in Misty's direction.

'Secret lover? What on earth are you talking about?' Even

as she spoke, Misty could feel a red blush creeping up her neck.

'You tell us,' said Alex, sharing a meaningful look with Karen. She counted their points of 'evidence' off on her fingers. 'We know you were getting presents from someone before Christmas.'

'And very nice ones too,' put in Karen.

'I've seen you twice making secretive phone calls from the phone box on Grange Road when we've got a perfectly good phone here.'

'Yes, *one* perfectly good phone between six of us. Half the time I want to call home, Jenna's on one of her endless calls to her long-distance boyfriend, or else one of the rest of you are on it.'

'And,' continued Alex, raising her voice over Misty's protestations. 'You've started wearing make-up to go to your lectures. You can't deny it.'

'Well, maybe there is someone that I like in the department. But if there was, then the last thing I'd do is introduce them to you two. That would likely put them off for life.' Misty forced herself to smile and laugh along with them, but she was shaken. She thought he'd been careful enough with Eric. *He* was certainly careful to the point of obsession. But perhaps there was no such thing as careful enough.

Karen dished up the first round of pancakes. Alex didn't add sugar, but other than that she ate it as enthusiastically as the others. Andrew might be a bit drippy at times, but she certainly seemed more stable since he'd been in her life. Perhaps Karen was thinking something similar, because when she changed the subject it was to ask about him.

'It's the housing ballot soon. You'll have to decide if you

161

want to go in with us again or are you planning on trying to ballot with Andrew?'

Alex looked thoughtful. 'I'm not sure yet. College aren't keen on letting couples share sets, but Sam Kershaw is sharing with his girlfriend this year, isn't he?'

'Yes,' said Karen, 'Matilda. I know her a bit. Wouldn't your parents kick off? The vicarage would go wild at the idea of me living in sin.'

Alex shrugged. 'I don't think mine could pull the religious card, not with a straight face. But they don't like Andrew. So, they keep making noises about how we're too young to really know what we want, and how dangerous it would be if we split up and it messed up our finals.'

'But that could happen whether or not you're actually sharing rooms,' observed Misty.

'Yes, and I could always just go home if I needed to. But I'm convinced we're not going to split up. We're going to stay together and we're going to move to London together and if you come and find us in ten years we'll be married. I think that's their problem really – Mum's especially – she can see I've got an escape route, and she doesn't like it.'

Misty and Karen remained silent for a few mouthfuls. Misty never quite knew what to say when Alex alluded to how bad things were with her mum. If she was brutally honest, she was never quite sure how convinced she was by Alex and how much she suspected that Alex was dramatising things.

'What does your dad say?' ventured Karen. 'Is he against it too?'

From nowhere, Alex burst into tears.

'Shit. Sorry, what's the matter?' Karen scrambled to get a tissue. Misty stayed silent.

'God, I'm sorry, what a state.' She blew her nose and composed herself. 'I've been wanting to tell you both for a while. I've told Andrew, but he thinks I'm being paranoid. The thing is ... I'm not sure, but I think my dad's planning to walk out.'

For a moment, Misty felt as if every drop of blood had drained from her body. Then it was back, her heart thumping and pumping it around with the force of an engine.

'What? How?' asked Karen.

'I overheard a phone call and then I sneaked a look at some papers on his desk. He's resigned from his fellowship; he's not planning to be in Cambridge after the summer. And he's in love with someone. I don't know who it is, but I heard him tell his oldest friend about it.'

'People get new jobs all the time. And that might not be related to the phone call. If it was in London or somewhere, he could commute – you might not have to move.' Karen was obviously trying to sound grown-up and pragmatic. 'I mean, people have affairs all the time. It doesn't mean they walk out on their families. And you said yourself you're not sure.'

'He wouldn't get a new job. No one else would employ him. No one good. He stays in Cambridge because of the kudos. If they got rid of him, he'd just stop working. I'm half surprised he hasn't already. And you're right. I could be putting two and two together and getting sixteen, but I can't stop thinking about it. I'm trying to decide whether to come out and ask him. What do you think, Misty, you're sensible?'

For a horrible moment she thought it was a trap, that Alex knew everything and was going to make her admit it and humiliate her in front of Karen. Had all the earlier conversation about her 'secret lover' been part of the set-up? But there

163

was none of Alex's usual mischievousness on her face. She looked guileless, and bereft. A weight of guilt and a flutter of excitement lodged simultaneously in Misty's chest. What if it was *her*? She knew full well that Eric considered his marriage to be over, but what if he was actually leaving Catarina for her?

'I think I need a glass of wine,' replied Misty. Then she remembered exactly what Alex's question had been, and terror joined the jostle of emotions fighting for space in her chest. 'No. No. Don't ask him.' She flailed around for reasons to back up her advice. 'I mean, if it's all a mistake, you'll upset him. And if your mum gets wind of it, she'll take it badly, won't she? Don't rock the boat. If he's got anything to tell you he'll tell you in his own time.'

And tell me? she wondered, inwardly. God, it would be crazy but fabulous. Being able to go out together, being able to *live* together. Imagine taking one of those brown paper parcels and turning it into her whole life.

Chapter 22

Karen
2019

As gently as Andrew tried to let her down, the humiliation shook her fragile confidence like a landslide taking out a sapling. She'd insisted he call her a cab and then burned with shame all the way back to Twickenham. Her first thought had been that she could never, ever, see him again. She ran through the scenarios that might lead to them meeting, and how she could guard against each one. Over the next three or four days he sent friendly several text messages, but she ignored them all.

Manda's pills were the only thing that numbed the embarrassment of the memory, and she found they worked even better with a glass or two of wine. It wasn't recommended, but she was an adult; she just needed to soften the edges at the moment. She told herself she'd stop using them soon enough. But her new start was always tomorrow, not today, and slowly another idea began to take shape in her fuzzy mind.

Perhaps, she decided, the reason that Andrew had rejected her was because he couldn't accept anyone. Or, to be more specific, couldn't accept anyone who wasn't Alex. *If you could*

bring back Alex, I'd give you the world on a plate. His wor
from their first meeting began to echo more insistently arou
her head. What if she could bring back Alex? That wou
salve her humiliation and earn his gratitude. And he'd o
her. The guy was a multi-millionaire. She'd be doing everyo
a favour.

And the more she thought about it, the more convinc
she was that the photo had to be Alex. It was fate. It had
be. She stopped googling Andrew and started googling A
instead. It was a renewed effort. She'd obviously had a br
look when she first saw the picture, but not with this sort
focus.

Tash came in one evening and looked over her should
There was a picture of the Valkyries that she'd got from
alumni site. She'd zoomed in on Alex, even although the s
didn't offer any information that she didn't already know.

'That's the girl from the photo in your study. Alex.'

'Yes, darling, I'm surprised you know her name.'

'I remember you told me about her. That she was anorex
and she died when you were at uni. I always thought s
looked beautiful in the photo. And fun.'

'She was both of those things. You would have liked he

'I know.'

Karen turned to look at her daughter. 'What do you mea

'Nothing,' said Tash, sharply. 'I ... I feel like I know her. B
it's just because of the stories you used to tell. Of course
don't know what she was really like.'

Karen frowned. There was something shifty and off-k
about Tash's reply. 'You always were a funny one, sweethea
She gently pushed Tash back and frowned. 'You don't lo
well, though.'

166

'Flu,' Tash said quickly. 'It's doing the rounds. I think I'm coming down with it.'

'Maybe you should stay off a few days. I can call school in the morning?'

Tasha went red. 'Erm, actually, Mum, I already did. You were sound asleep this morning so I just called in.'

'You pretended to be me?'

Tash nodded, shame-facedly. 'But only because I didn't want to wake you – I thought maybe you were coming down with it too.'

'I'm lucky to have such sensible, grown-up girls, aren't I?'

'Are you?' Tash sounded uncertain. 'I thought you'd go ballistic.'

'Come here, give me a hug.'

The hug was fleeting, broken off when Callie stomped in, dainty as a baby elephant as usual.

'I'm starving, Mum, what's for dinner?'

'Oh, is that the time? I got caught up in the computer stuff. I'd not planned anything to be honest, but we'll have loads in the fridge. What do you fancy?'

Her younger daughter had already opened the fridge and did not look impressed.

'Well, *not* leftover vegetable moussaka from, like, three days ago. Or mouldy beetroot. We've got lots of jars ...'

'Why don't I just do some pasta? I can blitz up a pesto, we'll have capers and artichokes in there, and there's some basil and parsley on the windowsill ...'

'I'm hungry now, Mum. It's, like, almost half eight. Can we not just get pizza?'

Karen sighed. 'All right, just this once.'

'Great! I'll have pepperoni please. The spicy one. And a cheesy crust.'

Tash made a face. 'I don't know how you can.'

'What do you want then, Tasha?'

'Actually, I ate earlier. Neither of you were around, so I ju[st]
fixed myself something.'

'All right. I'll give them a call. I get some extra garlic bre[ad]
because you'll probably want some when it gets here.'

'Yeah, probably. Thanks, Mum.'

Karen watched guiltily as Callie demolished the peppero[ni].
The poor girl must really have been famished. She had [to]
remember that they weren't grown-ups yet; they still need[ed]
her.

Chapter 23

Misty
2019

The walk from the station to the Neville house was familiar from the day of the party. It seemed quicker this time, but that was probably due to the fact that Misty was in flat pumps, rather than her party sandals. It was late summer now and getting cooler. Misty had come straight from the surgery. She was wearing a lightweight wrap cardigan, which she pulled around herself as she walked.

When she got to the house, she had to double-check she'd got the right number. Although it was still the handsome Victorian villa she remembered, it looked quite different from when she'd last been here and the house had been *en fête* and virtually gleaming. The empty bins were out, and the fact that the lids were scattered and there was no sign of the neighbours' ones, suggested the collection had been earlier in the week. The planting in the smart lead window boxes looked neglected and a pizza flyer flapped from the letterbox.

But even if the house looked empty, it evidently wasn't. The door swung open just as she lifted her hand to the knocker.

'You're Misty? Come in.'

It was Evie, the older daughter. Misty knew her voice from the phone call and vaguely recognised her from the party although her lank hair and the dark shadows under her eyes were new.

'Tash is upstairs in bed. That's where she always is these days. She says she's fine, but she's a million miles from it.'

'And your mum's out?'

Evie's face creased into a frown. 'Yes. I don't know what's going on with Mum these days. She keeps saying Tash is fine too. And vanishing off.'

'Vanishing off where?'

The girl shrugged. 'Well, you're here to see Tash, anyway, that's the important thing.' Misty couldn't help but feel there was a sudden defensiveness about her. She turned away, leading Misty upstairs and, presumably, towards her sister's bedroom. No point in hanging around, Misty supposed, but she had a sense that Evie was using the short journey as an excuse to turn her face away, to end the conversation and evade any scrutiny from Misty. There was no chance to try to engage her again, though – Evie had come to an abrupt halt outside a door with a starkly childish pink 'Natasha' sign. Gently, she pushed it open.

'Tash, this is Misty Jardine, the doctor. You met her at Mum's party.'

Misty stepped into the room, her experience immediately kicking in to make observations about the girl lounging on the bed. Her thin, loose clothing didn't disguise the fact that she was painfully skinny. Her skin had the rough, eczema-like abrasions that were common with anorexia, and when her forearms emerged from the pyjama top Misty could see the downy hair that grew to compensate as victims lost the insulating body fat that should help to regulate their temperature.

Tash was awake, her eyes wide open, appearing eerily large in their sunken sockets. Misty wanted to see defiance, pleading or even despair. Instead, she saw nothing; Tash's gaze was passive, betraying no emotion. Misty's heart felt heavy – that was the worst sign of all.

'Hi, Tasha, I'm going to sit down.' Without fuss, Misty lifted some books and clothes from the desk chair and swivelled it round, so she could sit by the head of the bed. She turned to Evie. 'Any chance of a tea? It's probably best if I have a bit of a chat with Tash on my own. Won't take long. I'll come and find you in the kitchen if you like?'

Evie looked as if she wanted to object, but she had nothing to match the polite insistence that came from Misty's years of experience. She nodded, and left the room. Misty turned to the girl on the bed.

'We met at your mum's party, do you remember? You were sitting here grumbling about the guests, if I recall. It looks to me as if things have got a bit out of hand since then?'

It wasn't so much a nod as a twitch of her head, but Misty decided to take it as affirmation.

'You going to tell me about it?'

This time, Tash shook her head emphatically and hunched round, turning away from Misty to face towards the wall.

'That's okay, if it's easier for you. I've helped a lot of girls in your position, Tasha. Everybody's different, of course, no one's story is the same. But I do have a bit of understanding of what might be going on for you.'

She paused, to allow Tash to respond, knowing that she

wouldn't. It was important to keep the gaps there, so the patients knew they would be heard. When they were ready.

'This makes you feel strong, doesn't it, Tash? It's hard to do – but that's the whole point – like climbing a mountain or running a marathon. If there wasn't a challenge there would be no achievement. You don't enjoy starving. You don't enjoy the pain and the cold and the weakness and everything else that goes with it. But you enjoy success. You enjoy being thin – the thinnest. You feel powerful. That feeling of power has got under your skin now, and you believe you can't kick it, although sometimes you'd like nothing better.'

Tash was so still it was almost as if she'd stopped breathing. She wasn't going to turn around, but Misty knew she was listening with every sinew. It was a start.

'The thing is, Tash, you have a disease. It's called anorexia nervosa, but you know that. You know that it's wasting your body. Perhaps you don't know that it's controlling your mind. That sounds dramatic, but it's the best way of explaining it. Girls like you *do* get better, and when they get better, they are so, so glad to have done it. That's the brave way, Tasha, and the strong way. And there are lots of people who can help.'

'I don't have it. There's nothing wrong with me.'

Misty jumped slightly at the monotone sound of Tasha's reply. The girl hadn't moved, when the response came, she hadn't been expecting it. What Tasha said, however, was exactly what Misty would expect to hear; it was what they all said. The ones who really believed it were the ones you had to worry about the most.

'Then talking to me won't be a problem, will it?' she replied, with deliberate brightness.

172

Tash turned, meeting Misty's eye now with a fevered intensity in her gaze.

'Some don't get better.'

Misty nodded, conceding the point, and noting to herself that Tasha's denial that she had the disease was just a defence mechanism. Still, in her experience a patient could believe one thing just now, another in five minutes and something completely different tomorrow.

'Some don't, Tasha, you're right. But you can. And like I said, when you have your life back – when you have your mind back – you'll be very glad that you were brave enough to let this go. I can introduce you to lots of former patients who feel that way.'

'They might be pleased with themselves, but what if the dead ones are happier?'

'What do you mean, Tash?'

'I know someone. She's happier than anyone still on this earth. She tells me. She tells me how I can float up like an angel.'

Tash paused, a note of challenge in her voice. She expected Misty to contradict her. Misty held her tongue.

'There's nothing to worry about up there,' Tasha continued, eventually. 'Maybe I'll fade away and be with her. And then I'll be happy like she is.'

She spoke haltingly in a rasping voice broken by coughing and pauses where Tash gathered herself. She'd slumped round onto her back, so Misty could at least see the profile of her face. Her eyes were fixed on the ceiling, but there was a gleam in them where before they'd been flat. Tears? Misty couldn't tell.

'What do you mean "she"?' Misty prompted gently. 'Who are you talking about?'

'She was a friend of my mum,' replied Tash. 'She's calle[d] Alex.'

Misty gasped, her professional demeanour toppled for [a] moment. Tasha must have heard. For the first time she rolle[d] over to look Misty square in the eye. Her expression wa[s] mocking, triumphant.

'I know you were her friend too, Misty. I've seen the pictur[e] of the three of you. I know you can't be trusted – Alex wa[s] very clear about that. So, you're wasting your time. I won't b[e] coming to your hospital; I won't be listening to your advic[e.] You can go now.'

Tash closed her eyes. Her breathing was still laboured fro[m] the effort of speech, and Misty suspected that she would hav[e] gone for a more dramatic gesture of dismissal if she'd onl[y] had the energy.

She allowed herself a moment to gather herself, closing h[er] own eyes and massaging her temples before standing up fro[m] the chair. Whatever she'd expected from her meeting with Tas[h] it certainly hadn't been that. Of course, Tasha wasn't speakin[g] to Alex. She didn't believe in beyond-the-grave communica[-] tion. But whatever twisted thing was going on here it wa[s] eerily close to the bone – 'don't trust Misty Jardine' woul[d] surely be exactly the advice that Alex would have given, ha[d] she been around to give it.

She wanted nothing more than to back out of the roo[m] to leave Tasha and the maelstrom of emotions her words ha[d] evoked and shut the door on the whole thing. But she was [a] doctor; she couldn't do that.

'I understand what you're telling me, Tash.' She kept h[er] voice steady and gentle, though it was an effort. 'I know yo[u] don't want help, but I can also see that you need it. I'm talkin[g] now to the bit of you that knows that too. I'm going to do everything I can for you. We're going to beat this.'

The girl on the bed was still, with only the faint rise and fall of her chest to show she was alive. But Misty sensed she was still there, still listening.

'I'm going now, but I'll be back, Tasha. Goodnight.'

She went to the bathroom – the same one she'd used before leaving the party, looking much less tidy now – and descended the stairs slowly, giving herself time to work out how much she would say to Evie. Biting her lip, she sent a quick text message to Eusebio too, confirming that she'd have to go back to the office to do some paperwork for a new admission. Sadly, this was not the false-alarm situation she'd hoped it might be.

Evie was leaning against the bi-fold doors, absorbed in her phone. When Misty came into the room, she nodded at a steaming mug on the breakfast bar and muttered, 'Just closing this down,' without looking up from her phone. A few moments later, she gave Misty her attention and the older woman tried not to let her irritation show.

'Well, Evie, you were right to get in touch. Tash is in a pretty serious condition.'

The girl nodded. 'So, what are you going to do?'

'That's a bit tricky, actually. I'd like to have her admitted to the specialist unit that I work in, where she could go on an intensive re-feeding programme and then, when she's ready for it, receive the psychological support she needs to start getting better.'

'Great, I guess. What's tricky?'

'Well, the first problem is my waiting list. I'm afraid there is much more demand for eating disorder services than there are places that can provide them. Having said that, Tash has deteriorated particularly quickly and I could certainly make a case for her being prioritised for admission, which could lead to her being allocated a bed in forty-eight hours, maybe a little longer.'

'That doesn't sound too bad.'

'No.' Misty's tone was reflective. 'The NHS is good at saving lives. But, when you get told you can be seen quickly, that's normally a good time to start worrying.' Misty paused. 'Evie?'

'Hmm?'

'The waiting list isn't the main issue with getting Tash the treatment she needs.'

'So, what is?'

'I don't think she'll consent to treatment. Put bluntly, she doesn't want to get better.'

'But ... surely you can do it even if she doesn't agree. I mean, you've just told me she might die otherwise.'

Misty took a sip of her tea, wondering how best to give Evie a crash course in medical ethics. She was only, what? Twenty-one or twenty-two? And not an official next of kin. But at the moment she was here asking the questions and Tasha's mother was ... where? Tasha's sister's perseverance may well have just saved her life. Misty would have to talk to Karen later, but that didn't mean it was wrong to talk to Evie now.

'So, generally, you have the right to refuse any sort of treatment, even if it's a barmy decision. You can say no to a flu jab because you don't like needles, say no to a blood transfusion because of religious convictions, say no to cancer treatment because you've had enough. But there's a different rule where people are deemed not to have capacity to understand the decision they are making. A very young child, for example, might not consent to an inoculation because they

176

just see the needle. They don't have the level of understanding needed to actually appreciate what's happening to them.'

'But then the parents decide, don't they?' Her face clouded. 'Is that the problem? Because Mum's sticking her head in the sand about everything? I'm sure she'll consent – once you speak to her and tell her how serious it is.'

'Well, it's not so easy with older children. Tash is fifteen, with no learning disability or anything like that, so normally she'd be deemed to have capacity to make these decisions for herself. Of course, anorexia is a mental illness. There's an argument that the disease itself erodes capacity. That once a person becomes as ill as your sister, they literally lose the ability to make sound decisions. In extreme cases, they can be legally treated without consent, but it's not an ideal solution.'

Evie's brow creased as she puzzled it over. 'But how can you tell, then, when a refusal to accept treatment is a real refusal? Do you always end up saying that because anyone would be crazy to want to die, the person you are treating must be crazy and you can ignore what they want?'

Misty was quietly impressed. Evie had grasped the fundamental difficulty with treating ED patients, who would regularly reject the treatment offered. The potential for a Catch-22 situation was something Misty remained painfully aware of. There was no easy answer. In Tash's case, as in every case she dealt with, she would strive to respect the patient's integrity and choices. But she'd been dealing with these cases for long enough to know that when you stopped a teenager from taking their own life they might recover and thank you with the passion of someone pulled from a burning building – or they might never forgive you. If there was a way of knowing which was which, then she'd yet to work it out.

'Well, that's the problem, Evie. What do you think? If you spoke to Tash a year ago, before all this had started, what would she say about it?'

Evie rubbed her eyes. 'I want to say that she'd want you to fight for her. That of course she'd do anything to be healthy ... to be alive.'

'But?'

'But do I really know her? I went off to uni a year and a half ago. She wasn't much past Little Mix and Claire's Accessories. Of course, I've been home for the holidays – some of them – but I didn't really make the time to check in with her. She's still, like, a thirteen-year-old in my head.'

'What would the thirteen-year-old say?'

Evie frowned for a second. 'The thirteen-year-old I remember would say, "shut up and eat some chips".' They shared a smile, although it only lasted a moment.

'You're a brave girl, Evie, and you've done the right thing for Tash by pushing for me to come here. I'll start getting things in motion – including trying to get hold of your mum and explain why all this is so important. But ultimately, we can't wait for her. We need to act, for Tasha's sake. You'll hear from me sometime tomorrow.' She paused, noticing the glisten in Evie's eyes, before instinctively reaching out to clasp the girl's hand in her own. 'You've been brave, Evie, you won't have to cope with this yourself anymore.'

'Thanks.' Evie's voice was a whisper. 'Just tell me, is she going to be okay?'

'I hope so. And I'll do everything I possibly can to make it happen.'

*

178

Misty walked away from the Neville house with her head throbbing and her heart hammering. Tash's fevered insistence that she was in contact with Alex was reverberating through her mind, harsh as the echo of a gunshot.

For years, she'd been telling herself that she'd left Alex behind. If she was honest, she never really had. Alex was why she was doing this job. Every patient she saved – every girl especially – was a reparation for Alex. They all helped, but she'd never earn enough credit to fill the yawning chasm of her guilt. Every patient she failed was Alex all over again.

She couldn't – she wouldn't – let Tasha Neville become another Alex Penrith.

Chapter 24

Karen
2019

Karen was on the tube. Northern Line. High Barnet Branch. To a foreigner, the glossy housewives and well-heeled commuters would look incongruous against the dilapidated rail-stock. Like every Londoner, Karen would usually be too wearily familiar with the undersized, carpeted seats and the battered fittings to actually bother to look at them.

Today, though, she was looking – really looking. She'd agreed to meet Andrew for dinner in Covent Garden. It would be the first time they'd met since the awful evening at the Lanesborough – a sort of peace offering, he'd said, even though they'd not fallen out. She'd left early so she could have a couple of hours spare to do this. The woman in the picture had been evacuated at East Finchley but that didn't necessarily mean she'd intended to get off there. It had been a northbound morning train, which still had five stops to make before the bomb went off. It might be that she was a commuter and she used that stretch of line every day, but most commuter traffic flowed into the city. It was just as likely that it had been a one-off, unlikely piece of fortune. Despite that likelihood, over the last few weeks, Karen had come up with the idea that she could find her. And become convinced that, in finding her, she would start to find some answers too.

She couldn't get Tash's funny comment about Alex out of her head. A day or two later, she'd overheard her daughter muttering something about Alex in the bathroom, but she'd clammed up completely when Karen had asked her about it. What if Alex was alive, and what if she was contacting Tash to somehow get at Karen? Karen didn't believe in ghosts. The more she thought about it, the more convinced she became that Alex must be alive, and that she had to find her.

Alex might or might not be alive, but Karen's guilt certainly was. For decades, she had buried her feelings about Alex's death – that crushing, soul-destroying certainty that she had been responsible. When she should have been looking out for her friend, she'd been encouraging her to play with fire – fuck it, she'd been the one handing over the damn matches.

It was hard to think about it even now. A sweat broke out on her brow that had nothing to do with the overheated carriages. She forced herself to slow her breathing, taking a long, shaking inhalation that matched the train's shuddering deceleration into the next station.

She'd spent her third year reeling and flunked her finals. The university had adjusted the results a little when, at the suggestion of her director of studies, she got her GP to produce a note saying she'd been adversely impacted by her friend's death. Even so, it was a poor degree and the plum job offer had been withdrawn. Her confidence was blown. Her start in London had been shakier than she'd expected, just about meeting the rent on the flat-share whilst she worked in bars and cafés and lived off baked beans. Jonathan had made everything better. Yes, she'd had a flair for the copywriting work, once she managed to break into it, but the slog had been hard and never truly felt worth it. When the chance to leave work had come, she'd been ready to settle – in every sense.

And now here she was, the poor widow from a fairy tale, without a job or a purpose, living in a house that would be repossessed in a few months. The only thing to her credit was her girls, and now it looked like she'd failed them too. She'd had so many chances, and done nothing with her life. She couldn't blame everything on Alex's death, but that was where it had started.

A fair number of people alighted at Finchley Central. She turned her head, straining to look along the platform, to check as many of the commuters leaving the train as possible. This was a busy stop, and beyond the site of the bombing. It made sense as a place to try. She recognised that the prospect of seeing 'Alex' here was tiny, but it would be much smaller if she didn't look at all. So, Karen was here to look, and look she would. Even if her thoughts ranged far from this stuffy train.

Most of all she felt as if she'd failed Tasha. She'd noticed Tasha becoming discontented – of course she had. Tasha was her child, so she'd been the first to notice the skipped break-fasts and the wrinkles in the skinny jeans and her hair losing its gloss. But she'd been paralysed, convincing herself that any attempt to intervene would be doomed to make it worse.

Karen had been delighted when Tasha took up with that boyfriend – Stanno, as she called him – Karen hadn't probed for his actual name. She'd hoped that would make her daughter happy, that the diet would stop before it took a hold. She'd tried not to notice as the relationship drifted off course, as Tash became listless and more obviously thin. Karen feared that *she* must be the problem – something about her was driving Tash to this, just as she'd driven Alex to it. Or perhaps Tash was picking up on her stress about the money and the house. If she kept herself out of the way, then Tash could get on with being a teenager. She'd always been sensible and resilient; she'd be fine. But that didn't seem to be happening. Although she couldn't bring herself to say it out loud, could barely articulate the thought, with her deepest instinct she knew that things were not right with Tasha and that she didn't have the tools to fix them.

If only she could find Alex …

She could get to the bottom of what was going on with Tasha, and she could change Andrew's world, which would, somehow, lead to him fixing all her financial problems. She could fix everything.

So here she was, scanning the trains, scanning the stations. Making herself giddy by trying to focus on each face on each crowded platform. Getting sweaty and uncomfortable, ears numb to the station names and the security announcements and the robotic advice to carry water.

Of course, Andrew was adamant Alex was dead and, logically, Karen knew that the alternative was too far-fetched to countenance. But maybe now she needed far-fetched. She needed a miracle, because without one her life was crumbling to pieces.

Chapter 25

Misty
2019

Eusebio was already sitting at a table by the time Misty entered the pub. He had two tall glasses in front of him, both slick with condensation.

'G&T. I managed to wait.'

'Just what I need.' Misty raised her glass in thanks. 'Have you ordered food?'

'Only some prawn crackers. They've decided they're Thai now.'

Misty made a face. Their local had a dubious track record on food offerings, but it was an easy stagger, quiet enough to chat, and you never had a problem finding a table. It wasn't usually this dark, although perhaps, along with the Thai food, that was part of the latest rebranding. Eusebio was wearing a black jumper and in the gloomy light of the bar, the whites of his eyes jumped out like cat's eyes in the road. He was still attractive enough to turn heads with his gym-vain figure and boyish features. Strangers could never guess his ethnicity – as plenty were rude enough to tell him – she suspected these days they'd struggle equally with his age.

184

'Tough day at work then? What was the story with the visit? You don't normally go out to their homes?'

She'd sent him a few messages over the afternoon and evening, knowing that he was expecting her home for dinner. He'd been going to cook for them, but as it became clear that she would be late and possibly too tired to be fully appreciative, he'd suggested they just meet at the pub instead. She gulped her drink, still trying to decide for herself exactly what conclusions she should draw about Tasha Neville.

'The girl's sick.'

'"Sick" as in bad day, or "sick" as in imminent danger?' From innumerable conversations over the years, Eusebio knew almost as well as Misty the high thresholds required to access treatment.

Misty shrugged. 'She's pretty bad. She's not going to die this week. Well, not unless she's got a heart condition we don't know about or picks up the flu.'

'Sounds not great, though, "suboptimal" as we are saying now, no?'

She managed a thin laugh. 'Yes. Suboptimal. And I have a bad feeling about her. It's accelerating rapidly and she doesn't seem scared of where she's heading. I didn't weigh or measure her, but I guess her BMI is at the sort of level we'd normally look at for admission, and on top of that I'm fairly sure she's having auditory hallucinations.'

'Hallucinations?' Eusebio raised a brow, his widened eyeball luminous in the dark.

'Hearing voices,' clarified Misty. 'It's actually more common than you'd think, but usually it's unidentified. They'll just hear someone commanding them not to eat, or threatening that, if they do, they'll get fat.'

'And this girl is different?'

185

'You could say. She claims she's been talking with her mum's old friend from university. A friend who died nearly thirty years ago ... from anorexia. I'm not sure if it's hallucinations brought on by the anorexia or if there may be a separate psychosis in operation too.'

'*Mierda*. And didn't you say the mum was at uni with you?'

Misty raised her eyebrows and took a swig of the G&T. She told Eusebio a lot about her patients – at least she did when he was around – but she was mindful of confidentiality and never named them, even when talking to him. She'd forgotten that they'd spoken at lunchtime and she'd told him about the call from Evie, briefly explaining about the party and how Evie had her number. Oh well, she trusted him. What was the point of living with someone if you couldn't open up to them about the things that bothered you most?

She nodded, lifting her glass to her lips again although there was nothing but ice in it. 'The friend who's supposedly "talking" to Tasha – it's Alex Penrith.'

Eusebio gave a low whistle. '*That* friend.'

Misty nodded. 'Exactly, that friend.'

'So ... now you are the big shot. The big success story. She's the reason you wanted to work with ED patients. I suppose you have her to thank.'

The prawn crackers arrived and he nodded at the waitress before wolfishly stuffing two in his mouth. Things were always simple for Eusebio. Black and white. Invariably positive. She loved that about him, but it was infuriating at the same time.

Before she had chance to reply he was pointing at her empty glass. 'Another one?'

'I think I could do with it.'

He went to the bar and she turned over the comment in

her mind. She had been successful – there was no denying that. But she'd never *enjoyed* her success. The failures always hit her harder and stayed with her longer. Probably she would have been like that whatever branch of medicine she'd gone into. It was her personality, or that was what she'd always thought. Success had come with a price – no marriage, instead a relationship with an attractive nomad who dropped in and out of her life like a pen pal. No kids, instead a roster of relatives and godchildren who tended to bore quickly in her unsuitable house and in her unattuned company.

The thing was, as she got older, she realised she wasn't going to find a cure for anorexia, nor bulimia, nor any of the other variants of disordered eating that seemed to be multiplying all the time. She'd helped plenty of people, but she was bailing out a rising tide. She could see it in the ward, but she could sense it all around. People were losing touch with food, losing touch with their bodies, with what it means to be human. She couldn't fight that, and she was weary of trying. But that didn't mean she could give up on Tash.

'Here you go.' Eusebio was back from the bar and he handed her a small can, bright with the marketing of some microbrewery. 'I got beers this time. Thought it would go better with the food. Who'd have thought this place would ever get so hipster?'

Misty raised a half-hearted smile. 'There's no escape from the beards and the coffee-geekery these days.'

'Yes, but they still have plastic stirrers on the bar. That'll be a death penalty offence in a year or two.' He paused, looking at her quizzically.

'I'm sorry, I'm not much fun. I just can't get that girl out of my head.'

'So what's different about her, except for the fact you know her mum?'

'This isn't my comfort zone. I treat the patients when they get through the door – I'm not the one banging on it and demanding that we let them in.'

'Well, should she be in hospital?'

'Yes, she's definitely ill enough to warrant it. She might not be top of the priority list – not quite yet – but she'd be pretty close. The fact she's young and this is her first major episode makes it even more important to get help. We have no idea whether she'll be able to put a break on it herself without outside intervention.'

'Then you need to make it happen. Get a court order – you've done that before, you've told me. People don't regret doing things, Misty, nearly so often as they regret not doing them.'

He was only telling her what she already knew. Regardless of any fallout from Karen, regardless of any difficult questions about waiting lists and funding priorities, she was going to get Tasha Neville inside the hospital.

Suddenly the beer tasted too bitter. It was hot and airless in the pub and she wanted to be somewhere else. She thought back to the party on that bright April afternoon, the three sisters – prim Evie, gothy Tash and little, bubbly Callie. Anorexia could devastate a family like an earthquake. No one knew that better than her.

Unexpectedly, Eusebio reached out, picking Misty's hand up and cradling it in his own hands.

'You're feeling this one, aren't you? But you'll do your best for the girl. I know it.'

Misty nodded, taking a moment to find her voice.

'I will, I would for anyone.'

'I know, I've seen how dedicated you are to your patients – all of them. You do a wonderful job, Misty.'

'Thanks.' She managed a weak smile. 'But I *owe* it to Karen more than anyone. I think once, very long ago, I let her believe something that wasn't true. I wasn't brave enough at the time, I just took the easier path.'

'Don't we all, sometimes? But whatever happened then has happened. Now she has a sick child, and you are the best doctor she could have. That's all that matters.'

'I hope you're right. My worry is – it's probably mad – but I can't help thinking that maybe this goes all the way back. I never promise parents I can save their kids, but I *have* to save, Tash, I just have to.'

Eusebio looked sceptical, but he didn't attempt to delve into Misty's strange conviction that the key to Tash's recovery was somehow rooted in events that took place years before she was even born. Misty was grateful. Instead, they talked about a Netflix show, about the gallery in Shoreditch that was driving a hard bargain with Eusebio's agent over stocking his new pictures, and about the couple down the road they were friendly with who had just announced they were getting divorced.

But even as the conversation meandered on, even as they picked at their noodles and settled the bill, even as she filled her lungs with the evening air and walked, slightly fuzzily, to their house, a chill unease persisted. It slid around in Misty's stomach, cold and slippery as the lumps of ice left at the bottom of her gin glass.

Chapter 26

Karen
1989

When she got the message, she wasn't actually revising, although she should have been. Instead she was staring into space, lying propped against a tree in a neglected corner of the Backs where the River Cam meandered picturesquely through the grounds of some of the grandest colleges.

It was April already. T. S. Eliot's cruellest month; not that that knowledge would get her off the starting blocks. Exams started at the end of May. Like everyone else, Karen was feeling the pressure and filling her head with quotes and dates and painfully rehearsed 'insights' that she hoped might be sufficiently original to catch an examiner's eye. Her grades had steadily improved through first and second year, as she'd gained in confidence. She'd even started to spark off Alex a little. She'd never be as brilliant as her friend, but she was more often able to use Alex's genius as inspiration to aim a little higher, whereas previously she'd just been cowed by it.

It was hard to believe that in a few months they'd be in their final year. Some people were already talking about job options, and a few had lined up placements for the summer holidays. Karen had no idea what she wanted to do. Her future was a blank and impenetrable fog.

Her slim volume of Eliot lay discarded at her side and an equally slim roll-up dangled from her fingers. She watched in the distance as students hurried backwards and forwards, stooped with the weight of their books and anxiety. Then, quite unexpectedly, one emerged, distinct from the bustle, and began to slowly work its way towards her.

'Karen! I found you.'

She opened her eyes, blinking against the sun that was now cutting low across the landscape.

'Yep?'

It was Jessica Simons, a second-year economist. She looked breathless. 'Misty Jardine phoned Benjy Cohen. She couldn't get you in your room. She says she's at Alex's house and Benjy was to tell you to come over there as quickly as you can. He's asked loads of people to look for you. Apparently, she sounded really upset, and something bad's happened.'

Karen was already getting to her feet. She stubbed the cigarette out and flicked it deep into a bush. Some of the students were getting totally overheated about the exams, but she didn't think it was something like that behind the panicked message. That wasn't Misty's style. Nor Alex's either, come to think of it.

Jessica helped her to stuff her books and odds and ends into her bag whilst Karen reached for the Doc Martens that she'd kicked off to feel the grass on her feet. When she got back to her room, she almost had to shut the door in the second year's face to get rid of her. She thought about ringing Alex's house. There was always the chance that the urgency of the message had got exaggerated in the telling. She even picked up the phone receiver, turning the moulded plastic in her hand once before setting it down again. She would go. If she got the bus, rather than taking her bike, then she could read more Eliot on the way.

*

'Misty?'

Her friend looked like she hadn't slept. Her hair was dull and sticking up, her eyes smudgy and shadowed. But it wasn't her appearance that caused Karen to question her, it was the fact she was opening the door to Alex's parents' house.

'Karen, thank God you're here. Come in.'

'What's wrong?' Karen asked as they made their way into the hall. But Misty simply shook her head, then led her along the familiar corridor to reach the kitchen. The smell of alcohol hit her like a punch, and she noticed an open bottle of brandy on the table, along with two used glasses.

'She's dead, Karen.' Her voice was a hiss, a whisper. Karen thought for a moment that she had misheard, but the look in Misty's grey eyes — intense, almost fevered — told its own story. 'Alex is dead,' she repeated, raising a hand to wipe away fresh tears that had flooded onto her cheeks.

'Dead? What? How?' Taking her lead from Misty, she found she was whispering. Nonetheless, both of them jumped guiltily when the door swung open and Catarina stepped blindly into the room.

*

'I knew it ... I always knew that this nonsense would kill my angel in the end.'

Misty had pulled out a seat for Catarina at the kitchen table, and Catarina had collapsed into it almost as though in a faint. Karen noticed that she was wearing a suit, which seemed odd for half eleven on a Sunday morning, but that was hardly the strangest thing about the situation.

When Catarina began to speak, the two girls could do nothing more than gape at her. It was a torrent of knives and razors – castigating herself, Eric, even Alex. Her hands twisted and tore at each other in such a frenzy that Karen found she had to look away. She'd always wondered whether she quite believed Alex about Catarina's Jekyll and Hyde nature, but the proof was sitting in front of her now, and made for an uncomfortable show.

'Where is Eric?' Karen mouthed to Misty.

Her friend nodded towards the front room. 'Through there. With the doctor.' Karen wondered if that was where Alex's body was. The thought chilled her. And if that was the case, why was Catarina not with them too? Surely not out of some misplaced obligation to be hospitable.

'She was such a happy little girl. I'll show you the pictures. Always smiling, always laughing. Always eating – ha!' Catarina shook her head, a tear rolling down her cheek. 'I don't understand why she would do this. Why she would not let us look after her. I am her mother. That was all that I ever wanted for her.'

'Um, would it be better if we went, Mrs Penrith? I would hate to intrude.'

Karen found herself echoing one of her own mother's phrases. Virginia was always hating to intrude, generally when she was being nosy, and in the past it had made Karen cringe. Finding herself in this situation, though, with no idea what was expected of her – or even really why she was here – it was her mum's words that rolled off her tongue.

'What?' Catarina looked at her as if she'd forgotten the pair of them were there in the first place. 'Soon, yes, perhaps – I'm sure Eric will want to say goodbye to you. He won't be long with the doctor I wouldn't imagine. Then I will go to my girl.'

Misty continued to weep. Catarina's words slid over her, whilst she stared, for the most part, fixed on a point on the wall ahead of her. Her hands trembled as she lifted them to her face. Karen had wondered why she hadn't just come back to college, but she could see that her friend was in no state to think of that, far less to actually do it.

The next ten minutes were a nightmarish purgatory. Karen watched the hands crawl round on the huge kitchen clock as Catarina continued to remonstrate and reminisce. The only comfort she would accept was the brandy, and with each glass she grew louder and more out of control, crashing glasses and the bottle around. Misty was sobbing and stricken, but seemed almost oblivious to Catarina being in the same room. Karen tried to put an arm around her shoulder but Misty shoved her roughly away. Karen herself found she couldn't cry. She couldn't accept that Alex – Alex whom she had sat with in the library just yesterday – was actually dead. It was all surely some absurd joke or misunderstanding.

Eventually they heard the front door being opened, and low-voiced conversation that was presumably the doctor making his farewells. A few moments later, Eric came into the kitchen.

'The funeral director will be round tomorrow morning. Probably about ten. We should think about who else we need to tell.'

He looked up with a slightly startled expression, as if he'd only just noticed that Misty and Karen were still there.

'Karen, I asked Misty to call you because I didn't think she should go back to college alone. I'll give you both a lift shortly. I'm sure I can trust you to be discreet, girls. I wouldn't want anyone hearing about this through gossip before we've informed the college authorities.'

'Right. No. I understand.' Despite the 'we', Karen couldn't imagine that such a mundane, practical thought had come anywhere near entering Catarina's head. The woman was stricken – her thoughts, understandably, consumed by the enormity of her loss. Eric, on the other hand, seemed oddly businesslike, although she supposed that grief had different faces, particularly a grief as raw and new as this one.

'We'll walk, thanks.' Misty's voice seemed unnaturally loud, as if she wasn't quite in control of it. 'It's not that late, and I'd like some fresh air.'

She slid off her stool quickly, and Karen followed her lead. But where Misty seemed ready to walk out without any further word, Karen faltered.

'I'm so sorry for—'

'Thank you, girls—'

Karen and Eric cut across each other in their fumbled attempts at politeness. In the end, neither finished their sentences. Eric strode through the hall and opened the front door for them, just as he had for the doctor only a few minutes before.

'We'll let you know about the ... arrangements, girls. And I'll call the master of the college tonight.'

With that, they were on the street. Karen wrapped her arms around herself – in the hurry to come she'd not brought a jacket. Heading towards the bus stop, they walked slowly under the cherry trees that lined the elegant roads around the Penriths'. It seemed wrong, somehow. The tress were still in blossom. A jet still streaked its vapour trail across the blue sky. None of the turmoil that Karen was feeling was reflected in the ordinary spring day around her.

'I thought she was better,' she said, as much to herself as to Misty.

Misty shrugged. 'She was doing better. That might not be the same thing. And maybe we were all mistaken about it anyway.'

'She's been thinner before. That's plain fact; you can see it. I don't understand why she'd die now.'

For a few seconds, there was nothing but the rustle of the breeze through the trees.

'Heart failure,' said Misty. 'Her heart stopped.'

'Because it was weak because … because of the anorexia.'

'I suppose so.'

'Shit.' Karen felt the breath seep out of her, out of her control. Her chest tightened as she though back to moments between her and Alex. Standing next to each other in their knickers, taking turns on the scales. Alex challenging her to eat nothing but chewing gum for forty-eight hours, Karen setting them both a punishing calorie-busting exercise regime in return. At the time, it had felt like friendship. In a world where so much was alien, threatening, or both, it was a way of being in control. Right from that first day in college she'd not quite been able to believe that Alex wanted to be her friend. She'd decided quickly that fitting in with Alex was her key to fitting in full stop. She'd never questioned too hard what she was doing to achieve that.

Karen liked being fit; she liked being slim. Of course, she'd gone hungry along with Alex and that wasn't fun, but she did it because she chose to, she'd never *needed* to. And that had been the difference between them. When Alex started to get involved with Andrew, though, dieting stopped being something they shared. Karen had been jealous, and that jealousy had prompted her to needle Alex in the way that seemed most obvious, without really thinking through the consequences.

Her stomach flipped nervously, although in a way there was nothing to be nervous about. The worst had already happened.

Perhaps this was how murderers felt, wondering if they were going to be caught. The thought took her by surprise. She didn't have Alex's blood on her hands – did she?

'It's my fault,' she said to Misty, so quietly the words almost vanished on the breeze.

'You knew she was ill, and you kept on telling her she was fat!' Misty turned on her, eyes flashing, like a cat suddenly baring its teeth and claws. 'Why did you do that? Why did you keep on doing that?'

'I ... I ... I suppose I wanted to make myself feel better.'

'Feeling better now, are you? Thought not.'

Chapter 27

Karen
2019

The platform was busy; polished brogues mingled with cheap scuffed school shoes, heels came in all heights and dimensions, pristine pimped Nikes bounced alongside scrappy plimsolls. They all deviated subtly around the woman sitting alone on the second bench.

Head lowered, Karen noted the trajectories of all the pairs of shoes avoiding her, taking in the dimensions of the force field that had manifested around the bench. She'd become someone that normal people avoided. Crazy lady. The was a noise – a snort, or perhaps a giggle – it seemed alien, not a noise that she would make. But the feet shrunk back further, crowded each other to gain another six inches, so she supposed it must have been her.

She was watching for Alex, of course she was. It was the only thing she could do. None of these people were right though. None of these pairs of shoes belonged to her friend. Her dead friend. The snort-laughing noise rang in her ears again.

Reaching in her bag, her fingers sought out the comfort of

the small plastic bottle the Americans used for pills. The last time Karen had emailed for some more Amanda had pinged back a raised-eyebrow emoticon and a message asking if the ones she'd sent a couple of weeks earlier hadn't arrived. She was unlikely to believe in another postal mishap.

Six left in this bottle, another small bottle at home. Maybe there was somewhere else she could source them from. For now, she let her fingers stroke the packet, telling herself that it was enough that they were there.

A pair of black heels caught her attention. They were smart – not showy, yet obviously expensive all the same – the sort of thing Alex would go for. She glanced up – smart suit, right height – but the face was all wrong. This woman was freckly, with a wide mouth and green eyes. And about twenty years too young. The girl flashed a nervous smile with her not-Alex mouth, and her awkwardness at making eye contact with Karen was written across her not-Alex face. She took a couple of small steps backwards, reversing into a heavy man wielding a newspaper. She turned to make a flustered apology, and Karen knew she was forgotten.

She told herself she didn't need to take a pill right now, but she could feel her nails flipping the cap regardless. She rolled the small tablet in her fingertips for a moment and then placed it on her tongue.

Breathe. Scan the crowds and breathe. She'd have to go home soon. The girls would be okay – probably getting on better without her. But she didn't want to scare them. She'd noticed two missed calls from Evie. And two from Misty Jardine as well, and two from Andrew – like a game of matching pairs. She couldn't imagine what Misty wanted from her. She knew that Andrew had brought her to the party because he had some idea of a reconciliation but, really, that was hardly likely after all these years. They all had their lives to be getting on with.

Maybe Misty wanted to rekindle their friendship. Why not? They could have a nice sauvignon and chat about the fact that Karen's daughter was trying to kill herself and Karen was too weak to watch it happening, oh, and on top of that they were about to lose their home.

She did want to see Andrew. He was the antidote. But she had enough presence of mind to realise that she couldn't let him see her the way these commuters were seeing her. She had to get her act together. Maybe she'd be able to call him tonight. Once she knew that Tash and Callie were okay and she'd had another pill.

The platform crowds had thinned now. There was no longer a distinct space around her; she no longer watched people deflect slightly from their course to avoid coming too close to the madwoman on the bench. There was space now for everyone to spread out. Less chance of finding Alex then. Although, she thought ruefully, if the chance was nil anyway could it be less in any meaningful way?

She stopped handling the pill packet and put her phone back in her bag, standing up just as the next train drew onto the platform. It was tempting to get on it, to believe that it could take her to a new place, to solve her problems. Instead, she summoned the resolve to walk along the platform and up the stairs, making her way to the other side, where the trains were going the right way to take her home.

Chapter 28

Tasha
2019

Alex was in the room with her. She was wearing the same clothes she had on in that picture on the wall of the study – a black and white striped dress and black plastic earrings. Her hair sat in crispy curls.

'I could scrunch yours for you,' she offered. 'It'd suit you.'

'Maybe another time, thanks,' Tash replied, hoping that Alex wouldn't be offended.

Her hair products might have been dated, but Alex was beautiful. Her skin sat light on her bones like gossamer, leaving every plane and curve of her body's architecture on display. In some lights, her bones themselves seemed to glow, luminescent through the whisper of her skin. As if they were made of opal or mother of pearl – something precious.

Alex had come to help her along. Alesha was her first helper, but she wasn't around online much at the moment. Alex would encourage her, tell her that she was doing well, that she was good at this. Evie was always the one who was good at everything. If they were sisters in a story, there would be some sort of consolation prize – Tash would be an amazing artist, or able to swim like a dolphin. But real life didn't work like that, so Evie got all the gifts.

'You got your dad, though,' Alex reminded her, looking up the copy of *Grazia* she'd found by the bed. 'He always loved you the most.'

Tash giggled. 'I know. Although he pretended not to.'

'Shame he carked it,' she added, blandly.

Tash's giggles evaporated.

The door opened and Evie came in. Tash hadn't heard her in the hallway and gazed down to see that she'd sneaked upstairs in her purple fleecy comfort socks. She was carrying a soup bowl and the steam was wafting off it, salt-scented and mouth-watering. Evie wasn't a cook, Tash knew it had come out of a tin, but the smell was still enough to drive her wild.

'I don't want it,' she said, through gritted teeth. 'Take it away from me.'

Instead Evie moved closer. Alex had vanished. Evie brushed *Grazia* onto the floor and took the chair beside the bed.

'Look, it just soup, Tash, it's fucking *diet* soup – there's nothing in it.'

She picked up a spoonful of the orange liquid and then let it dribble back into the bowl to demonstrate the watery consistency.

Tash shook her head. 'Go away, Evie.'

'Fine,' she said, standing up so quickly that the soup sloshed over the side of the bowl, scalding her thumb. She let out a little yelp before walking out of the room without another word.

'That was easier than I expected,' said Alex, now back in the chair. 'Maybe the bitch is finally getting the message.'

But the pair of them had underestimated Evie.

There was no mistaking the next set of footsteps on the stairs. Callie still pounded up them with the gait of a baby hippo, even, it turned out, when she was carrying a bowl of soup.

She didn't speak until she'd plonked herself down in the chair. Tash couldn't see Alex anymore, but she could feel her lingering resentment. Callie waved the soup spoon in her face.

'You *have* to, Tash. Sit up. Have some.'

The wobble in her voice was matched by slick tears pooling below her eyes. Tash turned her face to the wall so she didn't have to look at her sister.

'Please, Tash ... I l-love you. I don't want you to d-d-die. P-p-please ...'

It was the blubbing that made her lose it. 'Fuck you, Evie,' she shouted at the wall. 'You can't use Callie! What kind of monster are you?'

There was no reply except for the little-girl whine of her baby sister.

'Please ... just a little bit. J-just for me, Tash.'

It seemed like about five minutes ago that Callie was in a high chair and Tash was doing Weetabix aeroplanes for her. Those huge grey eyes. When Tash was eight there was nothing in the world as beautiful as her little sister. There still wasn't.

'I'm not going anywhere until you have some. That's a p-p-promise.'

She knew Callie meant it too. And she couldn't just throw it back at her like she might with her mum or Evie. She forced herself to turn away from the wall and started to inch upright.

Instantly, Callie was fussing around like she was the original Florence Nightingale, pulling at Tash's pillow so she could

203

sit up more easily, then handing her the bowl and spoon like they were precious relics.

The surface of the soup was greasy, and sort of ... splattered.

She turned to Callie. 'You cried in my soup?'

Callie looked mortified, then they both burst into hysterics.

'It'll save you putting salt in it.' She nodded, through her giggles.

Tash skimmed a little off the top and raised it slowly to her lips. She needn't have worried about scalding herself, though. The battle had lasted long enough for the liquid to have cooled to almost to room temperature.

'That's it,' said Callie, encouraging and excited all at once. 'And another one.'

Tash's lips were so dry that even the cool soup stung them, acid from the tomatoes finding its way deep into the cracks. The taste filled her mouth like a bud coming into flower. The intensity almost brought tears to her eyes to match Callie's.

She did what her sister asked, though, and took one more minuscule sip. Then another. Then another. Callie beamed and, despite herself, Tash felt good to make her happy. There was no sign of Evie. She was probably keeping out of the way deliberately, congratulating herself on getting Callie to do her dirty work.

'Well done,' said Callie gently. 'You're almost there.'

It wasn't true. Tash was only just over halfway through the bowl, and the gentleness of Callie's voice just about killed her.

'Thanks, Callie, you've done a good job. You can take it away now.'

Tash pushed the bowl towards her but she shook her head. 'Sorry, Tash. Not until you finish it.'

'No, Callie.'

'It's just one bowl.'

'I can't, Callie. I'm sorry.' Now Tash was the one sobbing her words out.

'You can. You will.' And Callie picked the spoon up from where Tash had let it slide out of her fingers and onto the duvet cover. Reversing their roles from years ago, Tash let her little sister feed her. Callie pushed the spoon into her mouth time after time, and Tash didn't have the will or the strength to push it away. As slow as death itself, they battled through that bloody bowlful, every sip polluting her body.

'I love you,' Callie said, standing up. 'I'll go and put these in the dishwasher.'

Tasha knew that Alex would be back, and that she'd be angry. She could already feel her in the room, could already hear her caustic laughter as she jeered at how weak Tash was, what a hopeless coward.

'Don't go now,' she said to Callie. 'Stay for a bit.'

'Okay,' she agreed, setting the bowl down and settling in the seat again.

Tentatively, Callie reached out a hand and began to stroke her sister's hair.

'Dad used to do this to me,' she said quietly. 'Mum says I only think I remember because there's a photo, but I *can* remember. Did he stroke your hair too, when you were little?'

'Yes,' said Tash, and then there were no more words.

Chapter 29

Misty
1989

'Thank God you're here. We're going out tonight. Dinner – if I have one more stodgy buttery pasta thing I might actually die – then dancing. We don't have to stay late, but, God, I need to get out of here.'

Alex had appeared in Misty's doorway. She was already dressed for a night out in a short and clingy black dress, and she'd had her hair cropped. It looked amazing, a brief tumble of black curls falling forward, then shaped in at the back. Her hand brushed the nape of her neck, giving away the fact she still wasn't used to it.

'I'm not going out tonight. We've got exams starting in six weeks in case you hadn't realised.'

'Yes! Six weeks. You can't revise twenty-four hours a day for six weeks.'

'What's up with you, anyway? Andrew stood you up?'

Alex scowled. 'No. I want to go out with *you*. We've not done anything in ages.' She looked at her nails. 'Plus, Andrew's got a rugby dinner thing.'

Misty did a quick calculation. It was tempting. If she worked until eight and really focused then that might be more effective than eating at the buttery working late. Her head was already swimming with anatomy. It was like trying to do The Knowledge but with all the street names in Latin. A break might well help in the long run.

'All right then. You said dinner?'

'Maggiore's.'

She named the upmarket Italian she'd taken Misty and Karen to on their first night in Cambridge. Misty nodded.

'Half eight. I need to work until then. I'll come and get you at eight-twenty.'

Alex gave a little pout of dissatisfaction but seemed to accept Misty's offer, walking away and throwing a 'bye' over her shoulder when her friend turned back to her books.

*

Maggiore's meant that Eric would be paying. It was, Misty thought ruefully, more than he'd ever done for her when he was actually present. But then she understood that, whilst lunch in a café was explainable, he couldn't afford to be seen somewhere like this with her. Hopefully that would all change soon, if Alex had been right about him leaving Catarina. For the last few weeks she'd hugged the possibility close, the most tantalising secret. She hadn't actually seen Eric. He didn't seem to be keeping his office hours and he'd returned her call only once, to tell her, very charmingly, that he was particularly caught up in things at the moment, and it would be better if they could cool off for a few weeks. He was thinking about her, too. The last thing he wanted was for her to do badly in her exams because she was distracted.

207

In Cambridge, she noted ruefully, even the adults took exams seriously.

When the exams were over, he'd promised, they were going to go away for the day, possibly even overnight, and talk about the future. That was when he'd tell her that he was breaking up with Catarina, she was sure. And what would that mean for the two of them? She was less clear about that, beyond a hazy vision of summer days filled with riverside picnics, being able to be together in public around the city, maybe trips to London, or even further afield. Alex, far less her own parents, did not have any part in these golden daydreams that were sustaining her through the slog of revision. If her thoughts strayed onto what their reactions might be, she very quickly pushed them aside.

The waiter brought an ice bucket and champagne as soon as they were seated.

'To friends,' toasted Alex.

'Friends.' Misty raised her glass. 'What about Karen, could you not persuade her?'

Alex shrugged. 'Sometimes it's nice to catch up one on one, isn't it? Plus, we're revising for the same papers, so we would inevitably have ended up talking about it, and I just really needed a break. And some olives.'

Alex had asked for her pizza without cheese, but when it came, she ate it happily, along with the side salad and olives she'd ordered. There was no sign of any ritualising behaviour, or any panic. Misty felt oddly proud of her. She was doing so much better than this time last year.

They talked about plans for the summer, Misty making vague noises about going home and finding some part-time work. Alex was going to do some work experience at a publishing house in London. She and Karen had already secured an eight-week flat-share and Misty bit back her jealousy, telling herself that everything would change when Eric stepped in anyway.

By half nine, they were sipping coffees. 'So, you really want to go dancing?' she asked, slightly sceptically.

Alex nodded firmly. 'Yes, and not at a scuzzy student night either. Thank God it's Friday and there will be real people out in town.'

'All right.' Misty smiled. 'But I'm not having a late one. Let's go.'

A few minutes later they were approaching the entrance to the city's biggest nightclub – not that that was saying much.

'Seriously, that pizza was so garlicky, I'm not sure the bouncers will let us in if I breathe on them,' said Alex.

'I've got some chewing gum somewhere. I'll have a look when we're in the queue. I hope it's not too long. It's freezing tonight.'

The cold must have put people off, because the queue was down to a desultory eight or nine people and after less than five minutes the bouncers pulled the rope back and let them all in anyway. They stashed their coats in the cloakroom and bought a vodka and lemonade each. Misty quickly decided that would have to do – the weekend prices were double what the students paid on Tuesdays and Wednesdays. The crowd was different too, older and dressed more sharply. Men obviously on the prowl rather than out for a beer and a laugh.

They manoeuvred free of the come-ons from a few different guys, and the hassling eased up when, despite Alex's earlier avowals, they merged in with another group of female students. Alex vaguely knew one of them, having been the year above her at school, and they were out for a birthday and happy to include the pair of them in their celebrations, including the rounds of Sambuca that the birthday girl was buying.

*

Of course, the idea of an early night didn't last long. Misty couldn't remember why they'd decided to go back to Alex's parents' house although, in the years after, she was to spend plenty of time trying.

She remembered thinking she'd lost her handbag, but then finding it again. Maybe they'd seen it as a solution to not having keys – but the other girls would have been in and in the worst case the college porters would have had spare keys – they had to hand them out for plenty of undergrads all the time. The students might be clever but it didn't mean they had an ounce of common sense. And why would they still have gone to the Penriths' after the handbag turned up? Drunken logic; there was no fathoming it.

Maybe they just got hungry and decided the pickings were richer at the Penriths' house, although that would be unlike Alex. She did remember waiting ages for a taxi, so maybe when they'd found one the cabbie was heading home and would only go south. Maybe, in a fit of drunken nostalgia, they decided they wanted to relive childhood Saturdays and watch kids' TV in their slippers the next morning.

Maybe Alex knew exactly what she was going home to find and had set it all up from the start. Misty would never know.

She felt convinced that she remembered most of the night – it's just that the memories were fragmentary. There was an image of parting ways with the group they'd latched on to, hugging and happy-birthday-ing under a streetlight, watching one of the girls limping along, clutching a friend's arm because she'd broken a heel. She remembered recovering her coat from the cloakroom, which felt like it came afterwards, but surely must have been before given they'd all been outside at that point. There was the joy of finding the lost handbag, and the grateful tumble into the musty-smelling Cavalier. Her feet hadn't hurt when she was dancing but they sure as hell did waiting for that cab.

The Penriths' house was in darkness when the taxi pulled up outside. They hushed at each other as they lurched up the drive, but to no avail. A light flicked on upstairs. By the time they'd reached the front door it was being opened by a grim and rumpled-looking Eric.

'What the—'

'Hi, Dad!' Alex grinned brightly and reached up, offering a wobbly doorstep hug. Eric gazed over her shoulder, catching Misty's eye and turning a shade paler. She didn't suppose she could blame him, given that she'd been the one to stop returning his calls. Funny how she could remember the awkwardness of that exchange of glances in exquisite detail, but had no idea how she'd ended up agreeing to turn up at his house in the first place.

'We were out in town ... thought it would be perfect ... nothing to get back for tomorrow and we can get the bus if you're busy ...' Alex was chatting on to Eric, seemingly oblivious to his lack of response. He backed inside anyway, ushering them into the hall. Misty nearly stumbled on a pair of fawn stilettos discarded by the door. Not like Catarina, who was so punctilious about her clothes even Misty knew about it.

'And how are you, Misty? It's nice to see you again.' Just

as Eric composed himself enough to venture a remark in her direction, Misty was overcome by the biggest yawn. The hand in front of her face couldn't hide her embarrassment.

'I'm fine. Very tired.'

'And a little worse for wear by the looks of it?'

She blushed, annoyance rising at the fact she'd put herself in this situation where he was able to condescend to her.

'Well, it looks like you girls will be wanting to go to bed, then. There's a spare room made up, Misty, the blue one, you know where …? Or you can go in with Alex if you both prefer. Doesn't matter to me.'

'Great. I'll get myself a glass of water if that's okay.' She turned to Alex, who had seemed oddly distracted whilst Eric and Misty were speaking. 'Coming?'

'No. We won't go straight up,' said Alex, continuing to look at Eric. 'Who's here, Dad?'

'What do you mean?'

'Mum's at her conference.' She nodded at the shoes on the floor. 'Who's here?'

Chapter 30

Misty
2019

For the third time, Misty stood on the threshold of the Twickenham villa. She had been nervous before, but this was a different level. Her hands were slick with sweat and she could feel a giddiness in her throat that she knew meant her heart was racing. Philomena Dempsey, her social services contact, was waiting, parked up in her battered Ford Focus, ready to argue with any traffic warden who might choose tonight to enforce the residents' parking zone. Misty fervently hoped she wouldn't have to call on her.

Taking a final breath, she rang the doorbell. She only had to wait a few seconds before she could see movement behind the frosted glass.

'Evie, hello. Is your mum in?'

Misty tried not to show it, but she was immediately taken aback by how bad the oldest Neville sister looked. Evie had black shadows under her eyes and a breakout of spots on her forehead and chin. There was no smile as she opened the door.

'Hi, yes, Mum's just got home. Come in.' She led Misty

through to the kitchen, gesturing vaguely at one of the bar stools but not suggesting that Misty should take off her outdoor things, nor offering a drink. 'I'll go and get her.'

Evie's departure was abrupt and she didn't come back quickly. As Misty continued to wait, she draped her coat across the back of another stool and looked around her. Like Evie herself, the kitchen was showing evidence of the strain in the household. Dirty dishes were scattered around, along with unopened post and all the detritus of a busy household. The calendar on the wall still hung on the June page, although it was now two weeks into July.

Finally, she heard the murmur of voices. Karen and Evie, from the sound of it, although she couldn't make out what they were saying. Then, in a flurry, Karen was in the room.

'Hello, Karen, it's good to see you.'

'Well, we're quite busy at the moment. I wasn't expecting you and it's probably not the best time.' Karen waved a vague hand at the mess in the kitchen, but it was quite clear to Misty that that was the least of her friend's worries. Karen looked dishevelled, almost unkempt. Her eyes were glazed and flickered around unsteadily. Misty couldn't be sure, but she thought there was even a slight slur to her words. Standing behind her mother, Evie was the picture of unease. Misty had huge sympathy for the girl, who was still very young and hadn't asked to be caught up in any of this, but, despite Evie's discomfort, she knew she had little option but to push on.

'I'm here about Tasha, Karen. She's very, very unwell, and we need to help her. You need to help her.'

Karen's eyes finally fixed on Misty's for a moment, and a look of confusion crossed her face.

'But what do you know about Tasha? You've barely met her.'

'I heard ...' she glanced at Evie, not wanting to give away the girl's part in it unless she had to '... that Tasha was ill. I came to see her a few days ago. You were out at the time.'

'You sneaked into my house behind my back?'

'I didn't know if you were in or not. I was just concerned to see Tasha. Unfortunately, it turned out those concerns were well founded. As I said a moment ago, your daughter's condition is serious, Karen. She needs treatment. I need to admit her to hospital.'

At those words, Misty at least noted a hint of relief on Evie's face, but her mother's expression was anything but relieved.

'She's fine. She ate soup tonight with the other two. A whole bowlful, Callie told me. I'm looking after her – that's my job. I'm her mother.'

Misty shook her head sorrowfully. 'It's gone past that, Karen. Tasha needs more than a bowl of soup here or there. She needs intensive re-feeding. She won't accept that at home. She won't accept it from her family. I need you to agree to her admission.'

'And if I don't?'

'I'd rather not go there ...'

'Well, tough luck – you're the one who's come marching into my house telling me I can't look after my own daughter.'

'Nobody's saying that, Karen, I'm saying she's ill. But ... at the end of the day, if I don't have Tasha's consent and I don't have yours the clinic will apply for an emergency court order. I've got the backing of social services. There is a very experienced – very sensitive – social work manager waiting for me—'

'What the *fuck*, Misty? Social services? Like I'm some sort of child abuser? No. No. No. This isn't happening.' She turned to her daughter, her voice lowering to a whisper. 'Evie, you need to go now, please. I need to speak to Misty alone.'

Evie threw a look over her mother's shoulder that told Misty she'd better not have made things even worse than they were already, but that was what it looked like from here. Misty let her go. Just now Evie wasn't the one she needed to get on board, her mother was.

'Karen—'

'Don't "Karen" me, Misty. You've walked back into my life after nearly thirty years to do what? To take my kids away? To destroy me? Just because you still blame me for what happened to Alex? I know you never liked me, Misty, but this is too much.'

'Please believe me, it's not about us. I only want to help Tasha. She *needs* help, Karen.'

'But why are you here now? With a social worker sitting in a car outside? Shouldn't that be the endpoint, rather than the starting point?'

Karen was becoming much more lucid now. Her eyes were darting less, and she'd finally taken a seat, crumpling into it rather than sitting down. Her question wrong-footed Misty – how had they come to be here? She could remember many conversations over the years with friends and acquaintances who were concerned their child may have an eating disorder – or at least be heading in that direction. In many cases, the worries had proved to be unfounded; in a few others she'd pointed them in the right direction to access treatment, then been happy to provide a sounding board for questions they didn't want to ask their own doctors, or worries they couldn't express in front of

216

their children. How had she got here? Why was she diving in to treat Tash? She pieced together the last few weeks in her mind, reassuring herself that she'd had no option.

'I get where you're coming from, Karen, it's a fair question. But you've obviously had a lot on your plate recently. I'm not sure you've been as aware of what's going on with Tash as you might have been at another time. And I did try to call you, several times.'

'Calls in the last few days, yes, but what about before that? Why did you sneak around with Evie, coming to see Tash behind my back? Why not tell me she'd got in touch with you?'

'Maybe I should have. I just ... it seemed for the best.'

'This *is* about Alex, isn't it?' Karen's question was challenging and somehow defeated at the same time.

Misty paused, stuck for what to say. 'I don't know, Karen. We hadn't been in contact for years before Andrew dragged me along to your party. Evie got in touch with me. I had Tasha's welfare as my top priority. Doctors don't just involve other people – even parents – there's patient confidentiality you know.'

Karen snorted. 'Yeah. Well, like you said, you've been trying to get in touch with me in the last few days. I don't buy it. You think I'm killing my daughter like I killed Alex.'

She needed to deny it, but the words got stuck in Misty's throat. Of course, she knew Alex's death was not entirely Karen's fault, but she wasn't blameless either. The little digs about her weight, the silly dieting challenges. It had all had an impact. For no reason other than Karen's own insecurity. That was what had brought her close to Alex; that was what their friendship had been based on.

'You see,' said Karen, with a note of triumph. 'I'm right. You blamed me all along, you're still blaming me all these years later and now it turns out she might not even be dead. That would mess up your neat little world view, wouldn't it?'

'Sorry?' said Misty, genuinely thrown. 'You don't mean that photo, do you? You can't think ...'

'You tell me, Misty.' Karen held up her fingers, ticking off the points as she made them. 'First, the photo. We all think it's uncanny. You and I haven't seen her, haven't seen each other, in decades but it stopped both of us in our tracks. Second, nobody saw the body. Even Andrew, and they were practically engaged, for Christ's sake. Her dad wouldn't let him see the body. Doesn't that suggest there was something odd going on? Third, she's talking to Tasha. She's talking to my daughter, Misty – *that's* who you can blame for Tasha losing the plot. The supposedly dead person who is actually stalking her. Not sounding so dead anymore, is she? Well, is she?'

Karen's momentary lucidity had vanished. Her voice had risen, and she was gesticulating wildly as she spoke.

Misty's mouth opened and shut. She didn't know where to begin. But Karen was unstoppable now.

'Let me tell you this,' she raged. 'I won't be judged by you, Misty Jardine. I've raised my girls and protected them and fought for them more than you know or would bother to find out. And I'm not about to give up now. *I'll* get Tash eating, because I'm her mother, and that's my job. And you can take your pet social worker and drive away into the sunset.'

'But—'

'Are you leaving or do I have to make you?'

Misty flushed red, a combination of embarrassment and

218

frustration. But she didn't have any choice but to leave. She fumbled her bag and her coat from the bar stool and walked unsteadily back to the hallway. Karen brushed past her, almost pushing into Misty in her haste to get to the front door and swing it wide.

Misty glanced up the staircase as she passed it, wondering about the state of the sick girl lying up there, and whether she had any idea of what had just unfolded in the kitchen.

'You've got no claim on my daughter,' said Karen, her voice colder than Misty could ever have imagined. 'Get out of our lives.'

*

Misty didn't stop or look back until she was able to throw herself into Phil's passenger seat and slam the door of the Focus behind her. She exhaled deeply, resting her head on her hands, elbows propped on the dashboard.

'That went well then?' Philomena was popping Wotsits into her mouth, silver rings flashing on her fingers. Misty fought back a wave of nausea.

'We need to get that girl out of there,' she said, her tone of voice as grim as she felt.

'It's a big step, Misty. You don't think you can talk them round?'

'My job is saving lives. That's what we're doing here. You need to push the button on the lawyers.'

Philomena carefully folded down the top of the crisp packet and replaced it in her handbag, pulling out a tissue and wiping her fingertips before reaching for her phone.

'You're sure? I'm worried you're too close to this.'

'That's why I brought you, Phil. I don't want to be some kind of vigilante mental health service, but there isn't time to refer her through her GP or whatever.'

'So, you're sure we go for a section?'

Misty nodded. 'Completely.'

Chapter 31

Tasha
2019

From: Stanno

Oi! Tash. Not seen u in ages. U home?
Can come round tomoz am?

To: Claire

Just got a DM frm Stanno. Weird. He just broken
up with someone or what??

From: Claire

Good to see you pop up!
Hope feeling better?
Dunno bout Stanno. Try Lola?

To: Claire

Lola [barf-face]. I no I've been a dick.
I am sorry. And to Sonal.

From: Claire

Just asked Henry. Stanno went to
Majorca with boyz. Just back.

To: Claire

Prob still hungover then.

From: Claire

Prob got crabs!

To: Claire

Itchy! [crying laugh faces]

To: Stanno

Will be in tomoz am. Come round if u like.

Tash spent an hour working out what she could eat. The las
thing she wanted was for him to come in the room only t
see her stand up and keel over. Alex sat on the chair grum
bling about how Stanno was just a distraction and probabl
only wanted to come around to boast about how many girl
he'd shagged on holiday but for once Tash ignored her. Sh
decided she'd go down to the kitchen and have some muesl
and skimmed milk if they had it in.

It was easy to get dizzy if she moved too quickly, so sh
eased herself up from the bed really slowly and walked ou
into the hall, praying that none of the others would hear an
start fussing after her. Alex stayed in the bedroom. She alway
did.

After the muesli, she cleaned her teeth carefully. Her gums were tender and she'd sort of stopped a bit because it hurt and it wasn't like there was any food stuck in there. But the last thing she wanted was to have stinky breath for Stanno, so she just took her time and went really gently round every bit of her mouth. Then she had a shower and washed her hair, grateful for the energy from the muesli kicking in just in time to stop her from feeling like she might faint.

'Are you in there, Tash?' It was Evie, checking up on her – no surprises there.

'Yeah, just getting out of the shower. I'll be done in five if you want in.'

'No … no, you're fine. Just, um, nice that you're up. Well done.'

Her voice sort of faded out on the 'well done', like she wasn't sure if it was the right thing to say or not. That was subtle for her.

She decided it would be a good idea to put some make-up on before Stanno arrived. Heading back to her bedroom, she chucked her stuff onto the bed and gave her hair a quick blast. The hairdryer felt like some sort of weightlifting device. She couldn't remember the last time she'd bothered to use it at all, and she gave up pretty quickly, twisting her hair up into a messy bun. She'd have to wear leggings and a T-shirt because she didn't have anything else that would fit. Thank God everyone else was wearing leggings at the moment, too, although she wouldn't if her legs looked like two municipal rubbish bins squeezed into black Lycra like some of the girls. More like chunder thighs than thunder thighs. Alex liked that one, though Tash had to explain what chunder was.

Her make-up was all scattered around in the top drawer

of her desk. She'd never cleared it out so she still had nail polish from Claire's Accessories from when she was, like, nine, in there. She scooped a few up and decided to pass them on to Callie, in case ... something happened. She wouldn't want her little sister to be too freaked out to take the nail polishes if she wasn't there anymore.

She picked out her MAC contouring set and her favourite lipsticks. Even Alex seemed in a good mood, pouting into the mirror behind Tash and complimenting her technique as she shaded in her eyebrows.

'Total betty,' she nodded, making Tash laugh.

Tash had to admit, though, Alex wasn't too far out. She'd never loved the way she looked as much as she did now. Their faces together in the mirror had a sisterly resemblance, with the same wide brow, luminous eyes and jutting cheekbones. But that had nothing to do with genes. That was a different sisterhood altogether.

In a last moment of inspiration, Tash put on the silver feather earrings that Stanno had given her, when they were going out. He might notice them; he might not. But it felt like an appropriate good luck charm. Then she opened the wardrobe and threw in her damp towel and other bits that were cluttered around her bed and the room. Finally, with some effort, she pushed open the window. She didn't want to bring Stanno up here; she was sure it smelt stale apart from anything else. But she might have no choice if Evie insisted on hanging around and sticking her nose in, so it was best to be prepared.

Finally, she was ready to go back downstairs. She grabbed her phone and headed for the kitchen. *Crap*. She could hear Evie *and* Callie chatting in there as she got towards the door.

Hopefully, if she asked them nicely, they might piss off before Stanno showed up. It sounded as if they were talking about Callie's interminable Ed Sheeran obsession. Tasha gritted her teeth and tried to come up with something jolly to say about the yodelling ginger nitwit. Just as she was about to turn the door handle, though, she heard a deeper voice. She paused – Stanno – he must have got there early and Evie had let him in without telling her.

He broke into an a cappella 'Shape of You' and she heard Callie joining in with the harmonies. Tash couldn't help but smile. Stanno had an awesome voice and, actually, Callie was a sweet little singer too. She knew they'd stop when she walked in and, suddenly, she was reluctant to bring the moment to an end. She wondered if Stanno was thinking of her as he sang the words, if there was a little bit of him still hot for her, or hot for the memory of her at least. The performance faded to some ooh-ooh-oohs followed by a bit of beatboxing from Stanno and giggles from Callie. She took a deep breath and opened the door.

'Nice performance, guys.' She grinned at them both, even taking in Evie for good measure. 'Stanno, you're early – thanks for coming and charming my sisters.' She flicked her hair and amped her grin up to max.

Nobody smiled back. The silence stretched out and she felt her own smile bleed away. Her hands flapped awkwardly around her hips, flailing for the pockets the leggings didn't have, as she tried to act normal. Stanno's mouth literally dropped open.

'Fucking hell, Tash.' He shook his head. 'I mean, fucking hell.'

Shocked by the language, Callie tore her eyes from Tash to

look at him. She looked like she was about to cry. Evie was just slowly shaking her head.

'My God, Tash, do you have any idea what you look like? It's … it's horrific. You're like a Bratz doll come to life.' Evie's voice was soft and held none of the usual spite that was so familiar from all their years of bitching and sparring. She said it flatly, just stating a fact. Tash felt tears come into her eyes. Stanno shifted in his seat, like he was desperate to leave but not brave enough.

'Too much make-up? I was doing some selfies for Insta. But the contouring's a bit full-on for real life, right? Maybe I'll just go back upstairs and tone it down a bit.' Even to her own ears, her voice sounded shrill, almost fake, but she was giving them all a way out and the expressions on both Evie and Stanno's faces relaxed just a fraction.

Tash turned towards the door but, flustered, she turned too quickly. The room started to swim, a familiar blackness closing around the edges of her vision. Evie was there in an instant and as Tash swayed back into her sister's arms Evie pivoted her awkwardly onto the nearby sofa. Then the tears that were threatening a minute ago broke free, carving channels in Tash's make-up. This was *not* how it was meant to go.

Before any of them could come up with their next move the doorbell rang.

'I'll get it,' said Evie, a grim expression on her face. 'Callie, give Tash some water.'

Tash's heart was hammering like a piston. Her whole chest was throbbing. Everything ached. She felt about two hundred years old. There was nothing she could do to stop the tears – she was too weak to even lift a hand to brush them away, so they pooled on her top lip and dripped off my chin and onto her jumper. Stanno was staring at her like she was an animal with a gruesome injury, his bottom lip curled in disgust. For a second, she wondered if this was it, if she might actually die here, on a sofa in the kitchen, with her mum AWOL and her ex-boyfriend pinned to his seat in horror at the sight of it.

She managed a sip of the water. Callie didn't let go of the glass and they lifted it to Tash's lips together. Callie's hands were shaking almost as much as Tasha's were. The throbbing eased a touch. Her heart rate slowed. Then the kitchen door opened and Evie walked in again. Tash thought she'd be carrying a delivery from Amazon or something, but instead she was followed in by a whole cluster of people. At the front there was Karen's friend, Misty, the doctor. She was walking with a middle-aged black woman with long cornrow plaits and lots of silver jewellery. Behind them were two younger people – one man, one woman, wearing dark blue tunics.

Misty spoke first. She crouched down and her voice was gentle. 'You remember me, Tasha?'

Tash nodded.

'This is Philomena, she's a social worker.' The cornrow woman smiled down at her. 'And these are two of my colleagues, Elliot and Javinder.' The nurses – she guessed they must be nurses – nodded at her too. 'We've come to take you to hospital.'

'I'm not going, I'm staying here.'

Philomena stepped forward and shook her head. Her eyes were kind but stern. She reminded Tash of a favourite teacher she had had in the infants. 'You need treatment, Tash, and you need it now. Staying here isn't an option anymore.'

'You can't make me.'

'I'm very sorry, Tash, but that's where you're wrong.'

She pulled a piece of paper from her bag and laid it on Tasha's lap. It didn't look that impressive, just a bit of typing printed out on plain paper, but with a couple of black stamps on it.

'It's a court order, Tasha,' Her tone was the same, as if she was saying they'd be doing finger painting today, and then have a story. 'It authorises us to remove and detain you at the hospital. With immediate effect.'

Tash glanced at the two nurses. She'd forgotten their names already but suddenly their purpose was starkly clear. They shifted slightly awkwardly, the Indian girl looking at her shoes. Neither of them looked particularly tough, but then Tasha would hardly be a match for anyone.

'I've packed some things for you, Tash,' Evie mumbled. 'I'll go and get the bag.'

'You were in on this?'

Evie caught her eye and then glanced towards Stanno. 'I didn't know exactly when, I'm sorry, T.'

Stanno stood up, mumbling, 'Um, maybe I should go, Tash. I'll, err, call you, yeah?'

'Okay,' she said, weakly. There didn't seem to be any point in trying to say sorry, trying to explain that it wasn't meant to be like this. Even in asking him not to spread this around the school. So she just watched as he edged through the huddle of strangers and walked out of her life.

Misty perched beside her on the sofa, taking her hand and talking gently about how well they would look after her in the hospital. After a minute or two they heard Evie on the stairs and when she came back through the door, she wasn't alone.

'Tash ...'

'Mum, I didn't even know you were here.'

It was clear that Evie had woken her up. She was wearing a jumper thrown over her pyjamas, her eyes were glassy and her face was still creased from sleep. The clock said 10.20 a.m. Tash didn't have the headspace to think about what was going on with her mother.

Completely ignoring Misty, Karen bent down and grabbed both of Tasha's hands in hers. It hurt, but then everything hurt now.

'I wasn't part of this, Tash. None of this was my idea. None of it is my fault. I need you to know that.'

Her voice was urgent and out of control. Philomena, the social worker, put a hand on her shoulder and gently pulled her back. 'It's done, Mrs Neville – we have the order from the court. Please don't frighten Tash when there's no need.'

Karen stepped back and Misty held out her hand to Tash. She glanced at the nurses and then took it, allowing her to help Tasha to – slowly, slowly – get up from the sofa. Evie was carrying her leather holdall. It had been a present for her birthday; this would be only the second time it had been used. They made a little procession out of the kitchen, accompanied by the sound of Ed Sheeran, still on repeat, and Callie's sobs. Tasha noticed that Callie hadn't gone to Karen. Instead, Karen followed at the back, like a zombie.

The car was some kind of cheap 4x4, a Kia or Seat or something like that, in a lurid purple. Philomena helped her into the passenger seat, while Misty hung back to speak to Karen. Tash couldn't hear most of what they were saying. No love lost, by the looks of it.

'If you're not helping us, you're helping her to kill herself.'

She caught that. Misty turned back towards the car and her reserves of calm seemed to be failing. Karen looked like she'd been punched. Evie handed Tasha's bag to one of the nurses and stepped back. Misty and her two sidekicks squeezed themselves into the back seat and Philomena started the engine.

Chapter 32

Misty
1989

'Fine,' said Eric, and turned around, leading them up to the galleried landing. Misty hadn't been in this part of the house since the party.

Wordlessly, Eric pushed open a substantial polished door to reveal a traditional drawing room, with velvet sofas and panelled walls. Curled in an armchair at the far end was a petite, unremarkable-looking woman of – in Misty's guess – about forty. She wore a black wrap dress – essentially the grown-up version of Alex's own outfit. Her feet – evidently the feet that had kicked off the fawn heels – were tucked rather coquettishly underneath her.

Misty was sober enough to know she was drunk, and even in her inebriated state she immediately processed that there was something very wrong about this scene. Glancing to the side, she could see instantly that her friend was livid with anger.

'Alex ...' began Eric, 'this is Elizabeth Anderton. Elizabeth is ... a friend. It wouldn't be in anyone's interests for Catarina to know that she'd been here.'

'What – you're worried she might get the *wrong idea*?' Misty noted that the sarcasm in Alex's voice made him wince, although Elizabeth herself appeared serene.

'How drunk are you?' Eric barked.

Alex didn't answer.

'As it seems you're determined to have this conversation. You may as well know that I'm not worried about your mother getting the wrong idea. I'm worried about her getting the right idea.' He turned to the woman. 'Elizabeth, as you will no doubt have guessed, this is Alex, and Misty Jardine, a friend of hers.'

Competing realisations jostled for attention in Misty's drunken mind. He hadn't introduced Alex as his daughter. It was clear that Elizabeth knew well enough already who she was, even though Alex did not appear to have met her before. More than that, she had a pretty clear idea what Alex did think Elizabeth was doing there. Misty's whole body crawled with unease.

'Alex ... I don't quite know where to begin.' Eric ran his hands through his hair, his self-assurance deserting him for once. He cast a distracted glance in Misty's direction.

'Misty, this is family business, maybe you could ...'

'No,' cut in Alex. 'She's staying.'

Eric looked agonised, but then he could hardly explain why the presence of this friend of his daughter's, in particular, was making the whole episode even more awkward for him. Alex sat down heavily on one of the plush velvet sofas. After only a moment's hesitation, Misty followed suit.

'Well, Elizabeth and I have known each other for a long time. Actually, we've been in love for a long time. My marriage to your mother – I suppose, it was like ... like a firework: an intense explosion that quickly burnt away to nothing.' His eyes were wide and pleading; his very desperation to make her see things from his point of view had lost him the battle already. 'Catarina had been through so much. I couldn't leave her in Spain. When we got married, we were down to the sparks, Alex. I did it out of duty – because it was the right thing – not out of love. I hoped it would work out when we were together in England. I hoped again when you were born. But ...'

He trailed off but there was little more he needed to say. Misty knew most of it from what she'd already seen and been told by both Eric and Alex. What she didn't know was all too easy to imagine. 'She'd been through so much' was an understatement when it came to her Catarina.

It was incredible that she'd managed to carve out a career in academia. Perhaps her background had given her a way in, some extra credit, but ultimately, she'd flourished on the strength of her work and her publications. In marked contrast to her husband, Catarina Penrith was an academic superstar.

Away from the university, though, and behind closed doors, she was broken. Tormented by nightmares and flashbacks. She relied on medication to sleep as well as heavy painkillers to numb the physical legacy of her experience. The smallest, most innocuous thing could trigger a recurrence of her symptoms. Misty knew that Eric had lived his adult life walking on eggshells around her, and Alex had grown up doing the same.

'Things have changed now.' Eric was still speaking. He had moved over to Elizabeth's armchair, perching on the upholstered arm and picking up her hand. It was funny, thought Misty. She was a bit younger than Catarina, but not by miles.

She was a very average-looking woman, with a dark permed bob, laughter lines at her eyes and a front tooth that was ever so slightly crooked. She was far from the stereotype bit on the side. *No*, sneered a cruel voice in Misty's head, *that was you.*

Eric continued to talk. 'Elizabeth was working abroad. Now she's coming home. She'd got a job in Bristol and ... and so do I. We're going to move there this summer.' His voice lowered almost to a whisper. 'I really hope you can be happy for us, Alex.'

'Fuck.'

Alex's hands went to her temples and she stared at the couple across the room. Time seemed to slow down. It was the drink, Misty told herself, wishing that she was drunk enough to have conjured the whole thing up. Amidst the silence, the fantasies she'd built on Alex's worries about her father crumbled and fell. It had all meant nothing. She'd been nothing but a cheap squeeze. One of tens or even more? A convenient amusement with his wife estranged and his real lover abroad. She felt sick.

'Alex, language, please.'

Eric sounded genuinely shocked. Well, good for him, Misty thought, he could join the club. 'I'm sorry, I'm pretty sure you're trying to tell me you're breaking up our family to have another go at the whole thing and see if you can do better next time round but no, you're right, it's out of order for me to swear in front of guests.'

'Alex ...' Elizabeth was speaking for herself now, her voice tentative, almost wheedling. 'Alex, your dad's moving in with me. I've got a flat in the centre of Bristol. It's a great city. You'll always be welcome.'

'We'd always planned this for when Elizabeth came back and you were old enough to cope with it, Alex. You've done so well at college, you've got over your health problems, you and Andrew are so happy. Really, I think it's for the best.'

'No ... no!' Her voice rose to a shout and, once again, Misty could see the anger writ livid on her friend's face. 'You can't leave Mum – she wouldn't cope. You know she needs ...'

Eric looked at his feet. Alex's voice changed again. It was cold, now, and steady. 'No. Wait. I think I understand. It's never been a question of waiting until I'm old enough to look after myself; has it? You've been waiting until I'm old enough to look after Mum. How am I meant to graduate and move away and live my own life? You know damn well she wouldn't cope – she wouldn't stand for it. I'm just your ... your insurance, your get-out clause. And who cares if it drives me back to anorexia because you've got out with a clear conscience.'

When he looked up from the floor his eyes were glistening. 'Of course not, Alex ...'

Elizabeth butted in, assertive for the first time – a sharpness to her voice that was at odds with her appearance.

'You're an adult, Alex, or near enough. And, more to the point, so is your mother. Who happens to be away in Nice at a conference all by herself like an adult, in case you'd forgotten. You will live your life and if she's indulged less everyone may well find that she can live her life too. Perhaps we'll all be happier.'

Alex turned on Eric. 'So *that's* the fairy tale she's been feeding you, is it? Of course, you want it to be true. Who wouldn't? But it's not and it never can be. You know that in your heart, you know you're abandoning me.'

And me, thought Misty, but of course she couldn't say

anything. Her dashed expectations, her grief, her wounded pride; none of them had any place in this tragedy.

Alex and Eric argued on, time passing unmarked in the dead of the night. The same points, the same posturing, it was probably less than an hour but felt endless. Eventually when Misty's stomach was churning and her head thumping with a headache that could have come from either the wine or the unshed tears, Alex announced that the two of them were going to bed.

Chapter 33

Misty
2019

The ward round, as ever, was a mixed bag. Jodi MacFarlane was being discharged today. It should have been cause for celebration, but Misty was already worried about a relapse. From the anxious look on Linda Sillitoe's face, she surmised that the elderly foster carer shared her doubts. Jodi had followed the treatment plan to the letter, putting on *just* enough weight to meet her targets – or near enough. She'd participated in the relentless hours of group therapy, encouraging others to be honest about the problems in their lives, about their difficult relationship with food. On the face of it, she was a success story.

But when Misty looked into Jodi's eyes, she was certain that it was still the disease staring back. They hadn't *really* managed to reach the frightened girl hiding inside, not this time. A hunch wasn't enough to keep someone as an inpatient, though. Jodi had ticked the boxes, so home she would go. And poor Linda would be the one to reap the whirlwind.

On Silver Birch, the male ward, there was better news. Hywel had been discharged a few days ago and little Ben was making great progress. She'd feared he might struggle with Hywel gone – the older lad had really taken Ben under his wing – but he seemed to be maintaining steady weight gain and was doing well in therapy too. He had individual therapy because the presence of a younger child would skew the group dynamic; they needed to be able to talk freely. But he still managed to be everyone's favourite. There had been some chat about Hywel and Ben going to a Liverpool game together once Ben got out, so hopefully that would be a motivating factor too.

'Can we chat, or do you need to complete the level?'

The kid pressed a couple of buttons and then put down his game.

'S'okay. It's rubbish anyway. You should get a PS for in here. Or an Xbox.'

'Hmm. We could put in a bid to the Hospital Friends. Maybe you could write me a letter, Ben?'

'Yeah, or I could ask my mate Shilpan to donate his old one. His family's loaded. They paid for the whole gym team to fly to Malta for a competition.'

'Well, if Shilpan has an old DS lying around we'd be happy to have it.'

He threw her a scornful look. 'You mean *PS*, Miss, a DS is handheld – for kids.'

'And you mean "Doctor", not "Miss", you're not in school, you know.' She smiled at him. 'Quits?'

'Yeah. All right.'

'So, how are you getting on with Elodie, the new therapist, then?'

He shrugged. She had no way of knowing if it was a problem or just typical teenage reticence, so she probed a bit further.

'Are you finding it helpful?'

'S'pose. We talk about the gym. And how I want to compete and how my body needs calories to perform at its best.'

'And what about how gym makes you feel?'

'I dunno. I've just always done it.'

He'd always done it and it came easily – he'd always been the best. Until the last year where he started competing nationally and not coping very well with being fourth or fifth. He was tall for his age, and growing. It was hard to keep the precision needed to make all those perfect lines and angles with a body that was suddenly alien to you. She could see well enough all the issues that would have to be unpicked – as, indeed, could her colleague Elodie. Getting a confused young boy to see them was the challenge, but Ben seemed to be doing well.

Her final stop was Maple. She didn't know who had decided to call all the rooms after trees. The patients referred to Maple as 'syrup'. She intended to change it, but it wasn't a priority. A throwaway reference to pancakes wasn't going to make or break anyone's treatment programme.

Maple was a six-bed room. The only person there when Misty opened the door was Tasha Neville. One bed was currently unoccupied; the other four girls were at therapy. Tash wasn't ready for that yet. She'd only been on the ward for three full days.

They'd once had a cover nurse brought in who normally worked in a learning disability unit. He described the new inpatients here as suffering from temporary autism. By the time they were admitted, their obsessions with weight and calorie intake had become all-consuming. Their mental horizon had narrowed so much that they were unable to bring anything else into focus. Tash was still in that zone. Soon, hopefully, the re-feeding would kick in and she'd start to pull out.

'Morning, Tash, how are you doing?'

The girl on the bed stared at her with malevolent eyes. Her limbs were pulled up, tepee-shaped, under the thin sheet, like twigs gathered up to make a fire. She looked fragile as a snowflake. Misty's mind flashed back to that afternoon at the party, when it had been easier than expected to get Tasha to talk to her. There wasn't going to be a repeat of that today.

She sat heavily on the edge of the bed.

'I think maybe we should try you in the therapy group next week. You only have to go to the session, you know. You don't have to say anything. Lots of girls don't at first.'

Silence.

'Well, when you want to start going let me know. Then you can start to work towards trips out, getting home. I'm sure you want that.'

Tash lowered her eyes, so they were staring down at her knees instead. Defiance replaced by a simple refusal to acknowledge her. Misty sighed. 'Well, I have to weigh you anyway – let's get on with it.'

She stood up and tugged back the sheet. Pyjamas with cartoon hedgehogs on them flapped around Tash's stick legs and arms. The girl looked at her and hesitated, the memory of her first day, when the ward assistants had had to drag her onto the scales, hung between them. Slowly, with hatred burning in her eyes, she pushed herself up from the bed and walked the ten or so steps to where the weighing scales had been wheeled in by a care assistant earlier. They were never left on the ward.

'Come on, then.'

Silently, Tash stood and walked the few steps over, before seating herself on the scales. The seat was forward-facing, so the patient couldn't read their weight. Misty noted the figure impassively. Tash was moving in the wrong direction.

'Okay, all done,' she said, keeping her voice cheery. Tash wordlessly resumed her position on the bed, pulling the sheet up over the points of her knees.

'Have you spoken to Laura or Natalie?' Misty gestured towards the two beds in the far corner before continuing to speak, knowing better than to expect an answer. 'Laura's thirty-seven. Natalie turned forty this year. You wouldn't know that from looking at them because all you see is the disease. Their bones are crumbling like women twice their age or more, but their faces look like kids' faces – as long as you don't look too closely. They lead kids' lives, too – they don't have jobs, they don't have relationships. When they're not in here they live with their parents. They've been going round in this cycle for twenty years or more. It's wrecked their lives. They won't mind me telling you – they'll tell you themselves given time.' She sighed again, fighting back the frustration that was such a natural part of working with eating disorders, but crucial not to give in to.

Finally, Tasha spoke. 'They've failed then.' Her tone was harsh, dismissive. 'I'm not going to fail.'

Misty took a breath. She couldn't let herself react, couldn't let her herself get emotional. That would be handing control to the girl, exactly as she wanted. No, Misty mentally corrected herself, exactly as the disease wanted. At times like these she felt like she spent her life doing battle with an actual demon. How could she even hope to win? And how much of her would it take in the end?

She kept her tone studiedly neutral. 'You're not making progress, Tasha. You've been here for three days and you're yet to start eating sufficient quantities or show any willingness to engage with therapy. We're going to have to insert a feeding tube. Tomorrow morning. It's not painful – we use a spray to numb your throat and the tube is very narrow. You'll have chance to ask any questions before the procedure. Once your calorie intake is up and your brain is getting the nutrition it needs, I hope you'll be able to make more positive choices about how you want your life to turn out.'

Tasha was mute again. Without another word, Misty replaced the clipboard with her notes in the holder at the end of the bed and left the room. She walked back to her office slowly, pondering over previous cases she'd had, desperately trying to think of some way that might work to reach her old friend's daughter.

Although this was the start of Tash's fourth day on the ward, Karen had been in only once. Evie had come each day, and yesterday she had her mother in tow, although it was very clear that Evie was the driving force. Karen had been both spaced and twitchy at the same time, displaying what appeared to Misty to be fairly obvious signs of anxiety. In a rushed conversation in the corridor, Misty had asked if she was getting any medical help. She couched it in general terms, observing that many parents with children on the unit had almost reached breaking point by the time they got there, that they had to look after themselves if they wanted to offer the best support to their children – both the ones who were being treated and any others.

Karen had replied curtly that she was fine, and that had been the end of the conversation. Putting up a wall – like mother like daughter – Misty mused. She could feel the beginnings of a headache taking hold.

Her thoughts were disrupted by chatter and footsteps around the corner. Glancing at her watch, she realised one of the group therapy sessions would be ending. Sure enough, she rounded the corner to see a gaggle of seven or eight patients, standing around and – from the sounds of it – chatting about *Love Island*. It might have been a high-school corridor or an office water cooler if you squinted to ignore the fact that two of them had feeding tubes taped to their cheeks and a third wheeled a drip stand.

'Hi.'

'All right.'

'Hi.'

The hubbub quietened as they walked towards her, none of them wanting to draw her attention. She sometimes wondered what it was like to work in the sort of wards where people were glad to see the doctors.

'Laura?'

'Yes?'

'Could I grab you for a minute? In my office – it's okay, nothing to worry about.'

'Sure.'

As she continued down the corridor with Laura trailing behind her the chatter from the rest of the group faded behind them. She wasn't sure what she was doing. The whole group therapy ethos meant that patient confidentiality took on a slightly different shape here than in other specialisms. Apart from anything else, the ED patients would relentlessly compare and compete however much anyone told them it was against some data protection law. So, she felt comfortable with what she'd said to Tasha about two of the unit's most long-standing regulars. But now she had some crazy spur-of-the-moment idea that Laura Smith could give her, the consultant psychologist, some key to help her break through with Tasha. Maybe she was losing it.

'So, what do you want to talk about?' asked Laura, once they were settled in chairs but without the cup of tea that would invariably accompany this sort of chat in any other setting.

'Natasha Neville.'

'The new kid in Maple?'

'That's right.'

Laura shrugged, looking bored. 'What about her?'

'She's only fifteen ...'

'That's not especially young for here. Ben's thirteen, we've had eleven-year-old girls before.'

'No ... but she's gone hard.' Misty picked her words carefully. She didn't think her personal connection to Tasha was making her treat her any differently. But she didn't want Laura to get any hint of it all the same. 'You know how it is ... almost all of the patients are conflicted, the pull to starve themselves versus the pull to be healthy, to get out of here.'

'Reasons to stay alive?'

Misty nodded. 'Exactly. There must be reasons for Tasha, but she's not letting me near them. I've rarely seen anyone so closed up.' She paused and looked up at Laura. 'It's a bit unorthodox, but I wondered if another patient might have more luck with her.'

'Playing at being big sister, you mean?'

Misty thought of Evie and felt herself grimacing. 'I sense

244

that Tash might have had enough of big sisters, now you mention it. Let's just say an older, wiser friend.'

'It's been a while since anyone accused me of having any wisdom.'

Misty shared an uneasy smile with her patient, and wondered if she was doing the right thing. Laura was a ruin. Misty knew that when she left the unit people stared and whispered. It didn't help that she was grazing six foot in height but it was her skeletal frame, patchy hair and wrecked skin that really drew the crowds. Staring and whispering might be the least of it. She'd heard rumours of an incident when Laura had been knocked to the floor and spat at on the tube.

There was always the danger with anorexia of patients egging each other on. It was one of the arguments used against inpatient treatment. But she was confident that Laura, at least, was past that. After more than twenty years in the grip of the disease she held no illusions about it being a positive life choice. Unfortunately for her, clear-sightedness alone hadn't proved a strong enough weapon to defeat her own demons, but on many occasions, she'd made really useful contributions to the therapy programme for younger patients in her groups. If Tasha wouldn't come to therapy, maybe Misty could fix things so therapy came to her.

'Well, if you'd look out for her. You know, try and strike up a friendship, I'd be very grateful.'

Laura shrugged. 'Fine, boss. It's not like I've got much else to do.'

*

245

Misty didn't move from her desk for a while after Laura left. It was past her clocking-off time. The charge nurse who looked after the unit on the night shift had been briefed and all the notes were updated. Of course, there was always work to be done, always more admin than there was time to do it in, but there was nothing she *needed* to stay behind for tonight. Plus, staring at her desk, lost in her thoughts, she wasn't getting any work done anyway.

Philomena and her court orders were all very well, but she knew that she wouldn't be able to keep Tasha alive in the long run unless that was what the girl wanted. Bottom line, most of the patients complied with most of what the unit required them to do not because of threat or coercion, but because they chose to. Everything about life in here – for patients – was designed to make it easier to make that choice and harder to continue to make the choices that the disease wanted them to make. But still, ultimately, it was a choice.

If they really knew what caused anorexia then presumably it might give a clue as to how to treat the really difficult cases like Tasha's. From her experience, as well as her learning, Misty believed that far more individuals carried the potential for eating disorders than would ever actually develop them. There was probably a genetic element – not one 'starvation gene' but a group of genes that could, in certain combinations, create a predisposition. If the predisposition was strong, it could take very little to trigger it – the simple uncertainties of puberty experienced in a society where food was plentiful and skinniness revered might be enough. In other cases, perhaps the environment played a stronger role – those boarding-school classes where four or five girls out of twenty would succumb, kids involved in high-level sport – like Ben

– or girls with mothers who passed their body issues on with added force. There were other cases where one traumatic event – perhaps something like the death of a close friend or family member – acted as a distinct trigger for the onset of an eating disorder. Most often it was probably a mixture of factors at work.

There was a knock at the door.

'Come in!'

'Hello, stranger, I thought you might still be lurking.'

It was Philomena. Misty waved at a chair and she sank her heavy frame into it, rubbing her eyes.

'Hard day?'

'No rest for the wicked. I was passing anyway and thought I'd come see you. Can't get that little girl out of my head from the other night. She doing all right?'

Misty grimaced. 'Not really. I was just chewing it over in my mind. Trying to work out what might have been the trigger to see if I can come up with some way of getting through to her.'

'You're close to the family, no? The mother? Maybe you should be passing her on to someone else.'

'No. This is the right place for her. I've disclosed the link to the managers. There's no conflict.'

Philomena accepted her assurances readily enough, but Misty knew she was right to raise them. She'd downplayed her relationship with Karen when she made her disclosures. But, she told herself, it was for all the right reasons. Tasha's best chance was here, in this unit, with her family close by, and with Misty fighting for her. She just hoped it was good enough.

She couldn't help but wonder if Karen had played a role

in starting Tasha off down this path. It was true that she'd instinctively lashed out at Karen after Alex's death. But then she'd been in a very difficult place, and prepared to blame everyone – Karen, Eric, Catarina and even herself. As she learned more about the disease and gained more distance from the events of that day, her feelings towards Karen would have softened. By that time, though, it was too late. After Karen graduated the following year, they pretty much lost touch.

But what if Karen herself had more of an issue with food than Misty had ever realised? And what if she'd passed it on in some way to Tash. The memory of Karen ranting at home – her delusions about Alex still being alive – sent a shiver through Misty. Perhaps it was just as well that Karen wasn't coming to the hospital. The thought of having to turn her away was not appealing.

'So, is the mother on board now?'

'Not exactly. I don't know what's been going on to push Tasha into this, but Karen certainly isn't doing much to help her recovery. She's only been here once.'

She paused, and Philomena waited, her large brown eyes were calm and impassive. Misty knew Philomena had a gift for making people confide in her – she'd seen it in action. This time, it was her turn.

'You know, Tasha's been having hallucinations.'

'Okay. Is that normal?'

'Not normal, but it does happen. Patients hear voices telling them to purge, or to exercise or that they're fat. Whatever it is. But Tasha's hallucinating a particular person. I've not come across that before. I'm assuming it's some form of psychosis.'

'Linked to the anorexia?'

'I can only assume so.'

'So, who's her imaginary friend then?'

Karen and Alex. Alex and Karen. The more Misty turned it over in her head the more it came back to that. Misty really wanted to put the past in a box and never open the lid on it, but the more she thought about it, the more she knew that wasn't an option. She took a deep breath.

'She's called Alex Penrith. She was at university with Karen – Tash's mum – and with me. She died in our third year, so Tash never met her. I suppose Karen must have mentioned that she died of anorexia. From what her sisters have said, Tash seems to have conjured her up as some sort of ... I don't know ... spirit guide I suppose. Alex is inspiring her to starve herself.'

'That's pretty twisted.'

'Yeah, well everything about this disease is twisted.' She gave a weak smile. 'I thought I'd seen it all by now.'

'So, you're thinking that if Tasha's subconscious has chosen to manifest this woman that she's never met, who's been dead for almost thirty years, that that says something about why she's developed this disease? And how you can get through to her?'

'I suppose so. Sort of. The thing is, Phil, Alex is the reason I went into ED. Alex is every patient who's ever been in here and I've been trying to save her again and again and again.'

'Because you feel guilty about her death? Why? It's not as if you were her doctor.'

'No.'

Misty felt herself turning cold. No matter how kindly her manner, no matter how patient her expression, Misty could never bring herself to tell Philomena the truth. Her entire career had been spent atoning for her role in Alex's death. Her silly fling with her friend's dad had been all about feeling grown-up. And, like most things people did to make themselves feel grown-up, it actually showed the exact opposite. She'd failed Alex – not by not stopping her anorexia, but by betraying her. Because she hadn't been there.

Whatever guilt Karen carried with her, whatever darkness she'd unwittingly passed on to Tash, she wasn't the only one. Unlike Misty, it appeared Karen had not tried to work through that guilt. Instead, she'd kept it buried and carried on regardless, raising her family, making a life for herself. But now, in the face of Tasha's own illness, she couldn't simply carry on ignoring it. Unable to face up to it, she'd turned away from her daughter. It was the equivalent of putting her fingers in her ears and singing 'la la la'. She couldn't cope with the truth – or what she thought was the truth – so she had to hide from it.

A sadness pulled on Misty's heart like a weight tugging a buoy. She could have prevented this. If she'd supported Karen, instead of blaming her, if she'd acted as a real friend, perhaps she could have prevented that lifetime of guilt from falling on her friend's shoulders. One thing was clear, though, she had to put it right. She owed it to Karen as a friend, and she owed it to Tasha as her doctor. If Karen and Tasha could start to repair their relationship then there was just a chance it could tip the balance for Tasha – to give her enough to live for.

'Misty?' Philomena's voice was gentle, questioning.

'Sorry, I got lost in my thoughts. You're right. Of course, Alex's death wasn't anything to do with me really. It just affected me – you know what teenagers are like.'

She tried to smile and Philomena returned it with a broad, warm smile of her own.

'Don't I? Anyway, the ones here are lucky to have you. You know where I am when you need me. Just remember to look after yourself too, yes?'

'Yes. I will.'

*

Phil left shortly afterwards and it was time for Misty to go too. The streets outside were darkening and her eyes were already heavy. She'd been lost in her thoughts long after her shift had officially ended, and would have to be back here in only a few hours' time. Before she left, though, she would do the thing she had to do. She picked up her mobile and found Karen's number.

Chapter 34

Karen
2019

Karen was sitting in the kitchen with a bottle of chardonnay, turning the American pill bottle over in her hands. The contents rattled, there were so few of them left. None of the bottles stayed full for long. Manda was worried and had stopped sending them, but she'd found someone else online instead. They charged a lot and yesterday her credit card had been declined. Thinking about where to get the next lot from made her so worried she wanted to take them even more.

Was it yesterday she'd been to the hospital or the day before? The pills messed with her memory too. She wanted to see Tasha – she was desperate to – but just being at the hospital made her even more panicky. And what if she made things worse? Her phone flashed and squirmed about on the marble counter, commanding her attention even though she'd set it to silent. Misty Jardine. That was the third one in an hour. She wasn't going to pick up to Misty. She didn't want another lecture from her about how she'd failed Tasha.

A niggling voice in the back of her mind worried that Misty might be phoning with news of Tash, that there might be

252

something wrong at the hospital. But she knew if that was the case then the social worker would phone too. And they would undoubtedly call Evie, who was revising upstairs. She had taken over the role of responsible adult around the place. Karen killed the call and, with some effort, pushed herself up to standing. Callie had been in a few moments ago looking for some dinner. There would be pizza in the freezer. There always was and that would have to do.

As she slid the pizza onto the oven shelf a thrum from the worktop told her that her phone was going off again. With a sigh she pushed the oven shut and turned to pick up the phone. She'd assumed it was another call from Misty, but instead it was Andrew Dyer's name that was flashing on the screen. Despite herself, a wry smile flickered onto her lips. She'd left a couple of messages for him that he'd not replied to. To be fair, she'd not been in the best state when she left them. Probably he'd decided to run a million miles from her and all her complicated baggage.

'Andrew, hi.'

'Hi, Karen, I'm glad I got you. Sorry it's been a few days. I got called away on business. Singapore. The time difference is really awkward.'

'Right. Well, was it a good trip?'

'Oh, just the same as a hundred others. Look, though, I was wondering if we could meet up tonight. I mean, I know it's last-minute and you probably have plans—'

'No. No. I don't have plans.' She paused, thinking automatically of the girls. 'But Evie does. So, I've got Callie. Hmmm ...'

'Well, could I come over?'

'Yes,' she whispered. 'Come over. Please.'

'Around half eight?'

She glanced at the clock. It was after seven already. God, how had that happened? No wonder poor Callie had been in sniffing around for her dinner.

'Yes, that's fine. Um, do you want food?'

'Don't go to the trouble. I'll pick something up on my way over, shall I?' He must have heard the slight panic in her voice and she blushed at the thought of how incompetent she seemed at the moment. A year ago, she'd have been able to pull a home-made tagine from the freezer or rustle up a soufflé and salad at the drop of a hat. Not these days.

'Thank you, that sounds perfect.'

After hanging up she whipped around the kitchen, making an effort to turn it into something vaguely presentable before dishing up a singed pizza to her youngest daughter.

'Aren't you having any?'

'I was going to, but I've got a friend coming over, so we'll eat a bit later.'

Callie chewed slowly. She looked thoughtful, but it may just have been the cardboardy toughness of the pizza.

'We always used to have pizza all together, with salad and garlic bread and stuff.'

'You never wanted to eat the salad! Now you're complaining about it.'

Callie just shrugged.

Within a few minutes she was off to the den to message her friends and watch vloggers demonstrating a million different ways to style your eyebrows.

Karen nipped into the little downstairs cloakroom to peer at her face in the mirror. Jesus, she was a wreck. Broken veins splayed across her cheeks, she had smudges ingrained under her eyes and her hair was limp and frizzed with a halo of split ends. For a moment she regretted agreeing to Andrew coming over, before a pinch of her old pragmatism reasserted itself. If he was only interested in her youthful good looks then he wouldn't be interested in her at all. God knew, she had reason enough to look a state, and he would understand that.

The doorbell went before she had chance to try to effect any repair work. She pulled the door open, patting her hair flat and already with a self-deprecating comment on her lips. The sight of Misty Jardine standing on the doorstep stunned her into silence.

Misty put a foot over the threshold, as if she was anticipating Karen shutting the door on her. The truth was that Karen's reactions were too dull for her to have settled on a course of action. Even as Misty proffered a wine bottle and a smile, saying 'peace offering' the cogs of Karen's mind were still clunking against each other, trying to work out what was going on.

'Did Andrew send you?'

'Andrew?' A look of confusion crossed Misty's face. 'Andrew Dyer? No, why?'

'Nothing. Never mind.' Karen remembered binning Misty's call before she answered Andrew's. Clearly, whatever it was Misty wanted to say, she was determined to say it.

'Can I come in then, Karen?'

Misty's spoke the words slowly, with an exaggerated gentleness in her voice. With a start, Karen realised she'd just been standing on the doorstep staring at the other woman. Flustered, she stood back and ushered her in.

'Come through then. Not for long. I'm expecting someone.'

She led the way into the kitchen and, on autopilot, pulled two glasses down from the cupboard.

'You steal my daughter and bring me wine – there must be a Hungarian proverb or something about that?'

Misty shrugged. 'If you say so – you're the well-read one.'

Karen put the glasses down, but one glanced against the edge of a coaster and toppled over. It rattled against the marble worktop but, almost miraculously, didn't smash. She squealed, then pulled herself together with some effort, righted the glass and began to carefully uncork the bottle. Misty frowned.

'Have you eaten? I brought the wine without thinking ... If it isn't a good idea ...'

'No. No, it's okay. I'm ... Andrew's on his way, actually, he's getting takeaway. I'm just ... just ...'

'It must be difficult.' Misty's voice was quiet. Gently, she lifted the bottle and the corkscrew from Karen's hands and finished the job herself, pouring two half-glasses before looking around for the fridge.

'Over there.' Karen nodded to the corner of the room.

'Oh, yes.'

As Misty found a space in the fridge, Karen looked at her through the eyes of a stranger. She was neat and efficient, exuding competence. Her dark hair was laced by a few bright strands of silver, which only seemed to emphasise that the richness of colour in the rest of it was still natural. She wore an asymmetric, blocky necklace, and glasses with chunky acrylic frames, the trademark of a certain type of professional women. When had they become grown-ups? How had that happened?

'I should be quick if you're expecting someone,' Misty said, still peering into the fridge. 'It's just hard to know how to say it.'

'Say what? It's not Tasha, is it? You wouldn't pitch up here with a bottle of wine to tell me something's wrong with Tasha.'

'No, no. Well, no more than there was this morning, but that's not what I'm here to talk about, at least not directly.'

'So why are you here?'

Finally, the fridge was closed, and Misty returned to her bar stool and picked up her glass.

'Alex.'

It wasn't what Karen had expected to hear. She held her tongue and waited for Misty to continue, but instantly, her heart rate had picked up.

'I think I owe you an explanation, Karen. An explanation and perhaps an apology.'

'Apology? For what?'

'I'm getting there. The thing is, nothing you said to Alex caused her death. You blamed yourself and I let you.'

Karen pushed herself back in her seat. It was an involuntary reaction, almost a recoil.

'You mean ... she's still alive, isn't she? Just like I said, you knew it all along.'

Misty's face was open and honest and competent. She searched it looking for a glimmer of intrigue; the smallest hint that there was a reason to hope. Gently, Misty shook her head.

'No. She died, Karen. She's definitely dead. You need to be clear on that.'

'But the body ...?'

'I saw the body, Karen, even if her family didn't let Andrew see it. There was a body.'

'So? What is there to talk about.'

Misty took a breath, held Karen's gaze, and began.

'The night she died we'd gone back to her house from a night out. Eric was there, with this woman called Elizabeth. He was planning to move in with her. Alex went mad about it. She didn't want to be left with Catarina.'

Karen made a face. 'I can imagine that. She always thought she'd failed by not going away to university. The idea of another thwarted escape would have been horrendous for her.'

Misty nodded, then continued. 'Exactly. She'd been doing well with her eating. I mean, a relapse is always possible, but she was in a good place. I did blame you at the time, but looking back, it wasn't a coincidence that it happened on that night. The anorexia must have weakened her heart, or exacerbated some underlying issue, just like we were told, but it was what Eric told her that tipped her over the edge that night. The shock and her panic about what it all meant triggered the seizure, or heart failure, or whatever exactly it was.'

'Shock? Is that real? I mean, real enough to kill? I always thought it was a sort of Victorian melodrama thing. Pass the smelling salts and all that.'

Misty looked uncomfortable. 'It's unusual,' she admitted. 'But it's the only explanation that makes sense. You know as well as I do that her weight was healthy, she was eating well, she was happy with Andrew.'

Karen nodded slowly, the fuzziness still clouding her brain.

'It wasn't your fault, Karen. Do you understand what I'm saying? She didn't starve to death. You didn't kill her.'

'You didn't think that then. You were furious with me.'

'Well, I was furious.'

Karen gave her a quizzical look. Something solidified like

258

a lump of lead in her chest. How could she reach Karen, how could she help Karen reach Tash, if she wasn't honest about the whole story?

'Eric's bombshell that night didn't just land on Alex,' she began, picking her words carefully. 'It shattered me too, because – silly girl – I'd thought he was in love with me.'

Chapter 35

Misty
1989

'The absolute bastard ...' Alex was seething.

Misty's head hurt. Suddenly, she knew she couldn't do it. She couldn't face spending the rest of the night with Alex, soaking up all of her friend's pain and sense of betrayal whilst swallowing down her own.

'I need a glass of water,' she said. 'And I might step out the kitchen door for a ciggie and some fresh air. This has all been a bit ... intense. And I think the hangover might be kicking in early.'

'Yeah, see you in a bit.'

Alex was barely listening. She'd discarded the black dress for some pink striped pyjamas that didn't reach her ankles, hopping around tearful and half-naked as she pulled them on, not caring that Misty was there. Now she was huddled in her bed clutching a teddy bear. She was grieving the end of her childhood. Misty might not be an English student but she could get the blunt symbolism. That was all fine for Alex, but *she* was mourning too. Not for her childhood, but for what she'd thought could be her future. She turned and left, gently pulling Alex's door shut behind her.

The upstairs of the house was in darkness, but the hall windows were uncurtained. A greyish light – from the moon or a streetlamp, she didn't know – was good enough for her to negotiate the hall and the stairs, once she'd given her eyes a moment to get used to it. Were Eric and Elizabeth still in the drawing room? Or would they go to bed – and, if so, where?

She crept back to the hall, feeling on safer ground as she went down the staircase that led to the basement kitchen. She risked switching on one of the side lights, filled a glass from the tap and sat alone at the kitchen table she'd shared with Alex and her family so many times in the past.

Her relationship with Eric played out in her head. What had it amounted to? A glorified crush? He'd made no promises. When Alex had confided her worries, Misty had taken them and run with them, spinning her own little fantasy which, as it turned out, was a million miles from reality. A lump formed in her throat and she angrily swiped away a tear. She wouldn't sink to self-pity.

Tomorrow was a new day. With a heavy sigh she picked up her glass, switched off the light and navigated back along the villa's corridors and staircases. Instead of going to the family rooms, though, she headed to the back of the house and the little blue guest room Eric had mentioned. On the bed there was a neatly folded nightshirt that she recognised as one of Alex's, as well as a tube of toothpaste and a toothbrush still in its packet. Eric must have put them here for her. What a ridiculous man, still able to think of niceties like that when he was in the midst of wreaking havoc. Still, she had to admit it felt good to go to bed with clean teeth.

*

Eventually she woke to a grey, drizzly dawn. The house was quiet except for the creaking of the radiators. The warmth had woken her, she suspected; neither home nor college had central heating.

Quarter to eight. Her head pounded and for a moment she wondered if she might be sick, but she propped herself up on an elbow and took a few deliberate, steadying breaths. It was definitely a hangover, but not a terrible one. It was tempting to put her head back on the pillow and see if she could grab a bit more sleep, but her bladder had other priorities.

'I've put some coffee on!' Eric called up the stairs just as she crossed the landing, putting paid to any hope of going unnoticed. Well, she'd have to face the day sometime; it may as well be now. She hoped that Alex had beaten her down to the kitchen, but she could hardly check.

'Morning, Misty. Feeling a bit fragile?'

Eric was alone in the kitchen, sitting at the pine table with a copy of *The Times* and what might have been a smirk hovering on his lips.

'Hello. I'm okay. Is Alex still in bed?'

'Yes. Sit down, I'll get you that coffee.'

She would have liked to argue, but didn't really have it in her. Nor did she ask where Elizabeth was – that was too thorny a subject to open up. Instead, she slumped onto a chair at the far end of the table from him.

'I'm glad I've caught you alone, actually, Misty. I just wanted to say ... you know ... we had some nice times together. It ran its course, I think.'

'Okay.' God, she could do without the heart-to-heart in this state.

'Good. Good.' He paused, fiddling with the fancy coffee pot thing they had. 'I appreciate you not mentioning anything to Elizabeth ... or Alex. Thanks for that.'

'Okay,' she repeated, busying herself with spreading butter on a slice of toast instead. It would either cure her or kill her.

She sipped the coffee and chewed the toast in morsels. It seemed dry, despite the indulgence of the butter rather than the scrape of margarine college would have offered up. The wall clock had an audible tick. Eric retreated to his newspaper, wafting the occasional page. It was the most interminable meal she'd ever eaten, yet miraculously her stomach was settling, and it was making her feel marginally more human.

After almost forty minutes she'd had two slices of toast and two cups of coffee. Eric had offered one passing remark about the newspaper weatherman forecasting higher temperatures for the coming week. She'd not taken him up on it. There was only so long she could drag the meal out, and still no sign of Alex emerging to break the tension.

'There's a bus at ten past,' she said. 'If I sort myself out now, I can probably make it.'

He glanced at his watch. 'Comfortably, I'd say.' There was a sigh and he folded the paper into his lap. 'Look in on Alex before you go, yes? I'm sure she'd rather see you than me at the moment. Elizabeth has gone and if Catarina's flight is on time she'll be back before lunch. Alex might want the option to miss her.'

She nodded and left the room without saying anything else to him. That was it then, she thought, ruefully, that was their goodbye.

263

She knocked gently at Alex's door but got no answer. The door was firmly shut. After knocking once more she turned the handle and gently pushed at the door.

Alex's pink curtains were drawn, and the morning light filtering through them cast a blush across the room. She was lying on the bed, not under the duvet, but on top, despite the chill night. Her candy-striped legs and arms were splayed out in the too-small pyjamas. Misty couldn't help but smile – it looked like the night before had hit Alex even harder than it had hit her.

Then her smile froze.

Something was wrong. Alex was too still, too pale. Misty took one step forward, noticing a tinge to Alex's lips. Not blue, exactly, but off colour. Her heart rate picked up, the urge to get closer now fighting with the urge to run away, to close the door and hope to hell that she was wrong.

She forced herself to kneel by the bed, picking up Alex's wrist with a vague idea of feeling for a pulse. No need. No point. The skin was cold.

'Eric! Eric!' she called over and over, her voice rising to a scream. Her legs buckled under her as she heard his footsteps on the stairs. When he burst into the room, she could do nothing but point at the body on the bed.

*

He didn't call an ambulance – he said there was no point when she was beyond saving. Instead, he'd called the family doctor, and led Misty gently back to the kitchen whilst they waited for him to arrive.

'I've missed the bus,' she said.

'You're in shock. You can't go back just now. I'll make you a sweet tea.'

She accepted it meekly, thinking that she ought to be the one to comfort him, but with absolutely no ability to even try to do that.

'Catarina will be back soon. Probably before the doctor. How am I going to tell her?'

He didn't seem to expect a response and Misty didn't offer one.

They sat together in silence until they heard the sound of a car pulling up outside. Eric jumped up from his seat and strode into the hall.

'It's her,' he said.

Misty followed him, but found herself hanging back in the kitchen doorway. The polished parquet flooring in the hall gleamed like it was auditioning for a Mr Sheen advert. The luxury of Alex's house still had the power to disarm her, and now the conker-bright expanse of that empty hallway was distracting her from the shocking reality that Catarina Penrith was about to walk in and discover that her daughter was dead.

'Darling, hello, I wasn't expecting a welcoming committee.' Reaching the doorstep, Catarina reached up to kiss her husband, but even from her place in the shadows of the hallway Misty could make out the questioning look in her eyes.

'Catarina, my love, come in.'

'Misty.' Catarina came through the door and saw the guest hovering at the far end of the hall. 'How nice to see you.'

'Come and sit down in the lounge,' interrupted Eric, shepherding his wife with an arm round her shoulder.

Misty didn't hear exactly what he told her, but a few moments later there was a strangled sob loud enough to reach her. At the sound of Catarina's footsteps, Misty shrank back, cowardly, into the kitchen. She could picture everything as the noise of Catarina rushing to her daughter's bedroom and weeping in anguish echoed through the house.

Rather than follow his wife upstairs, Eric came to the kitchen.

'You should be with them,' she told him, tonelessly.

'I will be.'

But the sound of Catarina's slow steps on the staircase came before Eric had moved. The woman who came into the kitchen looked twenty years older than the one on the door-step ten minutes earlier.

'I've called Dr Gilbert,' said Eric.

But Catarina was already turning to Misty.

'She told me you were going out last night. Was it drugs? What did she take?'

'No ... nothing. We were drinking, that's all – she wanted to come back here.'

'She died in her sleep, darling, neither Misty nor I heard anything. I think it was peaceful; she looks peaceful. Nick will tell us more.' He checked his watch. 'He'll be here any minute. I'll open some brandy – look, we all need one I think.'

Chapter 36

Tasha
2019

Breakfast-snack-lunch-snack-dinner-snack-bed.

Their days were eaten up with eating. She did what she could to play the system, but they'd seen it all before. There was a nurse in every room, so they couldn't exercise without being caught. They were watched as they went to the toilet or the bathroom. The staff even made people go out in wheelchairs so they couldn't burn calories by walking around. Their portions were measured and plates had to be cleared, with the threat of the feeding tube looming. Always.

The thought of that lack of control terrified her more than anything. She had little enough choice about what to eat – tomato pasta or chicken pasta, strawberry milkshake or banana – and sometimes lifting that food to her lips, feeling it pollute her, was harder than she'd have imagined anything could ever be. But not as hard as the alternative. The thought of the tube, of giving them the ability to pump whatever they chose into her, so that she was mainlining calories like a fat junkie. Yeurgh. It sent her into a panic. When she thought about it, she started to sweat and tremble and itch like she

267

needed to crawl out of her sorry skin. The panic was so intense it was probably the one thing she was doing in here that was actually burning some calories.

And, of course, it was working: her weight was creeping up, clinging to the lower line on their acceptable projections chart. The numbness was fading. She thought about her family – especially Callie – and felt bad about what she'd put them through. Alex was fading too. She sat by Tasha's bed for the first two nights. Then she was just a voice. Then nothing.

But she craved the numbness. She'd crawl over broken glass on bloodied limbs to get back there. To get back to not caring. But she knew she needed to play the game. She'd tried to outwit them and she couldn't. So, she needed to get out. She needed to put on the weight and say the right things and tick the right boxes. She'd keep it up at home whilst Evie was there and keep her off her case. The hospital follow-ups would tail off if she was doing okay as well; she'd heard the chat, the danger signs were when girls start dropping weight within days of getting out. They were short of resources – well, of course they were – so with the best will in the world they wouldn't be checking up as much as they might if they thought that she was holding it together. There would always be someone in crisis.

Then, with Evie out of the picture and this lot off her case ... kaboom. Free fall. Showing them she was smarter than they gave her credit for. Getting Alex back, getting numbness back. Saying goodbye to all the crap.

Until then ... well, she supposed she'd just keep drinking up her strawberry Ensure shakes like a good little girl.

The girl from the room opposite had cornered her for a 'chat' the night before. They were sitting in the day room, with everyone on their phones and one of the nurses watching *EastEnders*. This girl, Laura, had fished a pack of playing cards out of a drawer and asked Tash for a game of gin rummy. She thought about saying no but remembered that she needed to start playing things more tactically, so she agreed. They played for a bit and then Laura started going on about Ed Sheeran as if she thought that was going to appeal to her. It was as bad as being stuck on a car journey with bloody Callie. From there she had segued into talking about depression, and how her depression made her to want to stop eating. She was clearly fishing for Tash to start sharing her story or confiding her issues or whatever. Tash could tell she thought she was good; she was just dying for her to roll up a sleeve and open up a vein for her.

Instead of following her instinct to clam up, Tash batted her eyelashes and told her how nice it felt for someone to finally understand. Laura lapped it up.

Tash resolved to let her be a good influence, hit up the therapy like it was the hottest ticket in town and get herself out of here quicker than blinking.

It was a plan worth raising a glass to, but she supposed a mug of strawberry protein shake would just have to do.

Chapter 37

'I had an affair – no, that's too grand a word for it – I had a *thing* with Eric Penrith. We kissed, we had sex a couple of times in his horrible office in the chemistry department, he bought me gifts. I thought it was some great romance.'

Misty looked at Karen, trying to see if her friend was taking in what she was saying. Karen's fingertips rubbed her temples. She looked hungover, but she was definitely engaged with Misty's revelation, even if she was struggling to get a hold of it.

'What?' she asked. 'You mean when we were still students? When Alex was still alive?'

Misty nodded, shamefaced.

'Did she know?'

'No. I was petrified of anyone knowing. But then, that night ... the night she died ...'

'What?'

'Eric told us he was leaving Cambridge, moving in with Elizabeth – do you remember he remarried a year or so after Alex's death?'

270

Karen shook her head. 'I didn't know. Or else I forgot. You know I was a mess. I spent the third year drinking myself stupid and almost failing my finals.'

'Well, he told us. I don't know if Alex guessed Elizabeth would be there. She knew something was going on – maybe she wanted to bring it to a head. The next morning, she was dead and my disappointment was suddenly ... I don't know ... meaningless, worthless ... just blown away to nothing.'

Funny, it wasn't as hard as she'd expected it to be. All these years, she'd believed it would be simply impossible to talk about this to anyone. That she wouldn't physically be able to bring herself to do it. But here it was. Her dirty laundry was as sordid and matter-of-fact as anyone else's.

'But instead of taking my approach you hit the books and aced your third year and everything else.'

Misty pulled a face. 'I suppose. I felt so burnt by the whole thing. Alex, Eric ... the house, the money. I just went back to what I knew before – being the hardworking schoolgirl. Keeping my nose clean. I was devastated to lose Alex, though. I mean, I don't see how I imagined we would still be friends if my stupid fantasy life with Eric had played out, but I don't think I'd ever properly thought about it. I tried so hard to understand how she could have so much going for her, and still feel this compulsion to refuse to eat. I could never give up on trying to make sense of it – I suppose that's what I'm still doing.'

Karen looked quizzical. Gradually, over the time that Misty had been there, she had come into focus, sharpened up. There were traces of the old Karen in the woman who sat in front of her now. Although she still looked rough, the druggy glaze was melting away and the orange plastic pill bottle she'd been toying with lay discarded at the edge of the breakfast bar.

'I remember that morning. You barely spoke to me. You seemed just about able to go through the motions. I assumed it was the shock of her dying, and because you thought it was my fault.'

Misty forced herself to meet Karen's gaze and felt a jolt of emotion when the eyes that stared back at her were Tasha's. Was this helping? Could Karen let go of Alex enough to let herself be there for the daughter who needed her?

She took a sip of the wine. She'd only had a couple of mouthfuls, but she could feel it going to her head already. Empty stomach. As if reading her mind, Karen stood up and grabbed a packet from the cupboard, tipping some popcorn into a bowl.

'Andrew's meant to be coming with food. I don't know what's kept him.'

'Oh, so are you and he ...?'

'He and I are having dinner together.' It was clear from Karen's voice that she wasn't going to be drawn any further. She swallowed as if the next words were hard to get out. 'You've not said anything yet about how Tasha is.'

'I'm glad you asked,' she said gently. 'That was why I wanted to come. Things aren't good, Karen. She's not acknowledging that she needs to get better; she's not eating; she's not engaging with my staff.'

She studied Karen carefully for a response. Her eyes were intent, focused, but giving away no emotion. 'I'm expecting to start her on a feeding tube programme tomorrow. This will be non-consensual, best-interests treatment. Philomena – the social worker who was here when we brought her in – has obtained the legal consents. She will be in touch too. We want what's best for Tasha, Karen. I know you do too.'

Shakily, Karen nodded.

Misty began putting her phone back into her handbag and digging out her car keys. Tread gently – that was enough for now. A goodbye was forming on her lips when the doorbell buzzed.

'That'll be Andrew,' said Karen, unnecessarily.

Karen stood and walked into the hallway. Misty followed, still clutching her handbag in the diminishing hope that perhaps she could get away with a quick hello on the doorstep. She was still a few steps behind when Karen gasped and stepped back, blocking her view of the doorway.

Only a moment later, Misty was echoing Karen's shocked reaction.

Andrew Dyer stepped into the hallway, clutching a white takeaway carrier and ushering a woman through the door behind him. Misty blinked and blinked again but it didn't dislodge the impossible sight in front of her.

She was looking at Alex Penrith.

Chapter 38

Misty
2019

'Misty!' Andrew grasped her shoulders and kissed her with real warmth on both cheeks. 'I came to surprise Karen but it's a surprise to me that you're here. All the better, though – I'm so pleased to see you.'

Karen had turned pale. Instead of leading them back to the kitchen, she opened a door to the left, which led into a plush living room. A large bay window gaped black onto the street and Karen hurried to draw the curtains and switch on table lights whilst the others settled themselves awkwardly on the pale linen sofas. Misty noticed her hands trembling as she did so.

Despite Karen's flustered activity, Misty's gaze was continually drawn back to the woman who had come in with Andrew. A couple of times, the woman's dark eyes met hers for a moment before sliding away, embarrassed. The gawping was rude, Misty knew, but that didn't mean she could help it.

She was absolutely the image of Alex, the same stature, the same posture, the hair, the features – all of it matched Misty's recollections. This woman was exactly the woman her friend would have grown up into. But the timeline didn't quite stack up. This woman was what – forty-five, perhaps?

'So ...' Karen's voice interrupted Misty's thoughts. She moved to sit down opposite Andrew and 'Alex' her questions starting before she'd even got herself in the seat. 'Will someone tell me what's going on?'

She addressed the room but was looking at Andrew. He swallowed once, then began to speak.

'Karen, Misty. I'd like to introduce you to Rosanna Penrith. She's Alex's sister – well, actually half-sister.'

'And you were the one in the footage of the tube attack?' Karen asked the question; Misty's brain was whirling too much to allow her to open her mouth.

Rosanna nodded. 'Yes, I wouldn't normally use that route, but I had a meeting in Finchley ...'

Andrew had started talking again and Misty forced herself to tune in to what he was saying. '... Karen Neville and Misty Jardine. We were all friends of your sister Alex at university, back in the late 1980s.'

'It's still hard for me to get my head around it.' Rosanna gave a bemused smile. 'I knew my dad had been married before, but all these years, my parents never said anything about a half-sister.' She turned to address Misty and Karen. 'Andrew tracked me down online. When I finally agreed to meet him, he showed me the photographs. Everything fitted together.'

'You must be Elizabeth's daughter,' said Misty, quietly. 'I met your mother once. I can't remember her surname.'

'Anderton. Yes, that's right.'

'But, they married the summer after. In 1990,' said Misty, her mind working quickly. 'You're not ...'

'I'm not under thirty, no – wish I was! I was twelve in 1990 when they got married. Their affair had been going on a long time, I understand, but I was born in Philadelphia, and raised there until my mum got a job back in Bristol.'

There was a trace of an American accent to her voice – Misty noticed it now. How incredible to think that Alex had had a sister all along. There had been a child across the ocean, ten years younger, so alike, and neither with an idea that the other existed.

'What about Catarina?' Karen was asking Rosanna. 'Do you know what happened to her?'

Andrew interrupted. 'I've done a lot of research. She stayed at Cambridge for a couple of years, but then she went back to Spain. It was safe for her by then, of course. She ended up in a care home run by nuns.'

'I can't imagine she liked that,' observed Karen.

'Me neither,' said Andrew, ruefully. 'She stayed there many years before she died in 2006, so I wonder if she was struggling to cope in terms of her mental health and that's the reason she went in. But that's just supposition on my part.'

'So how did you find Rosanna?'

He grinned. 'LinkedIn. There aren't that many Penriths, you know. As soon as I stopped looking for Alex and started looking more widely, it was pretty simple.'

'And Eric?' said Misty, not knowing what answer she wanted to hear. 'Is he still alive?'

It was Rosanna who answered this time. 'No. He died quite young, at the end of the Nineties. He never told me about Alex. I knew he'd had another wife, of course, but I guess I sort of supressed that. He came to visit us a few times in Philly. I don't suppose it could have been for more than a

276

couple of weeks at a time, but in my memory, it's as if he lived with us there too. Our brains twist things to fit, don't they? Especially when we're young.' There was a murmured assent but it seemed that Rosanna hadn't finished speaking. She paused, turned her hand and looked at her nails. 'Actually, there is something I've not told Andrew yet.' She flashed him an apologetic look. 'Or shown you, perhaps I should say.'

'Yes, what is it?' He was eager. Misty observed that there seemed to be an easiness between them and wondered how long he had kept his discovery to himself.

'Like I said, Dad never talked to me about Alex. After Andrew got in touch, once I knew it was real, I asked my mum about it. She cried on the phone – she's not normally emotional – it was obviously really difficult for her. She said she was there the night that Dad told Alex he was going to leave her mum and move in with mine.'

'That's right,' said Misty. 'I was there too. Alex and I had been out. We went back late to the house and your mum and Eric were there. There was a bit of a showdown ... Alex wanted it, I think. She already suspected her dad was planning to move out. When she was asleep that night her heart gave out – the shock, it seems, coupled with the long-term strain of her eating disorder.'

But Rosanna was shaking her head. 'Dad lied ... That's what Mum was upset about. She went back to her hotel in a taxi. She knew nothing about it until just before the wedding. He said he wanted to go into it with a clean conscience.'

'Lied?' Karen and Misty spoke almost in unison. Misty gestured for Rosanna to continue. 'What do you mean he lied?'

'There was a pill bottle. The medicine had been Catarina's

– strong painkillers, opiates, she took when her old injuries were flaring up. It was beside Alex's bed. With a note ...'

Alex had killed herself. Oh God.

Misty gripped the arm of the sofa as though she was adrift in a storm. Of course, the part played by 'shock' in her death had always jarred. But the eating disorder was a fact; the underlying weak heart was so likely. Alex's face as she'd last seen her alive flashed in front of her – furious, desperate. Misty had thought she was being overdramatic, had been too wrapped up in her own feelings of betrayal to recognise the agony that her friend was going through. The realisation cannoned into her chest. She *could* have saved Alex. If only she'd realised. If only she'd opened her eyes.

'But ...' Andrew was craning forward in his seat. He'd lost his composure watching his stage-managed little production veer so drastically off course. 'But ... there was a doctor, a death certificate. None of that was mentioned.'

Rosanna shrugged. 'Eric didn't want it to be. He tidied the pills away. The GP was a family friend. Her heart was weak, apparently. Eric persuaded the doctors that a post-mortem would be unnecessary – and cruel for him and Alex's mother.'

'And that would look a damn sight better for him than the fact that her mother's madness and her father's desertion had driven a brilliant, wealthy heiress to take her own life.' Andrew spat out the words, as though they were too bitter to tolerate on his tongue. 'The tabloids would have been all over it. I can just imagine.'

They sat in silence for a moment before Rosanna tentatively reached into her handbag.

'I have the note. Mum kept it, with some of Dad's things. She never knew what to do with it, but she couldn't throw it out. I went down to Bristol yesterday for it – that's why I was waiting to tell you, Andrew.'

She held it out, and he took it, tears running freely down his cheeks as he began to read. Rosanna turned towards the two other women, almost as if trying to give him some privacy for his grief.

'I was wondering … if either of you had any more pictures,' she said, quietly, her gaze flicking between Karen and Misty. 'I always wanted a sister. It's … it's hard. To find you have one and then have her taken away.'

'Um, yes, we can find some,' said Karen, casting around as if pictures of Alex were going to jump out from the walls. 'And stories too – she was a wonderful friend, you know. So funny.'

She smiled, but the effort was too much for her, and her face immediately crumpled. Now she and Andrew were both openly weeping, and Misty felt a lump rise in her own throat. This was the real grief, the grief they'd been cheated of all those years ago.

Andrew coughed and passed the note to Karen and Misty. They read it together, heads almost touching, hair mingled. They'd sat like this years ago, Misty thought, sharing a magazine or gossiping in a loud bar. Not often. Alex had been the one in the middle, the glue holding them together. But there had been moments of friendship, and maybe there could be again.

The note was brief and confirmed Rosanna's story. Alex's handwriting was still so familiar, even after all these years. She didn't mention Karen – would she be able to take that as absolution? Misty hoped so. Alex told Andrew that she loved him and that she wished him all the happiness of the future they'd planned to share together. He was the real victim of Eric's deception, thought Misty. Not Alex, who was dead and unaffected by whatever came afterwards, but Andrew, denied this last message of love that might have helped him.

'Tissues,' said Rosanna, taking a plastic packet from her bag and waving it around slightly helplessly.

They all accepted. Andrew blew his nose noisily and laughed. Karen nudged the takeaway bag with her foot.

'I don't suppose anyone wants to eat?'

'Funny you should say that ...' said Andrew.

'I'm actually starving,' said Rosanna, giggling with the awkwardness.

'I'll get some plates,' said Karen.

*

Rosanna was nice. She had a friendly manner and had that knack of being self-deprecating without making it seem fake or affected. She worked in marketing. She'd recently gone back after maternity leave. It was a late pregnancy after fertility problems and IVF. Her precious daughter, Freya, was fifteen months old.

'She was all I could think about that day when the bomb exploded on the tube – or failed to. I knew I couldn't bear it if anything happened to me that would leave her alone.'

Misty pictured in her mind's eye the photograph that she'd stared at so many times. That look of determination that Alex had when she was about to go into an exam or a tough supervision. This time it had been the resolve of a mother to get back to her child.

'I nearly gave up after that morning. It seemed like a

warning. But we couldn't afford to keep up the mortgage on Dan's salary and I can see now it was just a panic. I'm hardly likely to get caught up in something like that again – and it doesn't make it any more or less likely if I'm in work. I'll just have to hope that lightning doesn't strike twice.'

*

The curry wasn't the best. By the time they got around to eating it most of the dishes were going cold, so they'd dished up the food before microwaving each plate in turn, which didn't help the quality. Misty appreciated the sustenance none-theless and, looking around the table, it seemed as though the others felt the same.

'I've never understood anorexia,' Rosanna said, suddenly and rather timidly, as she prodded some rice with her fork. 'I knew a couple of girls at school with it but no one I was close to. It would never have crossed my mind for a moment to stop eating. I guess she must have been very unhappy. I mean, even before ...'

'No.' The three of them spoke at once, the same word in different tones.

'Anorexia is a really complicated disease, Rosanna ...' Misty was covering ground she'd covered a hundred times. 'Alex was ... joyful. She loved people; people loved her. She clearly had problems, I suppose more than any of us realised at the time. But she was a wonderful human being. Andrew will tell you—'

She was cut off by the ping of her mobile.

It was the alert tone she used for the hospital. They very rarely called her off duty; and when they did it wasn't good news. The message asked for a ring back and she briefly excused herself before stepping into the hallway to make the call. There was the sinking feeling in her stomach that an out-of-hours emergency on the ED ward always brought on, but this time it was accompanied by a horrible sense of foresight. She didn't have to wait for the charge nurse to speak to know which patient was in trouble.

'It's Natasha Neville – she's gone into respiratory failure. The crash team are doing the transfer to ICU and I'm about to call the family, but I knew you'd want to be here if you can.'

'You don't need to call the family, Eveline, I'm with Tash's mum now.'

'Oh ...'

Ignoring the confusion in her colleague's voice, Misty glanced back towards the lounge.

'I'll bring Karen Neville in,' Misty confirmed to Eveline. 'Tell me, what's your gut feeling? Did the crash team say anything?'

'Not really. She started fitting and one of the other girls pulled the alarm cord and yelled for us. She lost consciousness but because we were there, we managed to keep her airway open. It could have been a lot worse if it had been a couple of hours later and everyone had been asleep.'

Misty's mind was racing. Tash had been stable, even if she wasn't putting on weight. If only she'd gone a day earlier with the tube, but she'd thought they had time. But then lots of people had weaknesses – pre-existing conditions, congenital defects. Anorexia put an immense strain on the human body and, even in a recovering patient, sometimes a crucial line was crossed. Still, if the airway had been maintained so her brain and organs had oxygen ... ICU should be able to stabi-

282

lise her and support her systems until her body was ready to take back control again – provided, of course, that that point came.

'Thanks, Eveline. You're on all night, yeah? I'll stop by before I leave and update you.'

'See you then. I hope she pulls through.'

'Me too,' said Misty, but as she walked the few steps back to the lounge doorway her feet dragged as if they were made of lead.

'Karen?' She had to raise her voice to cut through the hubbub of conversation.

'Hmm?'

'Can I speak to you for a moment? In private?'

'Okay.'

Karen looked bemused, but she slipped off her stool willingly enough and followed Misty back into the darkened living room.

'That was the nurse in charge of the shift on the ward, Karen ...'

'What? What is it?'

'Tasha's in intensive care; she's had some sort of seizure, or collapse. We need to go in.'

Karen's hands flew to cover her mouth and the wine-induced flush drained instantly from her cheeks.

'I'll get my bag. No ... wait, I can't leave Callie.'

'What about Evie?'

'She's gone out to a party up in town. I'll need to ask a neighbour ... or ...'

'Look, let's ask Andrew. We're going to have to tell them where we're going anyway. And we need to get moving.'

'Of course. I'm not thinking straight. Callie doesn't really know Andrew, but she won't wake up short of an earthquake, anyway. So, if he doesn't mind staying ...'

'I'm sure he won't,' reassured Misty, conscious that she didn't have the slightest idea what Andrew's plans might have been for later in the evening. 'But let's check – come on, we should go.'

'Misty.' Karen grabbed her arm as Misty went to open the door. 'Is Tasha going to die?'

Karen's eyes were huge with terror. Misty felt the fluttering fear that assailed her every time she knew that desperate parents when pinning hopes on her that she could only pray she would be able to fulfil. Alongside the fear this time there was something else, something approximating relief. Karen's reaction was, well, *normal*. Instead of running away from Tasha's illness, or denying it, she wanted to be with her daughter.

'I don't know much, and I can't promise anything. But ...'

'But what ...?'

'I've seen people pull through worse, Karen – you've got every reason to hope. Now let's get you there.'

She'd seen people fail to pull through, too, but she wasn't about to tell Karen that.

Misty couldn't see the expression on Karen's face as they rushed back into the kitchen side by side, but the appearance of the pair of them immediately silenced Andrew and Rosanna. There was a clink as Rosanna set down her glass slightly clumsily on a glass table top, then silence.

'It's Tasha, Karen's daughter,' said Misty, taking charge. 'She's being treated at my clinic and she's crashed. Karen and I have to go to the hospital. Right now. There's no one else here to look after Callie. She's asleep, but ...'

Andrew and Rosanna started to talk at the same time, both offering to stay if Karen wanted them to.

'Andrew?' Karen nodded her agreement to him. 'She's asleep, but at least she's seen you a couple of times so you'll be a familiar face if she does wake up. Call me if she does – I'm sure she won't. There's coffee and tea and ... well, just help yourself to anything. And you're welcome to stay as long as you like too, Rosanna.'

'Just a minute,' said Misty, thinking rapidly. 'Actually, Rosanna, is there any chance you could come? I'll explain in the car, but there's a just a possibility it could be helpful to have you there.'

'Um, okay. Well, there's nowhere else I need to be.' Rosanna's expression was confused but she got to her feet and began to pick up her things. After Karen and Andrew had had a few more exchanges on the practicalities, the three women headed for the front door.

Misty unlocked her Mazda and the flicker of the headlights guided the others towards her parking space. She felt hugely relieved that she'd driven and not come on the train. The chat died away as the three of them clipped into their seatbelts, each occupied with the thought of what might be waiting for them in the hospital.

Chapter 39

Tasha
2019

The darkness felt watery and physical, like a lake, or perhaps just a bath. She was sinking into it, letting it soak every part of her. She wasn't choosing to sink, but she wasn't fighting it either. She dropped down, down into warmth, safety, comfort; why would she resist?

Before, she'd been panicking. She couldn't breathe and her vision had gone dark around the edges. She could remember Laura being there, shrieking and raising a commotion. Over-emoting as usual. Then a load of nurses had rushed in and then there was a lot of light – hurting her eyes. They were moving her and shouting at her; slapping her cheeks and sticking in needles. Given that she wasn't actually moving a muscle for herself it seemed to take a hell of a lot of effort.

Then there was only the darkness.

Well, almost but not quite. At the edge of her consciousness there was something else. Noises – perhaps voices – she couldn't quite be sure. It was too much effort to try to make them out.

Gradually, she sensed movement through the water. She

was drifting, as though in a boat, being pulled along by a current. There was pressure on her hips and shoulders where her bones were weighing on the mattress through her too-thin skin, but perhaps it was the bottom of the boat she could feel. She pictured a gondola with a carved prow and an elegant profile carving a silent path through the submarine depths. The water was still all around her, slick and silky against her skin, even whilst the idea of the boat became more and more real.

The journey continued – for minutes, for hours, for days? She had no idea. She was timeless as Miranda, lost in her own enchanted tempest. Eventually, the peripheral noises grew weaker and, correspondingly, her surroundings seemed to solidify. Now, her fingers could feel the ridged planks that made up the base of the boat. There was an eerie, silver-green glow, the light of the moon under the water. Now her eyes could make out the carved prow, just as she had envisaged it, and a smooth turned balustrade along the side of the boat, topped with the blind eyes of rowlocks missing their oars. Around her, tiny iridescent fish were darting about, their quicksilver bodies seeming to materialise from the water itself and, just as quickly, dissolve away again.

Eventually, the boat began to slow. The change was almost imperceptible at first, but then became more obvious, as if it was struggling against an opposing tide. Finally, with a sudden jolt, the journey was over.

She pushed herself up, first onto her elbows, but then quickly up on her feet. The movement was easy and painless; she had left her weakness back on the surface. Out of habit, she paused to catch her breath. But, surrounded by the enchanted water, she found she had no need to breathe. There was no giddiness or frailty and, eagerly, she stepped forward. Immediately, she found herself on a beach, the boat bobbing in the shallows behind her.

She couldn't make out much in this murky underwater light, but she sensed that she was on a small island of sandy shore and rocky hinterland. If there could be such a thing as an underwater island.

'Tasha, come to me. Tasha, come to me.'

When she noticed the voice, she realised the same phrase had been repeated several times before it registered in her brain. She still had no sense of where it was coming from – the beach? The boat? It simply seemed to fill the water.

At the same time as she noticed the voice, there was a commotion way, way above her. There was a disturbance in the water and splinters of bright white light echoed down through the depths. Instinctively, she shrank back from it, a feeling of panic rising up in her throat.

'Don't look at the light. Then it can't hurt you.'

The voice came again, this time from the beach. It was Alex's voice, as calm and sardonic as if she was sitting by Tash's bed, bemused at all the stuff in the magazines she didn't know about, like phones and apps and gluten-free. Tash looked around, eager to see her.

A figure materialised in front of her – not quite close enough to touch although she reached her hands out in the blurry light anyway. The girl on the beach was tall and elegant, clad in a flowing robe that shimmered with the movement of the water. Her body had stature, but barely substance, and, with a gasp, Tash saw that the elegant tapered hands emerging from the sleeves of the robe had jointed fingers of polished, opalescent bone; they were the hands of a skeleton. She looked upwards and, sure enough, there was the girl's domed skull. The head was bowed, but lifted as if to meet Tash's gaze. Where the eyes should have been, there were just blank sockets. One of the tiny fish darted through, pausing for an instant before vanishing off into the deep.

'Tasha, I'm thrilled you came. Welcome to my kingdom. And soon, as they say in the fairy tales, half of it will be yours.'

Alex held out her arms, beckoning, almost touching Tash's own outstretched fingers. She knew that she should be scared but she wasn't. Warmth and security radiated out from Alex. All the good feelings in the water, Tash realised, had been coming from her. What's more, she was beautiful. Perfect, shorn of the flaws of the flesh. Tasha felt a surge of envy and desire – she wanted this for herself. She reached out still further, preparing herself to step into Alex's embrace.

But there was more disturbance overhead. The noises and lights were stronger now, the sand shifted under her feet and she stumbled backwards.

'Tasha ... Tasha, it's Mum. I love you, darling ...'

The words, already muffled by the water, were partially drowned out by Alex's hiss of frustration. Tasha staggered backwards. The sound of her mum's voice pranged her back from her decision. She knew that joining Alex here would mean leaving behind everything she'd known before. Behind her, the prow of the boat began jolting. It appeared animated, like a reined horse jerking forward. The light above grew brighter still. She knew that she could go, if she wanted to, that the boat would carry her up.

'And what's for you there?' spat Alex, full of contempt. 'There you're a fat and ugly teenage girl. Not clever. Not special. Not loved. Go if you want, but you know you'll regret it. This is your chance, Tasha, are you going to fail at this too?'

Her resolve stiffened and the boat steadied. But her mum's voice was still there too.

'We all love you, Tash, darling, more than you can imagine.'

The voice grew stronger, and suddenly, Karen's face was there too. Tash found herself in the boat again, lying on her back and looking up at her mum looking down on her. Looking anxious. Looking loving. Looking as if Tash mattered. Other faces began to swim into focus. An Asian man in scrubs with a stethoscope. Misty Jardine. And Alex Penrith.

'Alex?'

Tash could see the hope in her mum's eyes. 'Darling!' Karen glanced across at Alex, who was no longer a skeleton but had very real eyes, red from crying, and a neat layered haircut very different from anything Tasha had seen on her before.

Glancing back to the beach, she could see the skeletal Alex still there. The arguments had stopped. Alex was passive and still, exuding peace and warmth, keeping the water calm.

Above her, the new Alex spoke to Tash, her gentle clipped tones very different to the exuberant ones of the old Alex, but her face unmistakable from the photographs.

'Y-your Alex is a fake, Tasha.' She sounded uncertain, and looked to Misty, as if for guidance. Misty nodded back to her and she carried on. 'She doesn't want the best for you. She means to harm you ...' Alex was growing in confidence a little. 'There are people here who love you, Tasha. I've heard so much about you from your mum. She told me how you made everyone in the family breakfast for Valentine's Day when you were seven, and set the kitchen on fire. How she used to find you and Evie sleeping head-to-toe in one bed and you said it was because you were saving each other from monsters.'

Karen was smiling at the memory, although she was wiping a tear away at the same time. Tasha felt tears fill her own eyes, kissed away by the water as soon as they had formed.

'Callie won't be a child for much longer ...' the new Alex continued. 'You'll want to get to know her as a teenager, as an adult. I know how hard it feels. It'll be a battle that you won't always feel like fighting. There will be days when it's easier to sink down, to fade away.' The words made Tash conscious again of the warm, soothing water caressing her skin. 'But I promise you it's worth it. It's worth it a million times over. I had a sister I never got to know. I don't want that for you and Callie.'

She faltered, but the man in scrubs began nodding encouragingly, and Misty joined in, patting Alex on the arm.

'I-I'd like to get you to know you too, Tash. I really think we could be friends. Friends in the real world – IRL – that's what your generation say, isn't it?'

Her voice dropped lower and Tash found herself straining to hear it. She wanted to get closer and, as if at her command, the boat began to lift her. Slowly, she moved closer to the voice, closer to the surface. She wanted to stay underwater; she knew she was safe there, with none of the problems and uncertainties of her life above. But if *this* was the real Alex, what did that mean about the one down in the water? And there was another nagging voice too, her own voice, reminding her that her mum and Callie and Evie all loved her, and wanted the best for her, and that maybe, after all, they could be right.

It was too hard to choose, so instead she allowed herself

to drift, suspended. She concentrated on fighting back the panic that came with the thought of facing up to everything that had gone wrong in her life. The exams she'd not revised for, the friends who must hate her because she'd betrayed them, the new friends who must be laughing at her. She could get help, that's what Dr Jardine always said: there was help for her if she asked for it. She just needed to want it.

Before now, she hadn't ever wanted it. She'd thought it was brave and strong to push herself as far as she could. It had made her feel clever to pull the wool over the eyes of the doctors and the nurses.

Did she want it now?

They were pulling her. Alex was pulling her down to warmth and bliss and a welcome end to all the mess that she'd got herself into. But Alex wasn't real. The other Alex, joining with her family and the doctors to pull her up, she must be the real one. It would be hard to go up. Tash wasn't sure that she was strong enough. She knew now that she needed help, but did she want it?

Did she want it?

Did she want it?

Chapter 40

Misty
2019

Eight hours later, Misty fought to keep her eyes open as the taxi turned the corner of her street. All she wanted to do was sink into bed, but she knew she wouldn't sleep with her head spinning and the accumulated grit and grime of twenty-four waking hours settled on her skin. Instead, she would peel off the clothes she'd been wearing for far too long and run a deep bath. She imagined pouring in extravagant dollops of the expensive foam bath she'd got last Christmas and sloughing off the smell of the wards with their desperate fug of bleach and bodies.

It was getting on for five in the morning and the sky was dove-grey with pink seams; an expensive mantle thrown over the grubby chaos of South London's streets. She was meant to be in the clinic at nine, but she had put in a call to say where she was, and they would just have to get some cover and manage as best they could. She should be able to get in for the afternoon outpatient session, but she'd be no use to anyone if she didn't get some sleep first. Along the street there was the odd lit window on the first floors of the terraced houses, and she caught sight of a white cat disappearing through a cat flap, home from its nocturnal adventures. Her own house, of course, would be just as she'd left it before going to work the day before.

She exchanged a muttered goodbye with the driver and walked a few steps to the front door. The fresh air prompted a deep yawn, which she made no attempt to stifle. Somehow, she fumbled her keys in the lock and the door opened, catching her off guard. Struggling for balance, she stuttered over the threshold and was pleased not to stumble. She must be even more tired than she realised.

But when she got in there was another explanation. A large suitcase dominated the narrow hallway, a newspaper and leather jacket slung on top of it. The door hadn't been locked at all.

'Eusebio?' she called softly, not wanting to wake him if he was sleeping. But before the word had fully left her lips he appeared, fully clothed, at the top of the stairs.

'Misty! I thought you didn't do nights anymore?'

She grimaced. 'I don't. Long story. And I need to get back in after lunch.'

He glanced at the clock on the wall and grimaced back at her. 'You going to sleep?'

'I thought I'd have a bath first. How about you, are you jet-lagged?'

He shrugged. Eusebio ran on his own time zone. 'I know –' he was grinning now '– you run your bath. I'll get us coffees from Marcio's – and almond croissants – we can have a chat then I'll pack you off to bed.'

'Ah, that sounds like bliss.' She wasn't exaggerating. 'But better make mine a decaf.'

It took all the concentration she could muster to go through the motions of running the bath, collecting her pyjamas and towel, taking her hair down and dropping yesterday's rumpled clothes into the laundry basket. As she sunk into the water, she closed her eyes and the image of Tasha's face arrived, unbidden, filling her mind. She looked so young, so frail. Tiny in the hospital bed, and still as a corpse save for her eyelids, which flickered furiously but never opened.

Seeing the work of her ICU colleagues up close still shocked her. It was more like butchery, or even plumbing, than medicine. She'd never been good at that stuff during training; the quick decisions, the physicality of it. It wasn't for her, but she admired them immensely.

At times during the night, it had seemed as if they were dragging Tasha back from the brink using nothing but their willpower and sheer bloody-mindedness. But they'd done it. They'd got her back.

Dr Rashid, the senior house officer she'd never met before and may never meet again, was convinced that Tasha had chosen to fight; and that she responded differently after Misty and the others had arrived. Well, it wouldn't be the first time that medics had noticed a change in a supposedly unconscious patient when their loved ones arrived. But was she being fanciful in her hunch that it might have been Rosanna, rather than Karen, who had made the difference? They'd never know.

The warm water eased her bones and she breathed deeply, filling her lungs with steam tinged with bergamot and rose. Psychosis was an ugly word, especially for someone just on the cusp of life. But the starvation and metabolic imbalances suffered by anorexic patients were believed, by some researchers at least, to be capable of causing transient psychotic episodes,

295

particularly in younger teenagers whose brains were still developing so rapidly. Once the patient regained weight and the nutritional deficiencies were rectified, the psychotic symptoms would disappear. At least that was the theory. She could only pray it would be that way for Tasha.

The sound of Eusebio clattering upstairs with the coffees reached her even underwater. She pushed her feet against the end of the bathtub, arching her back and stretching with a groan.

'It's all right, I'm getting out. I'll come down.'

'Come to bed!'

She thought of pastry crumbs on the duvet, but then she smiled. Why not?

She climbed between the sheets, still damp, and relaxed against him, his outstretched arm curling behind her. As they sipped their drinks, she tried to fill him in on Tasha and Karen and the reappearance of Alex, or rather Rosanna, keeping it all as simple as she could.

'And now you will be treating this girl again? She will be admitted to your ward?'

Misty shrugged. 'I expect so, eventually. Her weight had recovered; she seemed to be doing okay. We'll have to investigate whether she was restricting again – you know they're always finding some new way to game the system on the way. If that wasn't the direct cause of the problem then there might be some separate, underlying condition that needs to be treated as well. And she'll need to stay in high dependency for a few more days, whatever happens. I'll check in with them, keep an eye on her.'

'Maybe you should trust them to do their thing?' His tone was reasonable, gentle, as always. He'd always tried to make her see when she was getting too hung up about work, but he'd never push her.

'You're probably right.'

He turned to look at her, his dark brows lifting and his eyes wide in surprise.

'I've learnt … it's all a bit complicated to explain. Tasha's mum spent her whole life blaming herself for something that was nothing to do with her. If anything, it was more to do with me. I've been trying my whole career to bring back Alex. I think I'm finally accepting that I'm not going to do it. And I can live with that.'

As the word came out of her mouth, she felt a weight lift from her shoulders.

'That sounds like good news,' said Eusebio, his voice even.

'I hope so.'

Gently, he lifted coffee cup from her and set it down on the bedside table, before turning back and bending his head towards her. He kissed her collarbone and she felt the sand-paper-roughness of his unshaven skin against her breast. She ran her fingers through his hair and she breathed in his smell with a sudden urgency.

She needed to sleep, but the closeness of death had quickened the life in her. Wasn't that nature's way?

Chapter 41

Tasha
2020

She was eating breakfast in a Cambridge café. What would a curious bystander see if they stopped to think about it? Two women, too different in appearance to be likely mother and daughter, but still acting with a familial closeness – laughing at half-spoken jokes, touching hands easily. Their clothes made them stand out from the tourists, the older one in a chic silk jacket and skirt, a smart cream hat placed carefully on the chair beside her. The younger one – Tasha – wearing a dress – floral but modern, as bright as her smile. She was slight but her outfit accentuated the swell of her chest and lent a curve to her hips. She carefully sipped a soy latte, but the plate of avocado toast that had been in front of her was thoroughly demolished. There was nothing to signal to a casual observer everything that she'd been through in the last few years.

'So, all this will be you, come October?'

Tasha looked around and made a face. 'I don't think so, I'm going to Reading, remember, not Cambridge.'

Rosanna smiled. 'Don't worry, it's not about the surroundings, it's about the experience.'

Tasha nodded. She *was* excited to be going to university, and pleased to have got there, given how far behind she'd got with everything in her GCSE year. The school had entered her for A levels on trust, based on her previous performance rather than her abysmal clutch of exams. And there had been so much catching up to do, she'd still thought that she might have to stay behind another year to improve her grades, but with a lot of support she'd just pulled through. Maybe if things had been different, she would have had a shot at somewhere like Cambridge, but she could see already that that sort of pressure wouldn't help her to thrive.

Rosanna had read History at Edinburgh. She did an office job now that had nothing to do with History, and she'd loved getting involved in Tasha's A-level stuff. They'd spent hours together, including the times when Tasha couldn't face going into school. Rosanna even got stuck into the French too, although she'd barely spoken it since A level herself. Without her, there was no way Tasha would be going to university this year.

'It's so lovely that they're getting married.' Rosanna beamed.

'Well, I suppose you only turn fifty-one once – why not get married?'

Tash glanced at her watch. Evie and Callie had gone for a quick walk around the town centre but they should be back soon. Dan, Rosanna's husband, was catching the first half of some football game while little Freya had a nap. The six of them would need to make their way to the college chapel in about twenty minutes.

'I remember my mum's fiftieth,' Tasha continued. 'That was

the first time I met Misty. I can hardly believe it now, so much has happened since then. And today my mum's the oldest bridesmaid in England.'

'Yes, it's sad that they lost touch for all of those years, but then ...' Rosanna faltered. Maybe she didn't want to point out that it had taken Tasha nearly dying to bring her mother back together with her old friend. Or maybe she was thinking of Alex, who never lived to see any of her friends get married, far less do it herself.

Tash's own mind had wandered back to that other party. What a child she'd been. She felt a million years older now. And a million years wiser, hopefully. The thought of freshers' week was daunting; what would she have in common with a couple of thousand kids her age, who had nothing more to worry about than who they were going to hook up with? How could she be all bubbly and extrovert, when some mornings it was more than she could cope with just to muster a smile?

'Here come the others,' said Rosanna, jolting Tash out of her reverie. 'We should get going.'

*

The service had been lovely. Intimate, dignified but personal too, with a funny poem read by one of Misty's work friends and a Costa Rican blessing. Now Tash was sitting with the other guests waiting for Eusebio to start his speech. A glass of champagne – she didn't normally drink – had warmed her. The smiles and festivity had kindled a fuzzy affection, which encompassed everything around her, and was perhaps exacerbated by the alcohol. She watched her mother on the top table, talking animatedly to Eusebio's elderly parents, who seemed roundly bemused by the whole proceedings.

Even as a daughter, with all the familiarity that brought, it was noticeable to Tash how much Karen had aged in the last couple of years. Just as Tash carried baggage that sometimes made it hard to connect with others her age who hadn't gone through similar experiences, so Karen carried the mental scars from Tash's disease. But, God, she was strong. She'd fought over the lost investments, doing it all herself because she couldn't afford solicitors. Roping in the financial services ombudsman and finishing up with a decent compensation payout.

In the meantime, she'd got a job with a local accountancy firm, doing their office management. Andrew had offered her one, but she'd turned it down. They were friends and he still came round from time to time, but that was as far as it went. He was here today, along with a woman who looked half his age and was shockingly beautiful. Tash resolved to introduce herself later and see what gossip she could wheedle out. Tash and Callie looked after each other when Karen was at work. Tash made the food and Callie made sure that she ate it. Callie was fourteen now, looking almost grown-up in a full-length sheath dress and with hair put up. Still in love with bloody Ed Sheeran, though, even if she claimed otherwise.

Eusebio performed well giving his speech, playing to his audience and getting in some good jokes. When he sat down, Tash was surprised to see Misty get to her feet. Previously she'd brushed off the idea of doing a speech, saying that it wasn't up her street. She leant forward, curious as to what Misty would say.

There were a few thank-yous, and an apology that her decision was spur-of-the-moment and the speech wouldn't be very polished.

'What I really wanted to do, though,' she continued, 'was raise a toast. When I was a student here, long before I met Eusebio, I had two very good friends. One of them is here tonight, as my bridesmaid. The other, as many of you know, sadly died whilst we were still at college. Without Alex, I wouldn't have found the career that I love. But Alex, directly or indirectly, has also introduced me to some of the most important people in my life.

'I wish she could have known that she has a wonderful sister and an adorable young niece. I wish she could have met Karen's amazing children. I wish we could all have known the children that she and Andrew might have had together.' Her voice stuttered. Tash felt a catch in her own throat and knew it was shared by almost everyone else in the room. Misty wiped the back of her hand on her cheek, but managed to carry on.

'She also never knew Eusebio, and that makes me very sad, because I think they would have adored each other. This is a happy occasion, and I don't want to let it become maudlin, but the fact that it has taken the pair of us about twenty years to get around to getting married is something that has not escaped comment. The thing is, I've changed in the last two years. I'm a little bit less obsessed with my work. I'm a lot more forgiving of myself. And, most importantly, I've realised that I deserve to be loved. All those things have led us to today and they've all happened, in a way, because I've finally been able to look back on an earlier part of my life, and forgive myself, and say goodbye. So, the toast I want to make is an unusual one for a wedding, but it's important to me. And I know I'm not the only one in the room who would share that feeling.'

Her hand was shaking visibly as she reached for the champagne flute on the table but, again, she held it together and raised the glass confidently to the room.

'To Alex!'

Epilogue

Alex
1989

Misty had gone to get a drink. She must be reeling. As if it wasn't obvious that she fancied herself to be in love with Alex's dad. As if the fact they had some sort of sleazy thing going on wasn't staring everyone in the face.

The thing that Alex knew and Misty didn't, of course, was that this happened every year with Eric. His colleagues despised him and the university only kept him on because they would hate to lose Catarina, and because scandal was unthinkable. Eric salved his wounded pride with easy-to-impress undergraduates. It was pathetic, but she could live with it.

Elizabeth was different though. Elizabeth was a woman of substance. It was clear that she had every intention of enticing him off to Bristol. Eric, blinded by optimism – or perhaps by his own need to escape – refused to recognise the consequences of what he was planning to do. Well, Alex would show him.

She'd have to act quickly – Misty could be back in minutes.

From the bottom of a drawer she carefully took out the note she'd written when she first learnt that Catarina was making one of her rare trips abroad and guessed that she would have the chance to confront her father. From her sleeve, she took a small glass bottle of pills belonging to her mother that she'd lifted from the bathroom cabinet earlier in the evening. She picked it up, turning it over in her hand before holding it to the light to inspect the contents. It looked full, probably a new bottle – her mum would have the current one with her at the conference. The label on the front said there were 100 pills inside.

How much would she need to take to overdose? She checked the printed prescription label again. 'Take two tablets as needed, to a maximum of four times per day.' She needed something dramatic enough to scare him. They'd probably have to pump her stomach at Addenbrooke's.

She scattered a few around so Misty couldn't miss the evidence when she came back upstairs. She could pretend to be knocked out even if she wasn't. That way she'd only need a few to help with the grogginess and make sure there was something in her system if they tested.

A voice in her head niggled that it might all go wrong. That however awful life alone with her mother might be, she wouldn't want to risk losing it altogether. She quickly swallowed two tablets, then two more, washing them down with some whisky from a quarter bottle she'd stashed in her wardrobe at Christmas. More pills rattled down into her cupped hand and she pushed them into her mouth – she'd make sure he got the message.

There was no pain at all. It was pleasant, like floating on marshmallows. Before long, she heard footsteps on the stairs. Misty was coming back. Instinctively, she smiled, though her face felt frozen and she knew it didn't reach her lips. All hell would break loose, just as soon as Misty opened that door.

But Misty kept walking.

Author's Note

Choosing to write about anorexia was not an easy decision. I don't have any significant personal experience of the disease, either directly or through close family or friends.

One day, sitting in a traffic queue, my attention was drawn to a young girl waiting at a bus stop. She was very pretty, although I suspect she didn't know it. She had a canvas school bag, which she was drawing on with a black sharpie. Her expression mingled a potent teenage cocktail of anxiety, defiance and boredom. There was nothing to suggest that she suffered from an eating disorder, but as the traffic moved on and I continued my journey, the character of Tasha began to form in my mind. She stayed there for weeks, vocal and insistent, until I began to take seriously the idea that I should tell her story.

I knew from that first day what lay at the heart of Tasha's story and knew that it wasn't the crime novel I'd expected to write. As I pondered and planned, I became fascinated by the idea that jeopardy in fiction need not come from shadowy strangers – and might not come from violence at all. Anorexia has the highest death rate of any psychiatric illness. Couldn't this terrifying disease make just as compelling an antagonist as a scorned lover or obsessive stalker?

Whilst I wanted to produce a gripping story, from the start I was determined to write sensitively and responsibly about this complex topic. I read and researched widely and tried to make Tasha's experience (and Alex's) an authentic one, without sensationalising the disease. I am grateful to the many people who have shared their experience via blogs and articles, and also to several medics who helped with my questions. Of course, there will inevitably be errors and they remain my responsibility.

In particular, I wanted to say a few words here about Tasha's hallucinations of Alex. Whilst delusions and hallucinations of various sorts are not uncommon in anorexia, I haven't found any case involving detailed, realistic hallucinations of a specific individual, as Tasha has. I allowed myself this artistic licence because it served the story, and, in my view, enabled me to express a deeper emotional truth about the allure of starvation to an anorexia sufferer, which is so difficult for those of us on the outside to understand.

Beat is the UK's eating disorder charity. If you would like to know more about eating disorders, to seek help or advice, or to donate, you can find them at www.beateatingdisorders.org.uk

Acknowledgements

It has been a delight to work, for a second time, with the talented and dedicated team at Avon. Thanks must go to my editor, Molly Walker-Sharp, above all, but also to all of her colleagues. They have all made the process of turning my imaginings into a real live book as easy and painless as possible and put up with ridiculous numbers of silly questions in the process.

I'd also like to thank my agent, Peter Buckman, and his team at Ampersand, for their on-going support and wise counsel.

Special thanks to Niall Moody, whose winning bid in a charity auction organised by Matthew Dyson meant he got to name a character in this book. The auction was in support of the fabulous work of The Christie hospital in Manchester and the name was Philomena Dempsey, after Niall's mother. Thank you for giving me such a fantastic name!

Turning to matters medical, I would like to pay particular thanks to a close friend of mine, Jo Rawstron, who gave me a lot of encouragement with an early draft of this novel and shared the benefit of her wealth of medical knowledge and experience of the hospital environment.

I'm grateful to the writers and readers – many from the

fabulous workshop group run in Bath by Beverly Stark – who have read earlier chapters or drafts of this work, made insightful comments and generally kept me sane: James Aitcheson, Jonathan Carr, Jo Furniss, Lyndall Henning, Katherine Slee, Beverly Stark and David Towsey.

Away from writing, I would also like to acknowledge my long-term colleague, boss and (I hope) friend, Catherine Mitchell. Catherine is supportive far beyond reasonable expectations, utterly unflappable, and an inspiration to me and any woman who wants to have it all (where 'having it all' means juggling demanding legal work, child-related-crises, creative endeavours and actual chickens, whilst retaining a sense of humour and almost always wearing matching shoes).

I'd like to thank all the friends who have been tirelessly cheerleading my books. I've had so much support and it's hard to pick out individuals, but Michaela Pashley has definitely gone above and beyond – many thanks!

I feel very lucky to have family who continue to encourage me in my writing, as in everything else. This book is dedicated to them. I particularly have to mention my mum, Jean, who has always been my biggest fan; my dad, Bill, and my brother and sister-in-law, John and Nicola. The pride in the faces of my two lovely children has been, without exception, the most rewarding part of this wonderful adventure. Thank you to them. Finally, my husband Mike needs a mention for hundreds of barista-standard coffees, as well as all his moral support.

The lovely messages I've received from readers of *If They Knew/The Mother's Lies* has been one of the highlights of this past year. Thank you to everyone who has bought my books, read them, reviewed them and shared your enjoyment. Thank you for buying this one.